THE BOOK CLUB

THE BOOK CLUB

MARJOLIJN FEBRUARI

English Translation by Paul Vincent

Quercus

First published in Great Britain in 2010 by

Quercus
21 Bloomsbury Square
London
WC1A 2NS

Men speak too much about the world. Each one of us here, let the world go how it will, and be victorious or not victorious, has he not a Life of his own to lead? One Life; a little gleam of Time between two Eternities; no second chance for us forevermore! It were well for us not to live as fools and simulacra, but as wise and realities. The world's being saved will not save us; nor the world's being lost destroy us. We should look to ourselves: there is great merit here in 'the duty of staying at home'! And, on the whole, to say truth, I never heard of 'worlds' being 'saved' in any other way.

(Thomas Carlyle, *On Heroes, Hero-Worship and the Heroic in History*)

I

The Meeting

1

The sugar jar fell off the table. Just when things were going so well for Teresa. She had nothing to do and that Saturday morning was sitting reading *De Telegraaf*, a large-circulation daily, in the bar of the orangery on the edge of the village. Evidently a revolt had broken out in Kabul against the arrival of UN forces, and the front page featured a photo of a grinning Taliban next to a Humvee that had been shot to pieces. Below was an interview with the film star George Clooney, who promised to do something about the situation − 'see Show News'. Teresa leafed through it, zigzagging across the home news pages, studied all the photos of Clooney intently, read the film reviews, and having reached births, marriages and deaths threw the paper onto the table with a sigh. No one she knew would be seen dead in that down-market publication. And today she wasn't in the mood for the family entanglements of total strangers. Taking her mobile from the brown Paddington bag on the chair next to her, she looked around her for the waiter and so caught the eye of a tall, skinny man who was bending over the reading table to choose a paper. 'Would two be company if I came and sat with you?' he asked, immediately pulling up a chair.

'Company isn't the first word that comes to mind,' said Theresa in a critical tone.

The man stiffened for a moment and then started laughing. 'I asked more or less out of politeness.'

'Hm,' said Teresa.

He leant forward, hands on the back of the chair. An idealistic primary school headteacher, she thought, and suddenly her cheerful spring mood deflated. Just as long as he didn't want a debate with her. She had had the same aimless conversations about the world news hundreds of times before, and now she didn't feel like it; she wanted to go home, get in the bath, submerge in the beneficent warmth of silver fir and lavender. And then, just at the moment when she grabbed her bag off the chair and threw it on the table with a resolute gesture intended to make it clear to the still politely smirking man that she wasn't in the mood for a chat, an incident happened that linked her life, her innocent female existence, to that of all those people who were written about daily in the foreign news pages. As if a thin sliver of this radiant spring day were x-rayed and behind the pearly white of the healthy structures shadows were suddenly visible that had not been there at a previous check-up. It was a moment of fundamental, moral revolution. The sugar jar fell off the table.

Or no, it did not fall off the table, but completely unreasonably the Paddington bag did not stay in the spot where

Teresa had thrown it, and slid at great speed to the other end of the reading table, where it lightly tapped the sugar jar, a glass sprinkler with an old-fashioned spout that was dangerously close to the edge. Because Teresa cried 'Oh!' very loudly and sprang to her feet, Victor Herwig looked up from his coffee. He recognized Teresa instantly – and also immediately took in her precarious situation, with the sugar jar wobbling indecisively on the edge of the table, observed awkwardly by the newspaper-reader, from whom no help could be expected, and because Teresa was quite simply Teresa, he decided to save her from disaster. He grabbed the bar with one hand and catapulted himself force-fully from his barstool, so that he came running straight towards her at the moment that Teresa in her eagerness to reach and rescue the sugar jar, swept her Nokia off the table with her left elbow, sending it crashing loudly against the wall and then swirling through the air in slow motion until it lay virtually lifeless at her feet. 'Oh!' cried Teresa. She changed direction, bent to the side to see the screen display a last unfathomable message, and then – just as Victor made his final leap and Teresa stood up in dismay with the fragments of the telephone in her hand – the sugar jar fell, after all, off the table.

2

The village lies peacefully at the foot of a ridge. A main road runs through the centre, but there isn't often a queue of cars at the traffic lights at the junction. Most people turn off the road a village earlier. If there is a jam in the rush-hour, most drivers spend their time looking at the shop windows from their cars. Those at the head of the queue at the lights can see the display at the patisserie: raspberry flans, meringues with kirsch, and each new season ingeniously arranged nature studies in marzipan. From the car you can scan the local property on offer in the estate agent's window. Every lost soul from the big city drools over the large photos of country houses and farmhouses with stables that stand out in full colour against the white back wall. And it's just as well that from that distance they can't read the asking price under the photos, since in that way they can dream for a moment of swapping their Amsterdam flat for a castle in the country. Then the lights change back to green, they accelerate and in ten seconds they're out of the village.

Not much happens here. But not much happens in the
rest of the country either, the villagers say in their defence.
And it's true. Dutch people who have ever been abroad, as
aid workers in the shanty towns of Brazil or managers of
financial institutions in Washington, are amazed on their
return at the triviality of the news, which has changed with
the arrival of the immigrants, but is still pretty shallow. The
important news invariably breaks elsewhere in the world
and at the most is eventually imported in simplified form.
In order to feel grown-up, the Netherlands is utterly
dependent on imported crime, imported conflicts and
imported religions. Apart from that, there's little of vital
importance.

The country may already be to some extent in the grip
of exotic alarm, but for the time being that has passed the
village by. It is hard to imagine just how unsensational this
place is, at least if you don't find cross-country races and
sheep-pens sensational and need hordes of people, discos,
neon signs or sultry back-street criminality. Here the theft
of the hub-caps of a Mitsubishi Colt parked outside the
chemist makes it into the local paper. Outside the village,
the big castle is occupied by the same noble family that
lived there a century ago; on days when her grandchildren
are rolling around the castle garden the baroness phones
the Michelin-starred restaurant two kilometres down the
road: 'Lisa, do you do chips these days?'

'There isn't much call for them,' says Lisa, formerly sous-
chef at L'Astor in Paris, hesitantly, 'but I can make some.'

'Wonderful,' says the baroness impatiently (after all, what

has the demand for chips at the restaurant got to do with her?). 'We'll have a dish of them. And bring a packet of cigarettes too.'

Apart from that it's true that absolutely nothing happens here, apart from tree martens eating the squirrels, farmers' sons driving into a tree blind drunk in the middle of the night, and in one of the hottest summers for years a bird being spotted in the countryside that supposedly spread a mysterious African virus. But it all blew over, the excitement about the inspections and the red tape round the field behind the cheese-making plant. Peace has returned and you could say that the village is bobbing along under its own momentum, far from the madding crowd.

It was a long winter here. At the beginning of April the snow still lay on the fields for days and in the preceding months the village was regularly cut off from the rest of the world. Teresa called off her appointments and sat warm and safe at home watching the traffic chaos on the late news. She hoped to see her husband John's car somewhere in the endless tailbacks. Not that she was worried; he had doubtless meanwhile been given a cup of instant coffee by the army, which had deployed at full strength to keep motorists alive. Once or twice she thought she saw him, but each time it was a different dark-blue Audi with a businessman at the wheel. What kind of tie had he taken with him on his business trip? For the life of her, she couldn't remember. He was fairly conservative in his choice of ties, so that man on the telephone with the broad stripes couldn't

be John. Every day after the news the weatherman promised further snow, and the authorities made a desperate
appeal to the civilian population to stay home. But John
spent so much time abroad that he looked down with a
kind of detached pity at those nice Dutch people who
thought they were having their own share of bad weather,
though this, as he said to Teresa when he called from Schiphol
to say he was on his way home, was absolutely nothing
compared with American winters.

'Winter in America is cold,' hummed Teresa.

'What's gold?'

'Wishing I had known enough of love to leave love
enough alone.'

'What are you going on about?'

'First try to get home,' replied Teresa in a motherly tone,
'then we'll see about America.'

Come to that, it would teach him a lesson to get stranded
half-way at night. All that travelling around with business
class information and satnav systems that constantly sent
messages to his car with the latest news on cloud levels,
precipitation, temperature, wind, storm warnings and the
outlook for subsequent days had turned him into a
meteorological show-off. Spending an hour or so in the
open air while the soldiers hoisted his car back up the
incline could do him no harm, and he'd have the chance
to feel how even Dutch frost can burn through your clothes
like wildfire. It wasn't his fault, though, not some reckless
trait in his character. He simply had the attitude of a born
city-dweller to the weather; he knew about it only by

hearsay. So she watched the chaotic scenes on the motorway for a little longer, but channel-hopped to TelSell when the news started repeating itself. She listened to the American who tried with religious zeal to persuade her to purchase a steam vacuum cleaner, toyed for a moment with the idea of ringing the sales number, but on second thoughts switched the television off and went to bed. He'd be OK.

That winter Teresa twice woke up early in the morning, looked outside and saw John sitting outside the gate in the car. Because the driveway was impassable and even the council's snowplough had given up half-way down the avenue, he had got stuck, car and all, a few metres from the gate, and had obviously become caught up in a hectic conversation. Dashboard light on, business reports open on the steering wheel. Gesticulating energetically in the dark. Both times he was already sitting showered and shaved at breakfast when she got up a few hours later. Had he slept in his car? Of course not. At home as always, he'd got back on time; he'd rung Berlin this morning; things were much worse there. The Germans had to climb up on their roofs to shovel the snow off because of the danger of collapse. You didn't have that kind of thing in Holland.

It was in that same long winter that John joined the book club. He'd just returned from a short trip and was sitting in his study reading the mail when Teresa's father Randolf dashed in with a book, wrapped in the paper of the local bookshop, which he slapped down on the desk in front of his son-in-law with a mighty thud. There was nothing else for it. The book club could use another sensible reader.

'Christ Almighty,' said John, 'what good would I be in a book club? I never read books. The last time I read a novel was Grisham's *The Firm*. And I bought it in a mad rush. At an airport. I thought it was the latest bestseller on Heathrow management.'

He pushed himself away from his desk and rolled his chair back a little, stopping a metre and a half in front of his extensive collection of current and authoritative professional literature. Then he tipped back his chair and folded his hands behind his head. Since he had last shaved early in the morning, a dark shadow played across his face, misleadingly giving him – for all his innocence and amiability – a rather suspect appearance. Because of his exotic appearance, even on days when he *had* shaved, he was asked confidentially by his business contacts where he came from. Holland. And your parents? Holland. That answer usually led to suppressed indignation in the people he was talking to; they felt they weren't being taken seriously and ascribed that to the arrogance of an immigrant who, starting from an underprivileged position, had worked his way too fast to the top of the financial world.

These days John enjoyed exploiting that confusion. By exaggerating slightly and giving away as little as possible about himself, he derived an air of superiority and menace from his supposed foreign origin. Because, in combination with his exalted position, his haughty intelligence created the impression not only that he was a perfect example of

the successful rise of immigrants, but could also lead his
business colleagues to believe that he had access to the
inner circles in countries where no Westerner had yet set
foot.

He ran his hand reflectively over his stubble and shook
his head.

'Novels! I'm far too much of a barbarian to talk about
novels with those posh lawyers of yours.' When Randolf
did not react, he sprang to his feet. 'Haven't you got another
club I can join to win my spurs here in the village? Isn't
there a dining club or something?'

'The book club is best,' said Randolf Pellikaan firmly.
'You're a very suitable candidate for a book club. Sooner
or later every person with a sense of responsibility joins a
book club. Look, here, this is what we are going to read:
Carlo Emilio Gadda, 3 December at 8 p.m. at Lucius' place.
Just get Teresa to explain to you where it is.'

3

Sooner or later every person with a sense of responsibility joins a book club – that is the firm conviction of Randolf Pellikaan, Teresa's father, a great constitutional lawyer and famous columnist. He is supported in that conviction by the culture surrounding him. There is only one way of understanding people's lives, their randomness, their transience and their lack of drama, and that is by telling separate stories outside history. Literature, as Randolf explains repeatedly when he wishes to justify his interest in novels, is indispensable for understanding the particular, the separate events of which life consists as soon as you distance yourself from the structure that philosophy imposes on it.

Sometimes he works late in his office in the law faculty and no longer has any idea from what recesses of his body he is supposed to dredge new supporting arguments for his still fresh ideas: his adrenal glands have stopped secreting, he's worked non-stop for weeks and he's dog-tired. This has all the characteristics of an artistic impasse, he thinks: the literary writer must feel something like this when no new ideas present themselves. And as a result of this, this sense of emotional and intellectual breakdown acquires a stature that he greatly enjoys in the midst of his silence. With a mixture of self-mockery and embarrassment he comes to the conclusion that his life comes closest to real life when he's totally wiped out. When he wobbles, when everything in him wobbles, when he feels the puniness of his own body and the tears well up in his eyes from pure exhaustion. In a while, as soon as he returns to his work, the legal hair-splitting at which he excels, the feeling of urgency will disappear and his life will again shrink to servitude and functionality. No, if you want to understand anything about life, you'd do better to sit motionless on your chair and talk about nothing. Or about death.

The problem is, Randolf never thinks about death. Or perhaps he does think about it now and then, but when he does it never carries the tragic and melancholy charge that death has in the work of great writers. And that's precisely why he admires those writers so, and at the same time utterly despises them. Because they are able to give weight to the inner experiences that every normal person has; they don't require any special merit, they don't perform feats of superhuman proportions, they just live the same life as everyone else and yet imbue it with extra significance. That is both impressive and disappointing. Come to that, he's never given very much thought to the contradictory nature of his feelings. He prefers to push his contempt for writers into the background, because when all's said and done it seems to him the least interesting aspect. His admiration on the other hand makes him one of the most fanatical members of the book club.

What is it that makes people reach for literature, Randolf asks the students at the start of his lectures. They look away uncomfortably and so he answers his own question: it's a longing for profundity. Because there's more to life that you might think at first sight, more than telecommunications, maximizing of profit, cultural globalization, genetic modification, worldwide migration: in short because there's more, sooner or later all serious people feel the need for depth.

They want confirmation. They want to hear that much in life is futile and much to no avail, that life is an incidental activity, a fleeting illusion, and that that's OK.

Although they themselves are of course also sensible people, with a bat-brain millions of years old that carries within it the corpuscular knowledge of dark caves and the deceptive shadows that the bright fire of truth casts on the walls, they still need books to tell them. Yes, they say, that's how it is, that's exactly how it is.

That's why a poet eventually comes to work at every office in the world and tells the staff about the fragility of their existence. Not because the staff themselves are ignorant on that score. But between the backlog of work piling up and lunches in the canteen they have to be reminded again of the feelings of despair they have when they're at home in bed; they have lost their memories of home the moment they go through the door of their office. Because here they're never alone, never at rest, never at ease. Here they never have time to think – about nothing.

That's where the poet comes in.

His language is more real than their language.

(Why are the words of the poet more affecting than your own words? In the oral exam one of Randolf's students replies: 'For the same reason that someone else's love-story is more affecting than your own. Because it's someone else's love-story. Because you remain outside it – with your dubious character and your second-rate body.')

And so, because the language of the poet is so much more affecting than their own language, the staff's hearts leap up as soon as their own feelings come up in the poetry workshops, although they've long been intimately acquainted with their own feelings, and precisely at that moment, they will say afterwards on their evaluation forms, somewhere deep inside a door opens.

When they are given the assignment of recording what moves them inwardly during the course, these are the things that surface; Randolf was once given the list by an office poet who wanted to know the first thing that came into the heads of the people on the course:

– Writing poetry is making us conscious of reality.
– Regard writing poetry as a method of management.
– In the south the hills are as silver as the silver fox, in the north as red as the coat of the red buffalo.
– Our management is made up of the kind of people who

when they hear the word 'abstraction' think of Russian painters.

- Desolate.
- An American gas station where you can buy apple pie.
- The dog had four pups in the back garden and simply left two of them outside all night.
- Article 4 of the Spatial Planning Act; possible compensation in the case of lawful government action.
- Discrimination is incorrect use of the *modus tollens*.
- In Ty Mawr there are two cottages, built of slate and granite, which would merge with the background if the window frames were not painted such a brilliant white and the doors such bright red: I shall move in there when I'm dead.
- Goethe is aiming at a synthesis between the qualitative and quantitative method.
- Every year is a wastepaper basket.
- As if, standing against the wall of the cinema, you are presented with the bill for dreams that evaporated long before you were born.
- Bloody Brigadoon.
- I have to control the impulse to throw myself face down in the verge.
- How are you? Please tell me, how are you?

It was the year when a British law practice made a great hullabaloo about appointing the first office poet, that Randolf Pellikaan became interested in the potential of literature. He'd been an avid reader all his life and had set up the book club with a couple of friends just after he left university. Yet despite his pious dedication to the world of high culture that novels represent, he himself would never have hit on the idea of also using them, the novels, as a source for his own work.

The British practice wrote in a press release – Randolf was sent the cutting from London – that it was really nothing special, the idea that an office poet was going to email poems round the office. You had to realize that in the past in many countries, Ireland and pre-Islamic Arabia, for instance, the law itself was transmitted by word of mouth; it was mainly poets who announced legal casuistry to the public in verse form. So the joint venture between lawyers and poets wasn't all that new.

Randolf liked the plan. The step those lawyers had taken had suddenly shown him that he too could also read classic literature with his own students without being accused of dilettantism by others. Kleist's *Michael Kohlhaas*, the humiliated citizen's sense of justice that has run out of control; *Billy Budd*, the inarticulate sailor unjustly condemned to death by an inflexible naval captain ('rules are rules'); Dostoevsky; Harper Lee; Auden: 'In the burrows of the Nightmare/Where Justice naked is'. He could see the course plan in front of him. And in that new flush of enthusiasm he decided to devote an MA workshop to the subject. With a select group of students he read poems, novels, discussed the underlying views of peace and law, of love and justice, and together they followed the rise of the office poets with great interest.

Well then, at a certain moment Randolf even did a blown-up print-out of a poem by the office poet Lavinia Greenlaw and pinned it pontifically on his office wall. In the poem – 'Galileo's Wife' – Galileo's wife travels around like a woman possessed looking for the edge of the world on her husband's behalf, but when she gets home all the thanks she receives for her pains is a slap in the face from Galileo. The great scientist himself has stayed safely indoors all that time: 'Every night he is at the university/Proving the existence of the edge of the world.'

Randolf is proud of the poem, that is, he's proud of having been chivalrous enough to hang it up. Not everyone in the university is prepared publicly to make room for criticism of the scientific enterprise. But if I've learnt anything from reading poetry and prose, he says, beaming at everyone who visits him in his office, it's self-irony.

Randolf Pellikaan is a passionate intellectual, he is shrewd, cautious, cultured, cheerful, ruthless, sentimental, dangerous.

Now, years later, he is still a supporter of the law-and-literature movement, although the initial excitement has subsided and all over the world with the fluctuations in the economy the status of poetry has again experienced something of a downturn. But Randolf continues to believe loyally in the importance of culture.

When his young colleagues, eager lawyers without much teaching experience, wrestle with the bored attitude of their students, he tells them they should simply become a little more like Robin Williams.

'I beg your pardon?' say his colleagues in astonishment.

'Robin Williams,' says Randolf, 'and the way he brought his uninterested students to life with poems in *Dead Poets Society*!'

O Christ, yes, they know the film.

'So we have to patrol the dorm at night too?' they snigger, and exchange meaningful looks.

'Laugh all you want,' says Randolf. 'The film may be old-fashioned and a tear-jerker, but you'll never be a good teacher if you don't understand its pedagogical message.'

Consequently, when he came across a DVD of *Dead Poets Society* a year ago, he immediately bought it. On Randolf's strict instructions the members of the book club all took turns to view it at home. Lucius, a founder-member, watched it at night in bed with a glass of armagnac. Slightly superciliously. But even Lucius can't get the scene out of his mind where two model parents discover their son's body. The son has blown his brains out in his father's study – why? Because he had been touched by literature, because he wanted to become a poet, an actor, an artist, but wasn't, that was why he took his father's pistol out of his desk drawer. And as he lies there, so young, so promising, such an unnecessary victim of the struggle between the ever-contrary Robin Williams and his conventional surroundings, while he is so hopelessly dead, his polite middle-class mother looks at him from a distance, rigid, turned to stone as if smitten by the hand of God, and says, 'It's all right.' It's all right.

'And that,' says Lucius when he's drunk at the end of a

busy week – when the book club is meeting at Gabrielle's place to discuss a book that in masterly fashion pulls together all the themes and tragedy of the twentieth century (or is it the twenty-first century?) – 'that could be the motto of our ideal book club. It's all right, it's bloody well all right as long as you love novels. As long as you commit murder with a licence, as long as you screw your students without its affecting your administrative duties.'

'I'm not in the mood for this,' says Gabrielle.

4

On the morning of that spring day when Teresa Pellikaan's mobile was to smash into the wall of the bar, her husband John had to go into town. He couldn't get out of it, he had to attend a Saturday-morning globalization debate organized by the Social Democrats in The Hague. They had assigned him to a forum on climate change and he would probably say something about the impact of climate on the market. 'What kind of world are we living in?' had been the indignant tenor of the contributions and John could sympathize with that indignation.

The next question – and there the situation became precarious – was what was John planning to do about it, that world that was growing hotter and hotter and across which the storms were raging more violently than ever? The moment that question was raised he would be on the defensive. What could he as a banker do about it? Nothing. And if he *had* been able to do anything about it, it would at the very least be a waste of time to come here and discuss the solution on a Saturday morning with a handful of Dutch parliamentarians and a few economists. John had enough access to the upper echelons of high finance – 'the 'hi-fis', as Teresa called them – to be able to save the world with a simple e-mail, should he have a brilliant brainwave.

Such misgivings led Teresa to call him crazy every time he sacrificed his time off to the social debate. But John was quite simply interested in such discussions. He accepted the invitations out of pure curiosity. Even if it was only to discover there and then whether he could turn the eternal questions round and round for a while and nevertheless elicit reactions that surprised him, put him on the track of something he didn't know. How is it you can manipulate an audience like that? one of the forum members had asked on a previous occasion. Because people like being manipulated was the answer, of course, but it had not been John's answer: John was just not a cynic. 'John is too much of a gentleman to be cynical,' was Teresa's comment. And she was right. So he gave a different answer: he was able to manipulate an audience because it wasn't his intention to manipulate them, he just wanted to create a dialogue.

But now, today, he would rather have stayed at home. Not that he was apprehensive about the content of the debate. If the atmosphere was right, he could reel off his story about the 'the butcher, the brewer or the baker' for the Social Democrats (all of them small shopkeepers), who are only too happy to supply us with food, not out of brotherly love, but because it's good for them. Most of those present would recognize the quotation from Adam Smith, and also the complex of conflicting views underlying it, about the pros and cons of the free market. Smith was always a good starting-point, John felt. The moment he started talking about the baker and the butcher, everyone thought they could pin him down as an inveterate free-market theorist, and it was precisely because his most fervent opponents were taken with the idea that they had invited him themselves, demonstrating their tolerance and broad-mindedness. In this mood of Saturday-morning togetherness, he might be able to slip in his wicked message that it is precisely the curbing of the market that represents a great threat to social equality. He could pester them with the unpleasant situation that climate change is forcing the world to check economic growth at the very moment when the Third World is finally ready for it. Nice topic. And business as usual. The only trouble was, he didn't feel like it today.

He emerged from his room, where he slept when he worked late, and as he knotted his tie by sense of touch, he walked into Teresa's bedroom across the landing. She was awake and sitting in bed with a cup of coffee. Her hair was a little tousled, which made her endearing more than sexy, and she had a thoughtful expression on her face. She didn't have her contact lenses in yet, and the newspaper, which she had evidently fished out of the letter-box early, lay untouched on the pillow next to her. John felt a faint surge of lust, a slight longing for her sleepy body under the duvet, but he wasn't going to risk his new Attolini suit. So he perched cautiously on the edge of the bed and looked at her with his head cocked slightly to one side, like a dog, which was usually surprisingly effective. 'Are you coming too?'

But Teresa grunted. 'No.'

'Come on,' said John. 'You look so much more like a socialist than I do, and then at least they won't make life so difficult for me today.'

That wasn't true at all. She didn't look like a socialist; she just looked young. More than that, she *was* young, twenty years younger than him. And acceptable to everyone, one of us under all circumstances, or at least not one of them. Her regular features were obviously a projection screen for many different desires; beautiful, but not in a frightening way; and Mediterranean, the genetic inheritance of a Greek mother, which gave her a cosmopolitan air. She looked a little like him, oddly enough, but softer and less aggressive. John, who in many social contexts felt like an intruder, always found it easy if she came along: she made him easier to talk to, more approachable. Apart from that, he really wanted her around today.

'Sweet of you, though I can't judge at all how great that compliment is,' said Teresa. She looked pained. 'But I can't come with you anyway, I haven't been at home for days. I'm absolutely shattered.'

'You won't have to do anything all day: we won't be eating in tonight.'

'But we will be eating in tomorrow. And you've no idea what a palaver that is. I tore a recipe out of the paper that I need spearmint for, and I first have to find out about spearmint. I have a strong suspicion that the recipe is going to get completely out of hand today.'

'Oh,' pleaded John, 'come with me. We won't go to The Hague, we'll go to Paris.'

Teresa slid back down and pulled the duvet up under her chin, Audrey Hepburn would say, 'I don't want to go to Paris. I want to die.' John simply took her silence as a refusal. He got up, waved to her and left her in bed, jealous at her day in prospect without him. He knew, since he had gradually become familiar with her movements, that after her Saturday shopping she would wind up in the orangery by the castle, and he would have liked nothing better than to meet her there, and have a gin after a morning of hard physical labour.

He went downstairs stoically, and as he crossed the hall towards the front door he went through in his mind at lightning speed – an old habit – all the things he mustn't forget: keys, money, driving licence, phone, iPod; when it got to the last item on the list something occurred to him and he went back to his study to get the CD of a new performance of Ravel's string quartet that had been lying there ready to be listened to for the last week. With the CD in his jacket-pocket and a pile of papers under his arm, he finally left the house, pausing for a moment on the threshold.

The day looked good, smelt good, and now the morning

mist had lifted there was a haze over the meadow that presaged good weather. It was going to be a little warmer than yesterday. Here in the garden there was a pungent smell of manure: cow dung lay among the rose bushes in chaotically scattered lumps. John scanned the boundaries of his land. The garden and all the land that went with the house, all in all almost two hectares, was enough to support a large herd of goats and cultivate emergency apple rations, should that ever be necessary, and that thought unfailingly reassured him. He got reluctantly into his car.

Judge not, he'd heard a clergyman say a few days before on the radio, judge not, that ye be not judged (Luke 6.37). Condemn not, and ye shall not be condemned. The therapeutic words from the Gospel. But precisely now when John was finally growing old enough to begin to let go, the world was tugging at him harder than ever. After the icy winter, spring had recently returned in all its glory. He would have preferred to have put in a morning's work in the garden, had he had a free moment. According to the farmer he'd bought his eggs from last week, it was going to rain later this week, so there was no time to lose. A magnolia needed moving, the redcurrant had to be dug up, and he wanted to saw a couple of branches off the beech in front of the house because they obscured the view from his study. But now none of that was going to happen, because he had to go into town. 'Back to the coal-face,' he said aloud, to cheer himself up. He sighed and took out the CD.

Just at the moment when he was fumbling in irritation with the case, which refused to open, the phone went. He recognized the number: Teresa's father Randolf, the great Randolf Pellikaan, conscience of the nation.

'Yes,' snapped John.

'John,' cried Randolf cheerfully to his son-in-law. 'I've suddenly had the idea of coming with you to The Hague this morning. I need to get someone to step back into line.'

'You need to get someone to step back into line,' repeated John, and despite everything he burst out laughing. There was undeniably something touching about Randolf's boundless vanity, and although John was used to warding off intruders and troublemakers, for some reason he could never handle his father-in-law. Their relationship was clear: if Randolf had to go to the debate to get someone to step back into line, there was nothing for it but to drive him there.

'Allrightie,' he giggled – he had accidentally adopted the word from Teresa, without knowing what the associations were – 'I'll be with you in two minutes.'

Now as he drove down the avenue, turned left onto the asphalt of the High Street and then a few avenues further on turned in the direction of Randolf's house, he was again cursing under his breath. He realized that he much preferred Teresa's company to her father's. Which was just as well, seeing that he was married to Teresa. But then why was he invariably lumbered with her father?

These days John did his level best to please everyone in

his immediate circle, not to be totally swallowed up by his work and his commitments, but he was not used to the oppressive warmth of the family and was still astonished at the small world Teresa inhabited. He himself had spent the first half of his life mainly abroad and as a result regarded himself as a citizen of the world. Looking back, he thought that his father had perhaps never fully realized himself as a diplomat: they had moved house just a little too often. Always beginning a new adventure with great enthusiasm until quite quickly a certain malaise or embarrassment made itself felt in the house and the whole family left for a new posting – but John had had a happy childhood and to his great satisfaction had derived from it a bird's-eye view of life, a panoramic consciousness that perceives all the individual events happening simultaneously at the same moment. It was an attitude to life, he was fond of telling himself, that left little room for discrimination: one city is just as good to live in as another, people everywhere give you reason to stay with them, till you finally leave. When Teresa met him, newly divorced, he had lived in a rented flat in Amsterdam, but was never there.

But now, for the last eighteen months, his whole life was suddenly concentrated in a village, and the village where Teresa had grown up at that. This marriage, his second, had given him an *entrée* into the world of families who have lived in the same houses for centuries, or at least in the same area for ages (guided walks through the grounds, open-garden days in May and September, meetings of the art club in the village church, country fairs, a chicken-run in the back garden, a second house in Normandy), and he liked it all better than he had expected. And his decision to join the book club had been a direct consequence of this satisfaction. Or rather, a combination of satisfaction, curiosity, the firm resolve to make his second marriage succeed, and a slight slowing down of his brain associated with growing older, so that he had said yes when Randolf turned up with a novel – and a few days later with all the novels that the book club had read and discussed in the past year. Yes, he joined the book club. And that was a lightly taken decision which from now on yoked him inexorably to his father-in-law.

'Funny,' he said in a good-humoured tone, 'how quickly you get into your dotage. In a year I won't want to leave the village at all.'

'So what? You mustn't underestimate the dynamism of this place,' replied Rudolf Pellikaan brightly. 'You haven't been banished. You've risen.'

The moment John drove up he had got contentedly into the car and now was sitting with his legs stretched out, the morning paper pressed at the ready under his arm, looking out. 'In Israel they call immigration "*aliyah*" – rise, – and emigration "*jeridah*" – fall. It's the same with this village. By coming to live here you've climbed up quite a way. And now we're driving down.'

They had left the built-up area and found themselves in open country. The provincial road was quiet; occasionally they met oncoming traffic that was in no more of a hurry than John was – these days cars thought for themselves; this morning they had adjusted their speed to the relaxed mood of the Saturday morning. As a driver you scarcely need to pay attention at all.

John drummed on the window with the fingers of his left hand and whistled Ravel's string quartet, which he could no longer listen to with Randolf in the car. The world was strictly organized: the mist had meanwhile vanished completely and the sky was bright blue, the ditches straight and a flight of crows flew over the meadows in formation, making a frightful noise. He looked at them critically. Initially he had tended to regard all birds as equally worthy of watching, but he had soon learned that you must not trust crows and magpies; they were murderers and were out to get the songbirds. Actually it had been the very first lesson he had learned here: that you had to take sides; if you were pro-squirrel, you were anti-badger; if you were pro-pigeon, you were anti-hawk. Now he looked suspiciously at the predatory silhouette of the crows and hoped they would stay clear of his garden. There was a blackbird in residence on his chimney that he had grown fond of over the course of time.

Randolf went on thinking aloud.

'It's quite understandable that you don't want to go back to town. The town is full of bad people. This area is where the good people live. That's always been so. A hundred years ago this was already a safe haven for the moral elite. Everyone wanted to get out of town, of course, but you could only afford to if you were a virtuous human being. And that still applies.'

'So am I virtuous because I live here, or do I live here because I'm virtuous?' John enquired.

'Both. It's a two-edged sword.'

The dreadful thing about Randolf was that he meant that kind of thing.

Make no mistake. Randolf is right when he talks about the dynamism of the village. Although everything has the appearance of deep calm, the world is run from this secluded corner. Above the villagers' heads are suspended communications satellites that cast no shadows, and over the years broadband connections have been set up that make no noise, so that no one can hear the traffic that roars through the village with thunderous force of exbibytes per second, but even though you can't see the lines, they're there.

The village itself may be no bigger than a waistcoat-pocket-size theatre – a single shopping street and a village square containing a bar, two banks with cashpoints, a paint shop and a bookshop with a sub-post office – but the world is wide and boundless.

Sometimes the inhabitants of the village act in the interest of that world. Then they take decisions and technocratic knowledge flows in the right direction, stabilizing the budget deficits in countries on the verge of bankruptcy and the level of prosperity increases across the board. At other times they do not act in the interest of the world. Then they sow death and destruction in faraway countries. You imagine that that sometimes gives the members of the book club sleepless nights; hoping no journalist or writer ever comes to the village and brings up the subject.

5

John is annoyed. At having to go to The Hague, at having no chauffeur today but again not having his car to himself, at the moral impassivity of the world along the route he is now driving to the motorway junction with Randolf.

He has to prepare for the talk he'll shortly be giving on climate; he doesn't want to talk only about the melting of the ice-caps and the rise in sea-level, threatening the Netherlands with inundation – he also wants to say something about the melting of snow and ice in the mountains, which is causing the Alps, up to now held in the grip of the ice, to fragment, crumble and, once freed from the vice of winter, to be strewn across the countryside and come to rest in the valleys. Soon the world will literally be turned on its head and the process has already been set in motion – shouldn't that cause some upset here in the vicinity of the village too? But here all is quiet. This area, which is already below sea-level, is amazingly unconcerned. Nothing has changed here for centuries, and if it's up to the inhabitants nothing ever will.

Randolf, who has opened his newspaper, reads out the headlines; when John snorts he glances to the side in alarm, but it looks as if it were a sign of amusement, and so he lays his head back against the headrest and reads on in silence. They drive on through the meadows without talking. John is annoyed, but doesn't know quite why. To be honest, you can't really expect the melting of the ice in the Alps to provoke an immediate uproar in a village in the middle of the Netherlands. Apart from which the area's indifference to things really is only apparent; as Randolf says, you mustn't underestimate the dynamism of this place.

A few weeks previously John was given a tour of the local country houses by his father-in-law. Randolf pointed out to him how cleverly people in those days managed to combine technology and progress with conventional morality. Some of the great houses have towers more or less as a matter of course, which at the time of their construction were meant to project responsibility and authority, but at the same time also had to house a large water-tank for the sanitation. In fact the whole construction of those Protestant mansions was an amalgam of plumbing work and charity, heating technology and piety. And that is perhaps the most characteristic aspect of this area: the ingenious interplay of virtue, as the acquired inclination to do good, and business talent. That is, you had to be a good person to come and live here in the countryside, and when you did you became better and better.

Thus far Randolf is right. You can say what you like,

but the fact is that in the past anyone who spent the whole year in town had obviously done something wrong, committed some gaffe so that he'd lost his money, or worse still so that he'd never had any, and this moral inferiority condemned him to live in the hopeless chaos of urban tenements and hovels. Out in the country was where the wealthy lived. And even when they travelled to The Hague at regular intervals in order to rule, that was purely and simply because they felt obliged to do something for the country – afterwards they came home as soon as possible. In the nineteenth century these pleasure-grounds wound their way for miles from the town past all the great country houses with their orangeries and hothouses for grapes right down to the river, and far into the twentieth century you couldn't buy foreign newspapers in the villages, because the world was so far away that thank God it didn't concern you in the least. A house in the country was a world in itself and owning it produced sufficient income to get by for ages without ever moving an inch.

The dynamism that Randolf makes so much of has appeared in the village since the virtual disappearance of people living on capital interest. Nowadays everyone in the Netherlands has to go to work. Even those people with enough money to be able to stay at home would feel ashamed if they just hung around jobless, and so the owners of the big houses are now out there in the world.

And that's why the future of mankind is now being decided from this village. In the last few decades, since the world has come this way, since the arrival of the papers has brought a wave of misery, the civil war in Darfur, the poverty in Kirgizia, AIDS in Malawi, the debt crisis in Bolivia, Europe has been seized by a sense of shame and moral panic that have led to a completely new attitude, one that that is easily recognizable in the men in the neighbourhood of the village, with their membership of ethical business networks and their bookcases full of solutions to poverty in the third world.

If you don't run into them elsewhere, you can observe those men on Saturday mornings doing the shopping. On Saturday mornings, for instance, there's always a customer at the baker's who during working hours is responsible for a budget considerably wider in scope that that of the Dutch state. Such men prefer to do the shopping themselves at weekends, since on their own testimony they know more about it than the rest of the family. They get fish from the fishmonger, sausage from the delicatessen on the corner, where the manager tries to persuade them to drink a glass of wine with him at the long table set up in the shop, which they do on some Saturdays, after which they go to the bookshop for foreign magazines. They potter around apparently aimlessly, have a chat here and there and order a few things. But however long they hang around in the main street, in their inside pocket there is always that invisible connection to the democratic movement in China, the Republican campaign in America, with women selling textiles in the market in southern Mozambique. What's more, when Lucius, secretary of the book club, had a Japanese colleague to stay, he rang John, who was at the cheese merchant's, to ask what the Japanese expression was for 'pocket of poverty', and John rang a Japanese acquaintance who was just sitting down to breakfast in a New York restaurant, after which he rang Lucius back, enabling Lucius to explain to the guest less than two minutes later what he meant.

When John comes home after a long day and takes a turn in the garden, bending over the magnolias and walking over to the rose garden to check whether the deer have eaten the buds, he is meanwhile conversing animatedly with men on the other side of the world, where it's already early morning. In the winter he enquires about the price of aluminium in Surinam and about forecasts for telephone networks in Korea, while flicking the old shells of beech nuts off the grass with the toe of his shoe. In the spring, when at sunset his neighbour's sheep come drifting past in the mist, he exerts pressure on an African regime in consultation with the United States. Then he whistles for the dog, which of course shows no signs of wanting to go home, having discovered something vicious and dangerous on the edge of the ditch, and as John stands with the knob of the garden door in his hand inhaling the smell of the grass one last time – it's late and a northwest wind is getting up – the phone vibrates again.

So you mustn't underestimate the dynamism of the village, but it isn't the case that that dynamism constantly galvanizes everyone: the intimate scale of the landscape makes the region just outside the coastal urban agglomeration an excellent holiday area, resulting in a large campsite in the woods, just outside the village across the provincial highway.

In the village you're not very aware of the campers, because they immediately adapt to their surroundings and are infinitely less rowdy than at home. And because those well-behaved campers come back every year, they gradually feel they know every stone in the village. But they don't know, because the villagers wouldn't dream of telling them, that the man next to them in the queue at the fishmonger's has the power to make decisions that will directly affect their jobs, their pensions and their future. The campers don't even have the slightest suspicion that a princess's horse is stabled at the farm on the woodland road.

In addition, to understand something of the geopolitical situation of the village the tourists from the city would have to know that the back-gardens of the houses are all adjacent, and if something has to be arranged, it will always be possible via those back-gardens to track down someone who knows a board chairman, an MEP or a lady-in-waiting, if direct access to the queen is required. But none of the visitors knows about the back gardens, since all things considered there's absolutely no reason for everyone to know.

John and Teresa live on the outskirts of this village, in a house that backs onto countryside. They look out across fields to the edge of the woods in the distance, and if they feel like walking a little down the garden they can see past the guest-room to the village church tower beyond. On their right lives a manufacturer of glass constructions for station awnings. And Dr Bennie 'The Nose' Driessen, head of a disaster identification team that is called in whenever there have been bomb attacks in London or mass graves are discovered in Cameroon, lives on the left. John raises his hand jovially when he sees Bennie setting off in his old Volvo, on his way to the front, but Teresa can't quite bring herself to do that, and just gives a little nod.

The village is secluded, like an old country seat, and is the hub of the new world. And Teresa? Teresa Pellikaan lives in the presence of this, but it passes her by. The information streams of the world markets run through her house, through her living-room, even through her bedroom. She observes them, but brushes them aside as completely uninteresting. She finds this world of big money slightly ridiculous and gets bored the moment capital is mentioned. 'You have money,' she tells John, 'you don't talk about it.' That is an old rule of proper behaviour that her mother instilled in her, and which is still an excellent guide.

'But someone will still have to earn that money,' John answers, in a rather irritated tone. And Teresa sighs at such superficiality.

She really can't understand what everyone is getting excited about. She herself travels round a bit, goes to museums, visits studios, gives advice on art-purchasing, returns home, plays the piano (and not without talent). And when she tots it all up, life and its pros and cons, she's bound to conclude that it doesn't amount to much. Nothing really special.

6

If anyone could save the sugar jar it was the journalist Victor Herwig. He was in full flow. Everything was going his way. He'd escaped from the stuffiness of the town and half an hour ago had finally returned to his home village, and he was happy. After the harsh winter, spring was breaking out enthusiastically here in the Netherlands; the moment he had left the motorway he had lowered the windows of his hire car and he smelt, no, he noticed immediately from his breathing, that the air was becoming fresher the closer he got to his old home. Because he had taken an early exit, he had first to wind his way through the meadows for a bit and the very sight of the tenant farms with their red-and-white shutters was enough to bring tears to his eyes after such a long absence. What a day for a reunion; what weather for rejoicing! The orchards in blossom, the bridges over the drainage channels renovated and given a fresh coat of paint, ducklings like little paper boats on the water, a red tricycle on the verge, the big castle, the sawmill, a buzzard in the sky, two young women standing talking in a neatly raked yard, with their hands fluttering round each other, and everywhere it smelled of the Dutch countryside. Ha! Great! He cried to himself in the car. Great!

And so now, half an hour later, he sat drinking coffee in the orangery of the small castle on the edge of the village. He looked around contentedly. He still remembered very well that when he was young the building had served as a summerhouse and furniture store, but while he was at university, after a great tug-of-war with the council, permission had finally been given for its conversion into a café-restaurant with a terrace at the front and a stately drive through the castle garden. Now twelve set tables, with white linen and starched napkins, awaited guests who would wander in in early afternoon to eat veal with lemon or a pastry followed by coffee. There were potted palms at the entrance, and on the wall opposite Victor hung a series of photos of the artist Marcel Broodthaers entering the Palais des Beaux-Arts in Brussels accompanied by a camel. Twentieth-century photos, which oddly enough made a decisive contribution to the nineteenth-century character of the café. All that was missing from the general atmosphere of transience was the creak of wooden floorboards and the inexpressible melancholy that could shroud objects in the nineteenth century, but that was because everything was new.

It was still quiet at this hour, and in the background some customers were mumbling as they ate apple cake at Thonet tables and a mild brand of world music was coming through the speakers. The man behind the bar was polishing wine glasses.

'This place hasn't changed much,' said Victor.

'Is it supposed to then?'

That tone clearly didn't belong to the world of the village.

'You're from Amsterdam,' said Victor.

'Hm,' said the waiter. 'You reckon so?' He put the glass down in slow motion. Cool, thought Victor indulgently, cool bar staff.

'You're not from here either.'

'Botswana,' said Victor. 'I got back from Botswana the day before yesterday. And before that from Liberia. I've been away quite a bit, the last few years.'

'Army?' asked the waiter, convinced that the Dutch army was ready to keep the peace anywhere in the world, and if necessary with a firm hand.

'Paper. I'm a foreign correspondent' – and that was a posh word that he never used, but one that in these early-modern surroundings suddenly seemed appropriate. 'I've worked abroad for a few years. Looking at economic developments, following politics. That sort of thing. Does the mayor still live opposite here in the woods?' The waiter shook his head in ignorance and slowly picked up a new glass.

Victor ran his hand through his hair, which he hadn't washed since his return and was still full of the sand of Africa; if he shook his head – he hoped at least – it would fall into his coffee. And not only was his hair full of sand and dust, he still had the pleasant feel of the tropical sun in his bones and stretched out his arms in front of him for a moment, fingers intertwined, palms facing outward. It was the last day he could still walk about like this; after that he would have to adapt and put on something warmer. He looked at himself curiously in the mirror behind the bar. With his hair slightly windswept, he had driven with the windows down, and with the collar of his shirt wide open he looked even more than usual like a young version of Harvey Keitel, and that vague observation in his subconscious awakened a vague desire for cigars; he felt in the pocket of his army trousers to see if he didn't have a box with him. He sighed. Only now he was sitting here did he have the feeling he was really back. He wouldn't be leaving again anytime soon, said Victor to himself again.

He was sitting, tanned and aged, on a bar stool in his old village talking to an arrogant waiter, and in this good-humoured mood he produced a magazine article that he had folded four times and stuffed into his back pocket this morning.

'Here, have you ever heard of her? Ruth Ackermann? She's written a novel: *The Summer of Canvas Shoes*. Seems to be a huge hit.'

'Yeah, it rings a vague bell,' said the waiter, despite everything affected by the glamour of the news, now he had got talking to a serious reporter.

'Wait a bit, I've got another piece, with a photo.'

Victor unfolded a second article. It was a report by the journalist Kiki Jansen. She would be following the promising young writer Ruth Ackermann on her triumphal procession through Europe and had just published the first instalment in the series. 'With Ruth Ackermann in Frankfurt!'

was the proud headline, stretching the full width of two pages.

Victor had fished out the article this morning from the pile of papers and post next to his bed waiting to be read. Everywhere, in all the literary supplements and all the magazines and catalogues, he saw the great hullabaloo about the fifteenth edition of the novel, which had only been out for three months, and for which not only had a large advance been paid before publication, but which had been published in three languages at once and in the meantime had become an international bestseller. A film version was in preparation. Victor had flicked to and fro in astonishment through the excited essays about the unrivalled Ruth Ackermann and her brilliant book, *The Summer of Canvas Shoes* – not because he suddenly felt a deep interest in the Dutch novel coming on, but because he suddenly recognized the name of the writer as that of a pathologically shy former classmate.

And two hours later, out of restlessness, nostalgia and pure journalistic curiosity – he still had a little holiday left before he started a new job – he got into the undersized car he had rented and drove from Amsterdam to the village where he'd been born and where years ago he had been at school with Ruth Ackermann.

The waiter studied the photo. It was a fairly interchangeable portrait of a young woman with short blonde hair and a rather bashful look. The waiter did his best to see something special. 'She looks nice.'

'You bet. Better than she used to. I went to school with

her for six years. Down in the village. She had quite a few problems back then, I think.'

It reassured Victor that she had become sufficiently stable to write a book, because the last time he had seen her things were definitely not going too well with her.

In a solemn tone the waiter read out the caption in a box next to the photo. '"*The Summer of Canvas Shoes*: loosely based on Dostoevsky's *The Dream*. The story of a young girl who is admitted to a psychiatric institution. There she meets a young man who proposes to her, but the following day maintains he has forgotten all about the proposal." Well. Sounds like world-class stuff.'

He gave the articles back to Victor. 'Of course she doesn't live here any more.'

No, Victor had got that far himself.

He stuffed the bits of paper back in his pocket, and while the waiter went to the other side of the bar to serve another customer, Victor asked himself for the first time that morning what he actually intended to do. How now, brown cow, he hummed through his teeth. Did he have a plan? An aim? Was there anyone else in the village he could go and talk to about Ruth Ackermann? His parents had moved away a few years ago and by now he knew no one else here. Looked at objectively he had scarcely more chance of finding anything out here than if he had simply stayed in Amsterdam.

This morning, as he drove into the village, he had dropped into the bookshop on the village square. He had bought Ruth Ackermann's book. That was a start at least. While he was paying he got talking to the young owner of the bookshop, who was of course very excited about the sensational fact that the famous writer had grown up right here. He told Victor that he was doing his utmost to organize a literary reading, but didn't think he had much chance. 'I ask you, why would a top author like that come and talk for an evening in the village church when she's also had exciting invitations from London and Hollywood?'

'Hollywood?' Victor frowned.

'It seems so,' said the bookseller.

'Can't you get someone from the village to act as an intermediary, someone who knows her well? Perhaps she'd be happy to come if you asked her nicely. Surely there must be people around who are still in touch with her?'

But according to the bookseller there were no people who had ever really talked to her. He had spoken to many customers about Ruth Ackermann over the last few months, but everyone had referred to the book club, and they had kept remarkably mum in response to all questions.

'Who's in this book club?'

'Randolf Pellikaan, Lucius What's-his-name, Jurgen Lagerweij, Gabrielle van Dam, Raoul Kemp. And a few others, I think. Does that mean anything to you?'

'Yes,' said Victor, 'that means something.'

Now he thought over that conversation again, he suddenly became curious about that book club's judgement on a bestseller like that, which according to the blurb on the back was the witty, splendid, utterly unexpected début of a great writer. But he could scarcely ring the bells of the glorious residences of the village dignitaries, who at most may have seen him cycling past when he was ten. And apart from that, what was he supposed to ask them? About Ruth Ackermann, yes, but she didn't live here any more. And it would be an immediate dead-end.

It was at that moment, as he was wondering again if there was anyone he could talk to, that he was startled by a scream – 'Oh!'. Immediately he turned round towards the conservatory, hidden by many potted palms, from where the sound had come, and quite coincidentally saw another former classmate, Teresa Pellikaan, bending over the reading table reaching for a sugar jar that was threatening to fall. He broke into a run.

And so it was that Teresa, in her ultimate moment of despair, suddenly saw a strange man charging towards her and grabbing wildly and then, no more than a fraction of a second later, standing looking crestfallen at the floor, where the sugar sprinkler had burst open on the floorboards. A huge mess of sugar grains had shot away for yards in all directions, so that you didn't need much imagination to see that it would be weeks before the floor no longer crunched under visitors' shoes, and years before the last grain had disappeared from the joins in the floor.

At the same moment the man pulled himself together. He shouted cheerfully through the loft space of the orangery: 'Teresa! Sorry! I tried to catch it, but I was just too late.'

He obviously hadn't had enough of charging about, as he kept moving, bent down, kissed her fleetingly on the forehead, pulled a chair out from under the table and then sat down with a bang. 'I see you've had coffee already. Phone broken? Let's have a look.' He immediately put out his hand and at the same time looked up at the nervous newspaper-reader who was still standing longingly next to Teresa.

'I'm sorry,' said Victor, 'were you two talking?'

'No,' replied Teresa. 'We weren't talking.'

Then she made a lightning calculation and took a chance on the stranger who with his impertinent expression looked so much more dangerous and adventurous than the frail villager, and who obviously knew her. In a burst of romantic improvisation she added in a severe tone: 'I've been waiting for you all this time. I thought we were going to do something nice.'

Victor, who had immediately regressed to his adolescence, as if they were back at school together and were plotting against one of the teachers, nodded. 'Yes, darling, so we are. Unless this gentleman has any more to say.' But the newspaper-reader realized he had lost the battle, mumbled 'sorry' and 'what a mess, all that sugar,' and slunk off.

'I . . .' said Teresa.

'Wait a moment.' Victor called the waiter, who had stayed at the bar looking bored when the sugar jar fell: 'Two white wines and the menu please. And there's sugar all over the floor.'

Then he beamed at Teresa and put his hand on hers for a second: 'You haven't the faintest idea who I am, have you?'

7

The publication of *The Summer of Canvas Shoes* had passed Teresa by. Quite a few things pass her by. Once, in the distant past, Teresa Pellikaan went to school with Victor Herwig and Ruth Ackermann, at present so widely acclaimed – six years together in the rundown classrooms of the local high school, gym lessons on the athletics track outside the village, school parties in the gym – but she can remember precious little of that time now.

Philosophers may say we consist of our past, of the sum of decisions and determinants, actions and involvements, but that simply doesn't apply to some people. If it does apply to them, they're not aware of it. They've forgotten everything. And it is not indifference, but a form of detachment.

On that day in spring when her phone smashed, Teresa was sitting in the café, as she did on so many Saturdays. Sometimes John picked her up, but today he was in The Hague having a discussion on climate change, and so she had all the time in the world. She had sought information from the greengrocer about spearmint, *mentha spicata crispate*, the standard cure for hiccups, and she'd been to the butcher's, had talked to Lucius in the delicatessen where he was tasting armagnac (would she like to try some? No thanks, not at eleven in the morning) and then she had bought a bottle of bath foam.

Now she was sitting by an empty cup of coffee reading newspapers. Usually this image – when she looked at herself from a distance, as she was fond of doing – recalled the poem by Yeats that she had learned by heart at secondary school and by way of exception had never forgotten. 'My fiftieth year had come and gone,/I sat, a solitary man,/In a crowded London shop,/An open book and empty cup,/On the marble table-top.' The poem wasn't particularly appropriate, since Teresa was only thirty, and she had no book lying open on the table, but the mood was right. Alone at the reading table, with a packet of cigarettes in front of her, and a recently purchased pair of Ralph Lauren sunglasses and a notebook in which she had jotted down something about kindling ('run out'), pentimenti in the underpainting ('that lady in Wageningen, enquire for M.') and the best way to worm a dog.

She could perfectly well have read a book. But the thought of John joining the book club: Oh God yes, she loved him, but he allowed himself to be steamrollered by her father in a way she considered unhealthy; how could he bring himself to join a society that stood for everything that was wrong with the establishment! Mr Well-Behaved. No, Teresa was no longer going to be dictated to by her family and the village dignitaries. She sat at the reading table and read a popular tabloid, initially with a provocative sense of triumph: look at me, reading about baby elephants at the zoo and a pop singer, who, dressed in a gold-lamé dress with a plunging neckline celebrates the joyful discovery of a new anti-wrinkle cream, and it all interests me enormously, e-norm-ous-ly! But gradually it became a silent, unconscious triumph, she had long since stopped thinking of her victory over good taste every time she opened the paper. Once absorbed in the news she was sincerely moved by the fate of the tiger cubs rejected by their mother immediately after their birth. She liked this silent Saturday routine and somewhere at the back of her head it was always accompanied by Yeats' words: 'And twenty minutes more or less/ It seemed, so great my happiness,/That I was blessèd and could bless.'

So it has escaped her, the appearance of the novel *The Summer of Canvas Shoes*, since, rebelling against her parents' slight literary hysteria, she seldom enters a bookshop. What's more, the name of the author wouldn't have meant anything to her.

For while Ruth Ackermann at the back of the class was heading straight for the psychosis about which she was later to write her bestseller, and while Victor Herwig at the front of the class, with a great deal of rumpus was making plans for a better world, Teresa had finished school without giving it much thought and afterwards had qualified *en passant* as a restorer of modern art. To her own surprise and irritation, since she didn't really like art, she now worked in a canal-side building in Amsterdam for a small and prominent bureau that gave advice on art to companies and rich individuals. Advice on art. Investment in art. Her boss was a charming young accountant who was well-known in better circles for knowing ways of preventing tax liability in a respectable way – and he did. Apart from that, he knew precisely what you had to do to transfer your collection ('in a tax-efficient way!'), to children or grandchildren, or whomever you wished, and within a few years this sort of advice ('estate planning!'), had more or less become his speciality. No problem there.

But Teresa wasn't the least bit interested in any of that. In fact, the idea that there was an index of modern art that could be offset against the Dow Jones struck her as ridiculous.

'We really are doing much better than the Dow Jones or the Amsterdam Index, Teresa,' her youthful future boss had banged on at the job interview. 'Come on, Teresa: Eight per cent down as opposed to forty per cent down since the beginning of the millennium, just look, just look!'

'Here,' he read out. 'Listen to this.' And he produced a newspaper article from his wallet. 'This has been scientifically researched. Listen. "War and recession are good news for the art trade. Researchers Jianping Mei and Michael Moses of New York University have demonstrated this with the Fine Art Index. This research project on the influence of four wars and twenty-seven recessions was concluded at the end of 2001. In black periods paintings turn out to produce more profit than shares." That must be significant, don't you think?'

But the reason that Teresa had finally agreed to come and work for the company wasn't because of that, nor was it because her energetic boss-to-be then went on to the thrilling story of how he'd once been commissioned by a Saudi Arabian customer to travel with a suitcase full of money – 'all above board, I'm not crazy' – to see Charles Saatchi in a vain attempt to buy a shark in a glass tank. No, the reason she finally put her signature to the contract and joined the staff of Art Property was because he told her how soon afterwards the shark had started to decompose.

Because that was what attracted Teresa in art. Not the technique of making nine million dollars out of £72,000 within five years, but the technique of preserving a shark properly in a tank of formaldehyde. Damien Hirst might have made an installation of a shark in an aquarium, to which he gave the rather flowery title 'the physical impossibility of death in the mind of someone who is alive', but he must first demonstrate whether he could also inject the formaldehyde professionally enough into the body of the shark in order to be able maintain the illusion in twenty years' time that death is an impossibility. If she were to be an adviser, with enough money in her pocket and the backing of such a renowned estate planner, she might be able to get close enough to those great works to learn how it was all done. To touch them . . .

★

For want of cats and dogs Teresa's maternal instincts had expressed themselves from an early age in a deep concern for defective objects, and nothing could upset her so much as breaking things to which she had become attached. The table in her study was covered with worn-out dictaphones, broken alarm clocks and radios that might still be saved, trays full of loose fuses, the purpose of which she would never know. When she saw a bollard for sale in the front garden of a house in Arnhem, set majestically on the lawn between the Venus di Milo and a plastic fisherman with a rod, she felt an urgent impulse to stop and take it away in the boot of her car.

'What in heaven's name are we going to do with a bollard?' said John.

'We could put it in the hall.'

'And then?'

'Say it's a Mario Merz, or a primitive form of interactive art.'

'Automobile art,' said John, who had developed a kind of detached intuition for the topics that concerned Teresa.

'Yes, why not?'

When he had just met her, and the first time he had driven with her, she had talked softly to her car at a traffic light. With her mind still on the committee meeting where she had got very angry about the purchase of a seventeenth-century work of art for the boardroom of a bank, she growled a little at the gear lever because it wouldn't go into first. 'Come on, lad, you can do it,' she had said, and when the lever shifted into place and the car pulled away, she had added a few growls of encouragement: 'That's it, you see. That's the way.'

John drove with her for the same reason that so many men went with Teresa and why they fairly persistently wanted to go home with her. He'd had his eye on her, had observed her from a distance during meetings on art acquisitions for his head office, but had not seen an opening until dawdling in the doorway after a meeting he heard her say that she was going to have dinner with her parents in her home village – and he had struck.

'What a coincidence, that village is exactly where I'm looking for a house. I'd like to have a look round some time.'

'I'll give you a lift,' she said. And he accepted, because you never know.

But John had not been prepared for this voice, that soft, calming sound that seemed be in direct contact with defective mechanisms, and was more deeply affected by it than he could ever have imagined: he was greatly moved by the realization that he was sitting next to someone who had the ability to approve of him without further considerations.

John, who by accepting a new job had just manoeuvred himself into a position where every economic wave in the Netherlands would be ascribed to his influence, and who had been accused by all the women in his life of working too hard, who through self-love had begun to believe in his own vices, of which egocentrism was obviously the worst, suddenly heard a conciliatory sound that he wanted to possess.

In the three-quarters of an hour that he sat next to her he dismissed all the objections he knew to a serious relationship with a young woman – Teresa was almost twenty years younger than him – and surrendered, just as the gearbox of the Renault Mégane had obeyed its driver's voice. And so John, when Teresa had dropped him in the village square and driven off obviously still deep in thought, had decided to marry her. In fact, he didn't need her consent, since she didn't give him the impression of being very interested in her surroundings or the people she mixed with. But she had a capacity for being admired, and that seemed to him a good basis for a marriage, together with that voice, which would put right anything that might go wrong at any time in the future. So in no time he had bought a house in her home village, married her and then quickly got back to work, because he had no time to lose.

So had nothing changed as a result of his marriage to Teresa? Yes, one new thing was that for the first time in his life he was able to be away for days or weeks in the reassuring knowledge that no one back at home would be getting het up about it. There was no room in Teresa's life for relationship problems – she had far too strong an aesthetic sense for that.

So they had begun fairly effortlessly on a perfect marriage. But a bollard in the hall was a sacrifice that John was not prepared to make just like that, and when he broke into a vague smile, Teresa realized that the whole idea had been absurd, so she relinquished her idea of her own bollard in the hall and was left with her old unsentimental desire to have the house full of lost and abandoned objects; a daydream like a Tom Waits song about broken bicycles and things no one needed any more.

So when her phone fell and broke it was more than a practical mishap. It was a minor catastrophe. The moment that Victor withdrew his right hand from her, she looked anxiously at the phone in his left hand. The unexpected romanticism of the situation was not lost on her, but through it all she was worried about the flap with the screen on it, which seemed to be hanging from a single point, and which might be saved if only the stranger took a little care with it.

Victor followed her gaze. He laid the phone carefully on the table.

'I don't think it's going to make it.'

God, he thought in alarm, how she'd changed. And not changed. She still had a fairytale beauty about her. But in the last ten years many riches had been added to that beauty. You could see that from her teeth, the pen that lay casually in front of her, the way her hair was styled, her bag, watch, shoes; she radiated money. And he could only conclude that she was either very successful – or very married. Both options made him uncertain.

'Hi, Teresa,' he said. 'I'm Victor. We were in the same class for six years. I didn't make much impression on you, and with good reason, but you certainly made an impression on me and I'm very glad and grateful to meet you again, even if it's under these sad circumstances. Broken phone and all that.'

'Victor,' she said. 'Of course I know you. Don't be so silly. I just had to get used to all the muscles you've developed. You've grown, young Victor. Become a man of substance. Look at him. That Victor.' She looked him up and down with a slightly mocking expression. 'Let me guess. You've just flown in from the Bahamas and you thought: I'll go and show them back in the village how brown I've got.'

'Actually I was hoping to run into you.' The waiter, who had forgotten the wine but had finally come along with the dustpan and brush to sweep up the sugar as well as he could, was threatening to leave again and Victor stopped him with a motion of his hand. 'What would you like? Do you want a salad too? Greek?'

He could have hit himself on the head. Wasn't her mother Greek? Or Russian? No, Greek. And you could see that clearly in Teresa herself, whose skin, in a pleasantly clichéd way, had the colour of Cretan olives, and from the deep black of her eyes. Great, Greek salad, you couldn't make it up. This was the point at which his Liberian friend Sam would ask: 'You asked her if she wanted a Greek salad?'; and with his eyes turned heavenwards: 'And what did she say?'

Well, right then, he was happy that Teresa continued to smile at him and had not used the vexed tone of those successful young women who derive their superiority from their condescension.

'And it was a white wine, wasn't it?'

He mustn't forget that he was a man of the world, with all the nonchalant self-confidence of the traveller, to whom nothing could happen, because he'd seen it all before.

Teresa was still smiling: 'OK, fine.' And she dropped her voice half an octave: 'Victor.'

So Teresa and Victor met for the first time in years and ate in this peaceful spot in a kind of nostalgic mutual affection. A castle garden in spring, on the edge of the village. Outside a peacock was crossing the grass, not yet on duty while no one was sitting on the terrace to admire him; he took small, indignant steps, and every now and then disappeared round the corner of the building, to see whether they had anything for him to eat in the kitchen.

A nineteenth-century country estate, with a nineteenth-century rack under the chestnut tree in which you could park your bike, although it was empty on Saturday morning; in the café only a few villagers, a few estate agents who had shut up shop early and, oddly enough, Victor Herwig was suddenly sitting there, suddenly grown up and looking like an explorer, with his sun-bleached hair full of sand and his green trousers with fourteen pockets. While in The Hague John was having an animated discussion on the Kyoto treaty, they were slumped smiling in their chairs, because it was so long since they had seen each other. Teresa still didn't remember much, but she did remember that funny boy at the front of the class who made a fuss about the injustice in the world, and now that funny boy took a newspaper clipping from one of his pockets, and the cutting was about Ruth Ackermann, who had evidently sat at the back of the class all those years and said nothing.

'Nothing?' asked Victor in disbelief. 'Can't you even remember her name? That's a bit odd. Don't you remember either that her mother tried to commit suicide by throwing herself in front of a train?'

'No,' said Teresa hesitantly. 'No. Not really. Though you'd think that something like that would be a high-point in your schooldays. Didn't she succeed?'

'No, not that time. But I heard, much later, that she'd had a second attempt. Pills. She was in a pretty bad way when they brought her round. It's a shame I left Ruth's book in the car, because if you ask me it's completely auto-biographical, and I was just thinking I'd like to ask your father whether his book club can't tempt Ruth to the village for a nice literary evening.'

Teresa shook her head. 'My father won't be much good to you. If that book really is about a love story, and a comic love story at that, my parents would consider it far beneath them. But I can ask John. He's also just joined the book club.'

'John?'

'My husband. John Vos.'

'John Vos? *The* John Vos? Yes? How the hell do you come to be married to him?'

Teresa looked at him cheerfully and then suddenly shot to her feet. 'Shit, he was going to ring. He's gone to a meeting, but he was going to call me when he got back.

We're having dinner with friends somewhere. And now of course he can't get hold of me. Sorry, this is all very nice, but I must get home.' She grabbed the brown bag, put it on the table open to stow away her cigarettes, sunglasses, notepad and the phone.

'Will you call me?' asked Victor. He took a card from his left-hand back pocket and put it in the bag.

Teresa stopped and looked him intently for a few seconds. 'That's impossible.' And more brightly: 'That's impossible. My phone doesn't work.' She brushed his cheek with her fingertips. And left Victor sitting speechless. When he got his voice back he swore with great feeling, but didn't know exactly why.

II

The Memory

1

The Summer of Canvas Shoes may be a successful book, and an international seller, but that doesn't mean it's suitable for the book club. They don't read just anything.

They read in order to travel, perfect their judgement, strengthen inner democracy, see themselves as protagonists in a plot, they read in order to discover all those things that are beyond their reach, the sublimity of nature, Kant's 'bold, overhanging, and seemingly menacing cliffs, thunderclouds piling up in the sky', the contingent nature of existence. They read to better themselves, in a non-material sense at least.

That is why there is never very much discussion about the choice of the next novel: there is a tacit agreement that the book must have content. As Randolf Pellikaan says, there are simply standards. And limits.

So none of the stylistic antics of postmodernism, with its frivolous focus on the limitations of language, and ab-so-lute-ly no chicklit. (Randolf once picked up this frivolous term from a student and since then has used it to denote more or less everything he doesn't like.)

And none of the standards they have laid down over the years has ever subsequently been consigned to paper, divided into for and against, and yet they are intuitively clear to everyone and don't cause problems; in the friendship that has built up over the years, most differences in taste have been smoothed over into consensus. So that the only female member the book club has ever had, Gabrielle, has no objections to Randolf's jokes about ladies' literature and chicklit, quite the contrary: as the senior partner in an accountancy firm she herself has a healthy dislike of everything that smacks of female ingenuousness.

In order to be able to judge things objectively Gabrielle has read some chicklit, a deep-pink-coloured novel about a group of women who jointly ran an internet business in second-hand haute couture, but the flirtations, the shoes, the precious secrets, the grubby intimacy of the girls' night out — she knows nothing of all that and doesn't want to be in any way associated with that mindset. And OK, it's possible that as a young woman she herself may have been predestined for such romanticism, but after working her way up from her academic environment into the world of accountancy, Gabrielle is very particular about her reputation as an unyielding and hard-working partner.

She knows that others think differently. At the Amsterdam branch of her firm they had a poet on the payroll for a year — and he read 'A Jury of Her Peers' with them.

It confused her. Because while that classic story by Susan

Glaspell, about two women in an old-fashioned kitchen in Dickson County, is undeniably a book about humdrum female lives, it still for some unknown reason stayed in her mind for weeks. It may be that she was touched by the description of that farm on a lonely March morning, with a fierce north wind blowing outside; when the glass jars of bottled fruit have frozen and cracked on the shelves in the pantry and Mr Wright's body is discovered in the bedroom upstairs.

The style of the story appeals strongly to the senses – you hear the wind whistling through the crannies in the house and you see the shabby furniture in the kitchen in front of you, the fire in the stove that has gone out, the dirty towel by the sink, the paper bag of sugar, the pieces of material to make a quilt. Somewhere upstairs the sheriff is going round with the district attorney, looking for a motive for Mr Wright's murder.

The two women are in the kitchen. The sheriff's wife, Mrs Peters, and the neighbour, Mrs Hale. They look round, clear up a bit, and gradually penetrate the wretched exis-tence of the woman who lived in this kitchen for years and must have been deeply unhappy and lonely. They can tell just by looking around. And so a conversation gradu-ally develops between these two women, who don't know each other, about that poor Mrs Wright, for whom they have had to pack a bag of clothes to take to her in prison.

Gabrielle smiled at the eternal contrast between the men, with their ponderous reflections on the law, and the women, with their simple stories of clean towels and home-made jam. She is intelligent enough to know why poets read such stories to accountants, and so she also smiles at how the poet sees her; he underestimates her, underestimates her emotional intelligence, her erudition, doesn't know that in the course of her studies she received a through grounding in the Platonic tradition of unity versus the Aristotelian tradition of diversity, the rationalists versus the empiricists, the tender-hearted versus the tough-minded; he thinks she's a bookkeeper. But although she has little confidence in the office poet's plan to sensitize her to the drama of everyday life, she is still gripped by the story of Mrs Peters and Mrs Hale, who as they rummage around in the kitchen find a sewing-basket with a dead male canary in it and so stumble amazingly on the real course of events leading to Mr Wright's murder.

'It's just as well the men can't hear us,' say Mrs Peters and Mrs Hale. 'Getting all stirred up over a little thing like a dead canary.' They are ashamed at the futility of their worries − as if the death of a little bird could ever be connected with such lofty matter as the pursuit of truth and the law. And even when the women put the sewing-basket with murdered bird and all into their bag, hence suppressing vital evidence, they do so as if it is completely unrelated to the legal quest being undertaken by the men in the other rooms of the house.

But well, the moral is plain enough and consequently the office poet laboured the point, so that the accountants should understand that crime is the result of murdered canaries and bad marriages, and is to be solved not with official forms and rules, but with sensitivity to domestic details.

Gabrielle later relates her experience as a reader, playing it a little for laughs, rather uncertain whether she hasn't been too sentimental, but the circle can't even see the charm of her legal anecdotes. The discussion soon moves on to the establishing of the pursuit of truth and evidence.

Only Randolf knew Susan Gaspell's classic story vaguely from a handbook on Law and Literature, and out of a faint sense of loyalty to a colleague he feels the need to make a friendly gesture to Gabrielle; he feels she has introduced the story into the discussions of the book club to make the female voice heard, and because he wishes to acknowledge its importance, he turns to Coetzee's novel *Disgrace*.

With relief, Gabrielle takes over the theme of rape in South Africa from him. That is violence on their intellectual level. Canaries are for the lower social orders. Sewing-baskets are for women.

2

The journalist Victor Herwig receives a phone call. It is the PA of the chairman of some umbrella organization, something with Arbo or board in it, Victor can't hear properly. The secretary has rung the paper, has been put through to Victor by the press room, and now asks Victor for his home number so that her boss can ring him back without involving the paper.

'He'll get right back to you.'

Now Victor has lost his concentration. He gets a cup of coffee, sits down again, looks at the telephone next to his computer. The man doesn't call. Men like that never do. Somewhere in the higher regions of society there lives a caste of important men who give their PAs pointless assignments, and those PAs have pointless conversations with innocent employees elsewhere, who then spend the whole day pointlessly waiting and pointlessly drinking coffee, until they realize that they're not going to be called back. After ten minutes Victor started swearing.

Because he didn't know what to do – he couldn't get

his thoughts flowing again, and had lost the shape of his own argument – he retrieved Ruth Ackermann's novel from under a pile of papers and leafed through the clippings that he had gathered in the meantime on the book and its author; he read again what Kiki Jansen had to say about Ruth Ackermann's European tour:

Wherever Ruth Ackermann goes, her fame has travelled ahead of her; readers recognize themselves in this book for many different reasons; it's hilarious, but at the same time, and that is the other side of the flipside, it gives a glimpse of the world of the psychiatric patient. A combination of modern youth culture and madness: *Bridget Jones* meets *One Flew over the Cuckoo's Nest*.

'The other side of the flipside,' grinned Victor.

He sat back in his chair and lit a cigar, an Ashton Virgin Sun Grown, from a box he had once bought for far too much money and had lugged around with him for ages and now had thrown into the back of a drawer in his desk. They were probably stale by now, but fortunately he didn't know enough about cigars to taste that.

He looked again at the photo of Ruth Ackermann and tried to recall her as she had been at sixteen. How old were they when they left school? Eighteen? He was nineteen, and so he hadn't thought about Ruth Ackermann for at least eleven years, and he was ashamed of that now, because he could remember her very vividly in her isolation, the deep misery that, looking back, indicated the onset of madness. Not that her misery had been constantly in evidence, she had always seemed well-composed, but he had once found her when she was obviously undergoing a crisis and it reflected badly on him that he should only now, years later, become seriously interested in the truth of the matter.

They had been, it occurred to him, a generation that had decided to do less well than their parents, because the spirit of the age demanded it. As if by agreement, they were as blasé as possible, didn't know much, pretended not to understand anything – and everyone seemed to keep to that agreement, except Ruth Ackermann, who was brilliant at a time when it wasn't the done thing, who translated Ezra Pound, who read Thucydides as if it were the newspaper. For that reason Victor was intimidated by her presence at the back of the class, but apart from that he had never given her much thought, having other things on his mind, the injustice in the world, his musical career that was on the skids, and he had only spoken to her at any length in the fourth year, when they had to report to the deputy head because they had both been hours late that morning.

'Were you late too?' said Victor, for something to say, now they were sitting opposite each other in the otherwise deserted school office.

'Yes,' said Ruth Ackermann.

'Why?' He was determined to be friendly with her, and obviously she was determined to be the same, since she snapped awake from her lethargic state and suddenly looked animatedly at him. At the time he had not been surprised by her frankness, but now he wondered what mood had led her to discuss what had happened with a boy she hardly knew.

'My mother committed suicide last night. That is, she tried to throw herself in front of a train, but she failed. We've been trying all night to find out whether she'd have liked to succeed, and we didn't get to the bottom of it. But anyway, she made an attempt. An attempt at suicide.'

'Why?'

'Because of everything.' And when Victor grinned rather sheepishly, she said by way of explanation: 'Josefien de la Mar? Actress? Jumped out of the window and left a note on the table. "Because of everything." Great suicide note. Because of everything.'

Victor was in the midst of puberty and the hormonal changes that directed and modified his brain had already communicated the fact that cynicism was OK, a sign of adulthood and of being equipped for the world. But though he reacted with an obligatory laugh to the explanation of the girl who sat imperturbably on the bucket chair opposite him, he still had the feeling that something was going on, something that he had raked up by accident and for which he had become responsible. He didn't know if he was supposed to contradict her cynicism, but decided at the time that there must be grown-ups around her who had matters under control. Ruth had meanwhile continued her train of thought and kept the conversation going.

'"Because of everything" is at least better than "because of nothing". That would be pretty shitty. If people ask: "Why did she commit suicide?", and then to hear that it was "because of nothing". Not exactly a crushing farewell.'

'Unless of course someone were walking under the window at that very moment.'

'What? Oh yeah. Crushed by Josefien de la Mar.'

'All your life you've hated Josefien de la Mar. "I can't stand Josefien de la Mar, I wouldn't want to be seen dead with her." And then: wham!'

'What a way to go,' said Ruth, rounding off the sequence.

They were silent for a moment.

'They might put a coffee machine in here,' said Victor.

'Yeah.'

With his right foot Victor pushed off against the wastepaper bin, a metal basket bolted onto a base plate. The wastepaper bin held firm and Victor tipped back a little. But his chair was too secure on the bar to be able to lean back properly in it.

'So,' he said. 'Your mother was standing in front of the train.'

'Well,' said Ruth, putting things in proportion.

'What?'

'She was standing on the rails. The train hadn't arrived yet.'

'Held up?'

'Something like that.'

Victor took his foot off the wastepaper bin, and because of the recoil shot unintentionally forward a little. He pretended the sudden movement had been intentional and sat half bent over, with his arms on his knees. There was something else he didn't understand.

'But what were you doing there?'

'She'd called me.'

'But she was standing on the tracks. Or does she have a mobile phone or something?'

'No, before. She'd rung before to say she was at the station and was going to jump under a train. She thought it was good manners to let me know.'

He ignored that facile joke, which was too forced to impress him and too slight to mask the gravity of the situation. He'd become interested in the whole situation in an extremely practical way.

'How did you get there so soon?'

'Bike.'

'You cycled the whole bloody way? In your pyjamas?'

'No, of course not in my pyjamas.' She was obviously getting annoyed, because the anecdote that she had wanted to tell in two sentences was beginning to lose much of its charm now her classmate was taking it far too seriously.

'A quarter past twelve: time for the last train. My mother rings, I put a sweater on, jump on the bike, ride to the station. And when I arrive the police are there.' She sounded as bored as possible. But there was something that Victor didn't understand.

'So why were you so late this morning?'

'Because we didn't go home last night. The police had . . .'

At this point, late as always, the deputy head came running in with the speed of someone who has more important things to do than tick off adolescents. 'Ruth Ackermann,' he said, 'come with me.'

When she came out ten minutes later, after the deputy head had let her go, she said wryly: 'He's rubbed me out. Erased me.' She was intelligent enough to shake her head at once at her own feeble joke and had swallowed the rest of her words and disappeared with a barely audible farewell.

But the image had made an impression on his romantic mind and that was what he had seen later when he saw her walking around in school: someone had rubbed her out by accident and she was trying to find a shape. At the time he himself had been very pleased with that image, which gave evidence of his insight into human nature and the essence of things. But only now, looking back, did he realize how damaged she had been. So shocked, so deeply hurt that she was no longer capable of normal communication and had solved the problem by writing brilliant essays about the human will and making translations of Antonin Artaud, so that when it came to the crunch no one need worry about her.

What as an adolescent he had seen as domestic problems had in fact been a state of emergency, a war-zone, a catastrophe; a few years later she had been sectioned and admitted to a psychiatric hospital, about which she had written a book that had won her international fame.

Why had he never asked her any more questions about her mother at the time? About herself? Looking back at the situation it seemed incomprehensible that he should have simply let the conversation pass.

It was six months later, he had just turned seventeen, when he was walking down the street with his mother and they bumped into Ruth Ackermann and his mother asked: 'What's her name again?'

'Ackermann. Ruth Ackermann.'

'No, not Ackermann. Is she called Ackermann? No, I'm sure her name . . . come on, what was that man's name? Well, I expect they'd change it after all that fuss. God, what a mess.'

At the time he hadn't reacted, because he didn't want to appear interested in a girl in his class in his mother's presence; that sort of thing would have led to great hilarity at home and weeks of teasing and snide remarks from his younger sisters. Yet the mystery had remained in the air and now it had returned. What fuss with her father? What had happened to Ruth Ackermann's father to make her mother want to throw herself in front of the train and Ruth walk around the school as if she had been rubbed out?

He could ring his mother and ask what she still remembered. But he didn't want her to arouse her curiosity and have her ask searching questions, and so he rang his father; for although his father certainly loved his children dearly, he took scarcely any interest in their lives and so you could talk to him with complete frankness. Victor rang his office – where he was as usual absorbed in such mysterious tasks as start-ups and greenfield projects – and interrupted him in a meeting.

'Hi, what is it?'

Victor decided to keep it short.

'Oh yes,' said his father. 'The chemist. Or, I could be wrong, I'm not sure if he was a chemist. At any rate he was the manager of a chemical plant. The manager. Yes. His name was de Winter. His wife's name was Ackermann.'

'Do you know anything else about him?'

'No. Actually I don't even know what's become of him. After that business on Haiti I never saw him again.'

Victor didn't feel like prolonging the conversation and decided to pretend he knew all about the business on Haiti. He could track down gossip and disputes without his father feeling obliged to show an interest in his son's investigations. He now had enough search terms. So he summarized the facts aloud again, got his father to confirm and repeat them and after a few more casual remarks he ended the call.

What was it that prevented him from searching further right then? Why didn't he start the search engine immediately and look for de Winter in his archives? Perhaps he sat there so undecidedly because he was on the point of learning something he didn't want to know. Because he had wanted to meet Ruth Ackerman as the successful first-time author she had become and not as the centre of shady dealings on Haiti.

His cigar had gone out; he immediately relit it, and with the cigar in the middle of his mouth, which gave him a feeling of professionalism and detachment, he began searching using the few catchwords his father had given him. The search didn't take long, the search terms produced thousands of hits and Victor chose one at random, so that he became the first to read a report on the website of some legal investigators.

> In the Bloem affair [it said] director E. de W. of Bloem
> BV was personally involved in the purchase of the
> consignment of contaminated glycerine which was
> then sold on to Haiti. Journalists have managed to
> obtain documents showing that E. de Winter himself
> conducted the correspondence on the sale. The corre-
> spondence in question contains among other things a
> rental agreement between de W. and a storage company
> in the port of Rotterdam, where the glycerine was
> stored by Bloem BV before being shipped to Haiti.
> At least eighty children died on Haiti as a result of
> the contaminants in the glycerine.

Victor exited the screen and at that very moment, almost an hour and a half after his PA had announced him, the board chairman called to invite Victor to a private meeting, and after that phone conversation Victor would have liked to have continued reading about the Bloem affair, but he didn't manage to for the rest of the day. He didn't manage to until the middle of the night.

3

Teresa had taken John to Washington. That is, she took him to the airport in his own car – he had already given his chauffeur the rest of the week off – and he sat beside her, with his seat tilted right back and the phone raised in front of his face. Phoning, humming, bleeping.

That phone had been worrying her for a while, and she wondered whether without telling her he was perhaps in contact with another world, somewhere far removed from the village and things. Because that incessant stream of reports that came in might of course be connected with his work, but more and more often she would find him in the middle of the night with his feet on the table, his mobile raised right up to his face with both hands, like a child with a Game Boy.

She became convinced that he didn't use this phone for business communications: since she had started paying attention she had discovered that he had two different phones and used the black clamshell model for bank business and the green candy bar one for the strange, mysterious bleeping.

And no, it wasn't that she suspected him of having an affair or going in for telephone sex. He was too relaxed and cheerful for that. But she began to suspect that he was playing games. That he was absorbed in a helicopter race against students in Finland and the United States. Or that somewhere in the solar system he was building factories on his personal planet, called Armazon. Or was competing with other solar systems in the hope of upgrading his people to a higher level.

So as not to feel totally excluded, she had enquired about the things that people did with each other in cyber-space, and it had reassured her that many players were grown-up like John, with regular jobs and a respectable social life – not outcasts. Not weirdos who had to make do with a fantasy world for want of a better one. She decided she might as well resign herself and not interrupt him with her own foolish concerns when he was obviously in the middle of purchasing a spaceship with a more advanced protective shield and a bigger hold than his last model.

Today he was wearing a new dark-red tie with strange primitive-looking symbols, most probably, Teresa thought, connected with his people on Armazon, whom he had to save from a collision with another planet.

Since she had become curious about his telephone traffic she occasionally wondered what else he was involved in. She knew that on his long foreign trips he occasionally kept his laptop in the hotel cold store, next to the grape-fruit and remains of the wedding cake. At least, that was where she had once found him when she rang and he asked in an adolescent impulse what she was wearing—

'And what are *you* wearing?'

'Lots, I'm in a cold store.'

'Can you get a signal?'

'Oh yes, I can get a signal.'

And in that way she knew that he was either lugging very old-fashioned gadgets around with him, or else ones that were so new that she still didn't understand why on earth they had to be kept at the right temperature in a cold store.

This morning he had walked to the terminal with his usual, hurried stride and given her a last brief jovial wave before disappearing through the door. Teresa raised her hand and drove off.

That morning Victor had travelled to Groningen. He'd thought he would be occupied all day chairing various discussion groups on global economics and the Social World Forum, but when he arrived he found the meeting had been cancelled. In the chaos they had forgotten to let him know, which would undoubtedly lead to the firing of one of the secretaries, so that he now had a free day and didn't know what to do with it. He wandered through the town for a while, had lunch at the museum and at about two o'clock decided to call Teresa. Having no car, since he'd taken the train from Amsterdam, he was forced to study the complicated rail connections to rural areas, and calculated sulkily what time he could be at Teresa's if he left now and changed at Utrecht for the slow train. She could pick him up from the station, and then he'd be there by early evening, and perhaps, if she wanted, they could have a bite to eat somewhere later.

At home in her study, Teresa had just put down the telephone and was looking with horror at the spider on the wall above her desk, which was too large to be spared, requiring her to get a vacuum cleaner – when the telephone rang again.

'Heigh-ho,' said Victor, and she already recognized his trademark greeting, which he always said twice and which in his case seemed to be the equivalent of the customary two kisses.

And although the 'heigh-ho' cheered her up, she hesitated for a moment before accepting his proposal, since she'd intended to devote the afternoon to her mail, making and fixing appointments, and she couldn't keep idling her time away with Victor. But as she looked up reflectively she saw the spider advancing slowly in her direction and the contrast between an afternoon alone at her desk and an afternoon outdoors with Victor was so great that she said yes, hung up, fetched the vacuum-cleaner and then set frantically to work to get as much as possible done in the little time remaining.

Teresa saw Victor standing on the pavement outside the station. With three days' growth of beard and his usual scruffiness he had a kind of all-weather, endearing bear quality: a quiet and calm she never saw in John, because

John was always alert, always on the go, intense and heading for something. She was suddenly unaccountably moved by this strange guy who was standing there waiting so confidently for her. She beeped and Victor ran over to her. 'Nice car,' he grinned, jumping in with both feet virtually together.

'John's.' She let the clutch in fast, hit the floor and pulled away in a tight arc, so as not to give the impression she couldn't handle the car.

'Does John let you drive his car?'

'Only today. I had to drive him to the airport this morning. He had a weird morning. There's some charitable organization that John's on the board of, and there's a problem. He was calling and emailing all morning. So he was a bit behind schedule and I drove him.'

'Yes,' said Victor. 'A big hassle. Some journalist found out that the outfit has used funds for other purposes than those intended. And now John's board wants to get the embarrassing revelation into the papers as soon as possible, because Hajenius is ill.'

'Who's Hajenius?' asked Teresa.

'Green Party spokesman on development aid. He'll ask questions in parliament when he gets to hear of this, but he can't because he's got flu. So John wants the news made public as soon as possible, before Hajenius is back on his feet and makes a nuisance of himself.'

'Oh. So that's the way it goes,' said Teresa. 'Strange.'

'Yes, my dear, that's the way it goes.' They were driving through the fields and Victor watched the cows delightedly for a while, but then decided the car was more interesting after all. He inspected the dashboard, switching the air-conditioning on and off, opened the glove compartment and took out a Sony dictaphone, which he immediately flipped open to see if there was a tape in it. 'So, are you still sleeping with John?'

'No, John's far too posh for that.' She glanced sideways to see what he was getting up to with the tape. Victor reinserted it obediently in the machine, put the machine back in the glove compartment and closed the compartment. Teresa looked straight ahead. 'That journalist phoned me – Kiki Jansen,' she said.

'Kiki Jansen! Queen of the mixed metaphors! Fine.' He opened the ashtray. 'She's got wind of the dirty linen and thought that you'd spill the beans to her.'

'Hm? I'm not going to spill any beans to her. I simply told her the facts.'

'And they are what?'

'That I find it impossible to remember Ruth Ackermann. So that for any inside information she should contact the school or the head, or something. Or the other pupils, whose names and addresses I don't have either.'

'Bravo. That's the spirit. And did she believe you?'

'Why shouldn't she?'

'Why should she? Of course it's incredibly odd that you should be in the same class as someone for six years and then not be able to remember a thing about them.'

He tugged at his safety-belt, to give himself more room, and then sat back in his seat. Let's drive to Paris, he thought. That was what his father always used to say when the mood was good and the weather sunny. Let's drive to Paris. He looked across at Teresa, who fifteen years ago in class had seemed so damned untouchable, and whom he was now sitting next to in the car as if it were the most natural thing in the world. Still untouchable, still miles away. Let's drive to Paris.

'What did you think of the book?' he asked.

Teresa grinned. 'Yes,' she said, 'Yes, I thought it was very good. It really made me laugh. And yet it was sad. Nicely written. Just a bit difficult to disentangle what was real from what existed only in the imagination of a psychotic girl.'

'That didn't matter much in this case. Come to that, it doesn't matter much in general. The point is what people regard as real. At least I've always used that as the implicit motto of all my articles – the Thomas theorem of the sociologist W. I. Thomas: "If men define situations as real, they are real in their consequences."'

'That sounds very postmodern. I'd still like to know whether something actually happened or not.'

'And how do you find that out?'

'That's where you come in. You're the journalist, not me.'

She shot down a side-turning. Victor recognized the house where the head of their school had lived.

'Do you mind if I drop in at the optician's? I need to collect my new sunglasses. They're broken again.'

Victor grunted. He closed his eyes and let himself be driven down the avenues of his youth by the most beautiful girl in the school, who had promised to have dinner at home with him in a little while. An hour ago he had still intended to talk to her, and show her the internet articles on the Ackermann affair and the scandal he had tracked down, but right now he decided to hold his tongue for an hour or two. If it had been about the affair, he could just as well have emailed her, he realized now. Obviously he had meant to see her from the word go. So why not enjoy it now he was here!

'It's here. Do you want to come in, or will you wait outside?'

Victor settled himself on the bench outside the shop. It might take a little while, said Teresa, because they were always busy and the frames needed adjusting, and heaven knows what, and Victor nodded and closed his eyes. Teresa swept into the shop and Victor fell asleep immediately.

When he woke a few minutes later, a group of fruit-flies were swarming around his head, causing the passers-by to look at him in some surprise. I'm in a bad way, he thought, the flies are already swarming round me. But there was nowhere to go. He had to wait until Teresa came out of the optician's, and as he couldn't just wander the streets, he stayed where he was.

His short moment's unconsciousness had done him no good. The shopping street with its ancient chestnuts looked as if an indistinct cloud had passed in front of the sun and he was suddenly not sure whether Teresa would shortly emerge from the shop. He looked around and shivered. Since he had returned here a few weeks ago for the first time in years, something about the village had changed. It was connected with Teresa, and with Ruth Ackermann; it was connected with the hole in the ozone layer that caused the spring to pass faster and the blossom to fade faster; it was connected with an unexpected surge of longing, with hormones, with morality, with John.

The last time he had been here he had met John. A few days after his reunion with Teresa in the café he drove back to the village, and brought her a copy of *The Summer of Canvas Shoes*; had she already bought a copy? No, she hadn't bought a copy, thanks, come in for a minute and you can meet John. And in the half-hour he had spent in that big, intimidating house where his old classmate now lived, John had sounded him out expertly and then urged him to join the board of the music association. As Victor sat here on the sofa, he stretched his arms along the back, left foot crossed over right. No, he decided inwardly for the umpteenth time and with profound irritation. No, there was no way he was joining the board of that shitty music association, to let himself be humiliated by soloists coming to the provinces for a trial run. He retained a little of the awe he had felt for music in his childhood. He hadn't sunk so low that he was going to join a board to count money, when he had once been destined for something great.

With his eyes closed he thought of the stalls you can see in markets abroad, with the chicken that plays noughts-and-crosses and always wins – in some way the rules of the game always hinge on something other than you in your innocence imagine.

Victor, who had gone to high school to find out the meaning of the words SCANIA VABIS on the back of lorries (danger, may swerve, said the Latin teacher), hadn't devoted much time to his studies apart from that, but had pinned all his hopes on improving the world and on a musical career, both of which aims had eventually come to nothing. He had at the very least an aptitude, maybe even a talent, for music, but his hands couldn't keep pace with his musical intuition, and what good was the precise musical image in your head if your fingers weren't capable of translating that image into the right finger positions?

In the past, before he had lost heart, he would look in horror at the macho types from the student orchestras, the neighbours' sons, studying medicine, who practised cello-fingering on the lapels of their jackets. The low double fingerings on their belts, the fast runs along their shirts, the flageolet tones under the knots of their ties. In performance they would always have the right fingering, the right-wing shits, their bows dangling from their eye-specialist's fingers, their scissor-shaped, scalpel-fingered heart-surgeon's hands. To avoid humiliation he had preferred to consort with the trombonists, who played their parts without any other pretensions, packed their trombones in their cases and departed to the bar to drink beer and immediately forget the performance.

He still had a preference for unpretentious conversations. I'm a simple person, he sometimes said to himself, I use my intelligence in order not to make myself more complicated.

Recalling the conversation with John about music, the rage flared up again. Yes, most people he knew liked classical music, they sighed at the *Hohe Messe*, they wept the moment they heard the *Requiem*; but all things considered, what good did that do the world? If you examined people's behaviour it wasn't their musical sensitivity that most struck you, but their wickedness, or perhaps not real wickedness, but a rancid scum of hypocrisy, lack of concern, superficiality and sneering *schadenfreude*. If you tried to fathom human behaviour, you had always to keep that thought at the back of your mind. But some people have no back to their minds. Who was it who had once said that about Nixon? Said what? Who had said what? Kissinger? Yes, it was Kissinger who'd once said of Nixon: 'Some people have such a thick skin they don't need a backbone.' Some people have a kind of fender in front of their faces, and so don't need a back to their minds.

Victor was now convinced that Teresa wouldn't be coming out. And even if she did, she wouldn't be able to save him from the raging storm rising in his head, that was not only to do with John, but also to do with the Bloem affair, on which he had gathered information he would have to keep from her, because she was too innocent.

Victor had thrust his head forward, as if he could hear all the misery in the world. Not only had his musical career failed, but improving the world had come to nothing. Teresa had teased him endlessly about it the last time in the café, reminding him of the plans he had made, at the front of the class, when he should really have been translating Tacitus, or separating compounds with low molecular masses, or whatever strange assignments they had had back then. Victor had laughed about it himself at the time, but today his mood was grimmer and he looked around with an implacable gaze.

Might he have thought during his turbulent years abroad that everything was better in his home village? It was as big a mess as anywhere else. Now he had thrust his head forward, he could hear, some way off in the rural area, people trying desperately to protect the fields and woods from the guerrilla tactics of the authorities, who wanted to flood them, leave fallen trees lying around and uproot exotic trees, and from the whole process of nature purification that xenophobic forestry officials and environmental civil servants wanted to implement; a coup by the conservationist organizations that had seized power – nongovernmental power – and wanted to submerge the country in a primeval state without democratic controls, without any controls, so that all that would be left would be mud and oak trees with toad-trails and badgers. And all the ecologists did was write reports about the primal scream of the landscape that desperately needed to be heard here – it would take a hundred years, a hundred godforsaken years before something of the ecological richness would return to those areas that had been allowed to run wild, and until that time you would have to spend a hundred years fighting your way through the monotonous destitution of weeds and undergrowth. The primal scream of the landscape! Megalomaniac talk by conservationists with purification agendas.

At the ministries there were two opposing camps, said

Victor's inner voice to anyone willing to listen. On one side, the knights of the swamp put the true primeval cattle out to graze and then let them starve if nature required it, so that unsuspecting walkers suddenly came upon carcasses and vultures in nature reserves, hungry sheep with overgrown horns, sick primeval horses and wolves. On the other side, the infrastructure builders ensured that in the vicinity of those disastrous cesspools councils merged, village centres were linked by built-up areas, and the high-speed rail connection came ever closer, so that because of the increased scale, the integration and the rerouting of the provincial road network, the rural area was becoming urbanized at the speed of an express train and everything was closing in menacingly on this small piece of land that had been doomed to submersion by other civil servants.

In this way the Netherlands was turning into one great wilderness, criss-crossed by motorways and railway-lines carrying mysterious shipments, not only in the goods vehicles and goods trains that crawled through residential districts at night, but also in aircraft, which when they crashed immediately turned out to be full of polonium or beryllium; when you prodded something it immediately turned out to contain radioactive material, when you took a lid off a lava-flow of noxious decay came bubbling out. And wrapped round these mysterious movements, like a rose petal round a thistle, was the day-to-day life of people who took their children to school in the mornings, went to work and formed part of an ignorant world.

Victor breathed deeply and tried to calm down.

For as long as he could remember, he told his inner audience, the Netherlands had been a marriage without arguments. There were never problems on the surface, never any slamming doors, it was a *marriage de raison* without histrionics. And in such a marriage (as relationship counsellors would tell you without exception), in such a marriage there is no purpose. And now there were suddenly problems and nobody knew any more how to kick up a fuss, how in this packed country you could disagree without casting a cloud over relationships and muddying them and ruining them forever.

So the wrong problems came floating to the surface; if you drove through the country, from the coast to the German border, you would have covered a distance equal to that between two ranches in rural America. But whereas in America the drive from your place to your neighbours' place would be uneventful, with not a soul to be seen and country music on the radio, in the Netherlands in the short space of one and a half hours you drove past all seventeen million Dutch people, with their opinions, their disappointments, their reproaches, their hurts and neighbourly disputes, their outlet stores, their posters of politicians on the billboards, their tailbacks, their traffic fatalities, and their crosses marking traffic fatalities. Modern piety forfeited some of its dignity next to some busy motorway; the way that every religious ritual imported into the Netherlands immediately lost its innocence and became over-emphatic – because of all the seventeen million onlookers – creating a lack of humility and self-effacement, a lack of the breathing space that the simple rituals possessed elsewhere, amid vast expanses. The wrangling in the Netherlands was so loud, the swell so powerful and the uproar so fatally draining, that even immigrants kept a base in the homeland they had left; the hubbub was so exhausting that even asylum-seekers occasionally had to return to the country they had fled, to get their breath back.

It was impossible to make the world better. He had only to look for Ruth Ackermann's father on the internet for them to reappear in his memory, the administrators who messed up and immediately afterwards got another top job. He only needed to be back at work for two weeks for him to find them in the archives: the railway-lines, the runways, the residential developments, the shopping centres, all built with fiddling and machinations and completely egotistical indifference. He sat up straight and glared furiously at the health-food store opposite.

This age had a fascination with official terrorists and caricature murderers disguised as cartoon characters who stabbed their victims or planted a bomb under a train. But all those unassuming citizens could just go on murdering: the nurses and doctors who didn't show up to help dying children in centres for asylum-seekers; the family guardians who didn't respond to phone calls from stressed-out fathers with homicidal tendencies; the doctors who because of irreconcilable differences of temperament in their teams let their patients bleed to death; the deskbound murderers, the boardroom murderers, the counter and window murderers, who collectively had more deaths on their consciences than any terrorist cell, but were free to come and go as they pleased, pious Christians or right-minded humanists.

Not doing your job, keeping mum, looking the other way, appealing to regulations that you know are worthless, hiding behind bosses you know don't give a damn about the world. And then in your leisure time gathering to discuss the world on the basis of films and books, collectively judging murders from the past over coffee, that typically condescending view of the world, America, Germany, that extensive network of book clubs, whose members swoon over stories about the oppression of women in China and torture in Franco's Spain and at the same time can't be bothered to cough up a little more for fair-trade coffee or eggs from decently reared chickens, and are too pathetic to pay more at the butcher's, with the result that Dutch pigs – sweet, intelligent animals, with the sensitivity of young girls – are piled into camps, shipped off in livestock trans- porters and slaughtered in factories.

And all this filth, the endangered children, the servitude of animals, masked by a love of culture, so that the national museums and concert halls had gradually assumed the func- tion of moral whitewash organizations, where members of the cultural elite could show they had a soul and the next morning in their headquarters continue clinching lucrative deals with criminal regimes, civil servants who sold weapons to criminals, business people who claimed to be committed to world peace and meanwhile channelled Colombian drugs money to clean accounts. And no one ever breathed a word. Everyone tight-lipped, total collective dissociation, intensified by the silence of journalists who continued to make much of their devotion, but woe betide you if you asked them to stick their necks out, the whole conspiracy of secrecy, avoidance and denial and complete loss of empathy, all social pathology, a family of ego states in which the hurt child would always win out over the caring parent – collective pampered infantilism.

Victor Herwig sat on a bench and saw Teresa saying goodbye to the optician in the doorway. She turned and came towards him. She had put on her new sunglasses and was radiant in the sunlight that as if by magic was again filtering through the leaves of the old chestnut trees. He realized how his irrational thoughts had run away with him, and with all his might tried to come to his senses in the few seconds it would take her to reach him. Think snow, he said to himself, think spring rain, and he thought of the morning when he had met her, of the ducklings, the sawmill, the wooden floorboards, the photograph of Marcel Broodthaers with his camel. He thought of Marcel Broodthaers' poem about the world, 'Everything is egg. The world is egg. The world was born of the great egg yolk, the sun.'

Teresa smiled at him. He tried to stand up, and almost stumbled. We are the world! cried a voice in Victor Herwig's brain. We are the children!

In Teresa's kitchen, which was actually John's kitchen, a luxury operating theatre in stainless steel and white marble, everything looked so neat and tidy, and Teresa was so friendly and at ease, that Victor was ashamed retrospectively for his depressed thoughts and the futility of his comments. Him and his cogent observations. Him and his deep dialogues on Existence. And what was he going to do about it? Which people would he lead out of the wilderness? Victor Herwig. The poor man's Moses.

After the visit to the optician's they had gone for another drive, as Teresa wanted to show him the restaurant of an old castle; then they had walked along the fringe of the woods in the dusk, and now they were in the kitchen, where Teresa planned to fry up something quick, but she looked around her rather indecisively. Victor opened the fridge.

'I'll look for another job,' he said. 'But at the moment I'm a little late in the season. I'll have to wait for the next season.'

Teresa rummaged in a cupboard. 'There'll be nothing next season that you can't already buy this season. Except for blueberries perhaps.'

Victor didn't really understand the meaning of this mysterious remark. He thought she might be making an erotic allusion, but let's admit it, in his present state of mind there was very little in which he did not hope to discover one. He thought about it for a moment, but by then it was already too late to ask about it, because that would be attaching too much weight to the matter. He took lettuce and a bag of tomatoes from the vegetable drawer and got the breadboard out from behind the toaster.

'Don't use the breadboard for the tomatoes. John is very

particular about those things.' Teresa went into the hall, opened a door and he heard her descending the cellar stairs. He took a glass off the draining board and poured himself some wine from a bottle that was on the table, emptied the glass in one, poured himself another and started cutting tomatoes. Teresa came back into the kitchen with a large oven dish in her hand.

'Christ, Victor, you've used the breadboard!'

'Sorry.'

'Sorry won't get us very far. I'm not saying this for the hell of it. John is terribly proud of his chopping boards. He's got a jar of oil somewhere for rubbing into his boards. He'll notice at once if there are carbohydrates on the protein boards.'

'Well then. My mistake,' said Victor casually. 'But if you're not allowed to make mistakes, we'll never make any progress, tell John that.' He put the lettuce on the kitchen table, retrieved his glass from the worktop and sat down.

And while Teresa, with her back to him, started beating eggs, he reflected on the subject a little further. 'Our mistakes have traditionally been the only essential component of our identity. Because everything that we get right, all our virtues and merits, are actually virtues and merits of the gods, who implement their divine plans through us. But a god cannot use human frailties to realize his plans. That would be most unseemly, and so our faults are ours and ours alone.'

Teresa, who was putting plates, knives, forks and serving spoons on the table, replied absent-mindedly: 'So don't gods make any mistakes?'

'No, in fact it's highly doubtful whether the gods act at all. At least Aristotle wonders how you're supposed to imagine it: for example, how are you supposed to compliment the gods on the fact that they don't make mistakes? That would be cheap praise, considering how little they are inclined towards the vice and evil desires we human beings are prone to.'

Teresa now looked at him slightly more attentively and reflected carefully. 'So you can't reward a god either?'

'Neither reward nor punish. Someone who does nothing can't expect much response. Would you like some wine?'

'No thanks, I'm not drinking today. So the gods don't do anything?'

'Maybe not, and if they do nothing, we can't have opinions about them.'

Teresa turned on the hand–blender, made a terrible din for one minute and when silence returned summarized the conversation. 'So you *can* punish people, but not reward them, because their virtues are not their own?'

'Rewarding is a superfluous moral concept anyway. People aren't given a higher salary because of their high moral standing and they're not rewarded for their innate virtue: rewarding operates along quite different lines than morality.'

Victor felt as if he had just turned everything he had ever read into an unacceptable hotchpotch, but Teresa wouldn't mind, so he ventured a provisional conclusion: 'Man's character consists of the space allowed him by the gods.'

He realized that as far as she was concerned the topic had now been wrapped up. Unfortunately this little intellectual exercise had greatly increased *his* concern as well. Actually he needed to talk to Teresa about Ruth Ackermann's father, and while he kept putting off the confrontation, his mood suffered noticeably. He so wanted everything to have an aim and a purpose; perhaps he had been spoiled and had to learn to accept that he knew nothing about his fellow men or their behaviour. If he wanted simply to live like everyone else, and that was what he ultimately wanted, he would do better to resign himself to the fact that the world is both good and bad and that that is simply how things are, just as the world cannot be changed.

What he wanted now was to stay here and be reassured by Teresa, who knew nothing about all of this because it didn't interest her. He could simply be honest with her and say: 'I need help.' A few hours and a bottle and a half of wine later he had got to the point. 'I've missed the last train,' he mumbled scarcely intelligibly.

'I'll drive you home,' said Teresa.

4

Teresa had to go to a party with John. At Gabrielle's place.

'What Gabrielle?'

'Gabrielle from the book club.'

'Christ,' said Teresa, 'do we have to socialize with these people now as well?'

'A terrible ordeal. Come on, put on your nice suit from Germany and be friendly.'

That was why he'd married her, she suspected. Because she was convenient. Easily portable. You introduced her to the host, set her down somewhere with a glass and she came up trumps every time. And because Teresa herself was fully aware of the importance of this role, she had indeed opted for the Dior suit that she had bought on impulse in Germany: black, with frills on the pockets that she couldn't quite fathom, but oddly enough it looked great on her, making her look like Jackie Kennedy, John said, though she hoped she was more Wynona Ryder, but anyway, the effect was pretty astonishing and Gabrielle nodded benevolently to her when she entered.

'Gabi,' said Teresa. She knew Gabrielle liked that. It had an intimate ring. Thank you for inviting me, nodded Teresa. Thank you for coming, nodded Gabrielle. It all went well, and Gabrielle, pleased that Teresa had turned up in full regalia – you never knew with Randolf's daughter – immediately took her under her wing and determined to introduce her to as many people as possible this evening, so that they had a good impression of Teresa when she came up in discussion on a subsequent occasion. She manoeuvred her towards the living-room.

Teresa, who had never visited this house, looked around in dismay. The room surprised, no, overwhelmed her. Used to the functional distinction of modernism she was entirely unprepared for this exuberance of tones and shades: sofas covered in plaid patterns, in a strange combination of colours of which Teresa could not immediately decide whether they were grotesquely ugly or on the contrary very unconventional, crazily checked armchairs and heavy, ruby-red velvet curtains lifted up on either side by a twisted gold cord. On all the walls were still lifes, illuminated by brass lamps attached to bent brass rods. The paintings were probably authentic and quite old, Teresa guessed from a distance, but because she knew nothing about the genre and because the rest of the interior was alien to her, she couldn't possibly determine the quality of the work. She shook her head involuntarily. This wasn't the interior of a chartered accountant, but of a woman with a deep-seated desire for pyjama parties and romance on a tiger-skin in front of the fire. Gabrielle must have a hidden extremely frivolous side, a girlishness that Teresa had never previously detected.

'How do you know Gabrielle?' asked a young accountant. Teresa sighed inwardly. But the Dior suit immediately did its work, and while she looked round fleetingly for John – he was standing some way away in a circle of men he obviously knew – she started smiling and with practised ease launched into conversation with the young man.

How did she know Gabrielle? She had to think for a moment before answering, because she actually knew very little about Gabrielle, although she had known her for a lifetime. Randolf and Iris Pellikaan had dug her up somewhere in the village, as a trophy of solidity and ambition, but beyond the book club there had never been that much contact between the two families.

'Do you know her son Walter?' Fine, the young accountant had caught her and had no intention of letting her go again; if he went on like this she would be forced to say something aloof about her husband John over there: yes, the man with the dark hair and raised eyebrows, yes, that's my husband. But for now she replied willingly to the question about Walter van Dam, with whom she'd been at school. Yes, she knew him.

Years ago she'd once seen Gabrielle's son Walter walking down the street between two policemen, who were bending his arms back in a paternal grip. It had been a weird moment, because in a flash Teresa felt an obligation to help him escape, while at the same time realizing she did not know which side to take in this conflict. But she couldn't tell all that to the young accountant, so she said something friendly about Walter van Dam's artistic ambitions and also passed in silence over the last thing she had heard about him, namely that he had now been banned permanently from driving, because, so Iris said, he had attracted the attention of the police by driving through the city blind drunk at ten kilometres an hour, with his left foot stuck out of the window to check on progress. 'You're joking,' said Randolf.

The matter had been raised because Lucius had refused to act as an intermediary, which had led to some cooling off in relations between the friends, but that had blown over and Teresa had heard no more about it.

There was now no trace of such bickering to be seen in the rooms of the big house. Gabi had really gone to town. There were caterers and everywhere young men with trays and girls in aprons were serving glasses of champagne; in the background long tables with covered dishes and hotplates were set out. In the kitchen a stack of glasses fell over with a violent crash, and although everyone looked up and stared vaguely in the direction of the kitchen, no one really seemed to notice, except Gabi, who went into the kitchen smiling affably, and emerged a little later smiling equally affably, which gave Teresa an uncomfortable feeling. She didn't feel at home here, in this atmosphere of strict affability.

While Teresa listened to the young man as he explained how much he owed to Gabrielle, she suppressed the impulse to feel the sofas and perhaps even sit on them; she looked again at John and saw him still in his circle a little way off, with his eyebrows raised and his head bent forward a little so as to be able to hear what the others said. He seemed to be interested, but Teresa, having observed him on such occasions for a few years, by now suspected that his thoughts were elsewhere.

Marriage is not the place to get to know each other in depth. Teresa had gradually realized that she would probably never find out what he was thinking of at such moments. Because although she was used to conversations full of double meanings and hidden messages – she was fairly adept at finding the key to other people's secrets – she had few intuitions when it came to her husband's inner life. It was true that he seemed a lot more straightforward than most people she knew, but there was always that distanced twinkle, a kind of inner exuberance that she could not place. At first she had thought for a while that in company his thoughts wandered off to his youth or to Miles Davis, John Coltrane, Bob Dylan, or whatever those old fogies were called, but he wasn't that nostalgic, and apart from that there were the recent messages on the green mobile.

She had recently heard from friends about the internet games that she believed John was playing, and she had been told that huge sums circulated in the sale of planets that didn't even exist. But to tell the truth she did not see John as the kind of man who would build his kingdom through purchasing; it was more likely that he would try to show his leadership qualities by being brave and proactive. In Gabrielle's colourfully checked and richly upholstered interior she imagined him in his thoughts perhaps running through the wood disguised as a medieval knight while outwardly appearing to all those present in the full authority of his social position.

Teresa knew that she mustn't get in his way this evening. She would have to spend the next few hours alone, without a husband to give her a social identity. So she decided to do her best; she preferred not to disturb the rose-tinted image of the world that others might have and so she played the role of the somewhat naïve wife of a banking magnate; when the young accountant took her to the buffet, she ate as much as possible from the dishes, so as not to spoil the atmosphere of hospitality and friendship. As Gabrielle came in her direction with a couple she absolutely had to introduce her to, Teresa looked at the raspberries, lying in the dish like little animals, and found it pitiful to eat them.

As soon as she was able to separate herself from the chatter for a moment, Teresa walked out of the room into the conservatory. They were all nice people this evening, but my chrysanthemums are nice too, she said to herself rather wearily, and now she wanted to hear something sensible – she decided to turn the television on and watch the news.

She sank deep into the floral-patterned sofa in front of the television, immediately relaxed and in a domestic pose, with the hand grasping the remote held languidly in front of her, she channel-hopped; she no longer felt like news, watched a music channel with dancing teenagers, passed some crime series and wound up at a feature film on a desert. When she stopped to see what would happen, a deep-black African woman could be seen topless in a Bedouin tent. The woman was kneeling between the legs of a white man in khaki trousers sprawling back in a chair and Teresa kept watching her gleaming breasts, which heaved casually and proudly to and fro in the middle of the screen. Then the woman bent forward, opened the man's fly and with a practised movement stuffed a breast into his trousers.

Although she had stayed with the film out of a vague erotic curiosity – she was bored enough at this party to be prepared to descend to anything that was down-to-earth, the subconscious or her own lower parts – Teresa was completely unprepared for this move. She bent double and groaned audibly. The people standing talking nearby looked and John stared at her from a distance with some concern, so that Teresa pretended she had a coughing fit, switched to another channel and sat up while coughing ostentatiously.

Lucius came into the conservatory with a bottle of wine and two glasses and sat down beside her.

'Got a cold?'

'You know what it's like with these air-conditioned buildings. I've been indoors all day in the cold.'

'All that work is good for nothing.'

'I won't do it any more. I'm stopping work as of today.'

Meanwhile, she had recovered sufficiently to lean back again and gratefully took a few sips of the wine Lucius had poured for her. She thought for a moment while he surveyed her with amusement.

'Tell me, Lucius, do you know anything about Ruth

Ackermann? She was at school with me and now she's written that famous book, *The Summer of Canvas Shoes*. Have you read it?'

'No. I've heard about it. Haven't read it.'

Teresa was cautious. She adored Lucius, the only one of her parents' friends who didn't take himself too seriously, but for that very reason she didn't know how reliable and discreet he was, and because she was afraid he would immediately pass on her questions, she decided not to talk to him too openly about her uncertainties and concerns.

'I got the impression my father didn't want to talk about the book. Well, I can understand that it's not exactly your kind of book, but I had the strange feeling he didn't want to say anything about Ruth's family either. Surely he must have run into the parents at some time? At a parents' evening, for example. Do you know anything about it?'

'I've attended precious few parents' evenings in my life.'

'No, of course that's true. But I thought: perhaps you have an idea. My father's such a terrific snob, you'd think a famous author would be bound to interest him. Or maybe just the opposite. It's complicated.'

'Human society is complicated. Come on, don't get too worked up about it. Your father is a mystery to everyone around him.' He placed a confidential hand on her knee, and she felt herself calming down. 'Are you coming outside for a smoke?' he asked. 'Gabrielle has a wonderful back-garden. Terribly English. I don't know how she does it, but it looks undeniably lush. As if Capability Brown had peed so copiously in the rose-beds that the roses tower above your head. Come on, I think you'll appreciate it. Bring your glass and I'll smuggle the bottle out with us.'

And when Teresa remained pensive, he said: 'I'll talk to your father about the book by the Ackermann girl some time.'

In John and Teresa's home John's working hours determine the daytime–night-time rhythm. The moment the lights go out, the thermostat goes down. The heating is not turned off by an automatic timer, because John wants to keep control of what happens in the home. Sometimes, when John feels he's done enough for that day, they go to bed together. It doesn't happen often, but he can look forward to it for days, and when it happens, he knows that that he must fight his way through an ocean of serious conversation before he can become intimate, since he knows she has a youthful aversion to anything tacky. When he still thought she was like other women he had occasionally told her he loved her, but that didn't go down well. And he told her she was beautiful and then she looked at him sarcastically, lips pouting, yeah, yeah, yeah, she said, 'when the light hits me just right, I'm as beautiful as General Grant on a fifty-dollar bill,' and John, not recognizing the quote from a 1960s film about a Volkswagen Beetle, had just grinned rather sheepishly and then grabbed his mobile telephone off the bedside table to check his messages.

So now, late on Saturday, when they were at home in bed after Gabrielle's party, John began reading a book and waited to see if Teresa would say anything. And Teresa had brought up her own book and sat next to John in bed reflecting on her conversation with Lucius.

It only struck her now that that he hadn't replied at all when she had asked about Ruth Ackermann, but implicitly, she suddenly realised now, he had conceded she had a point. Obviously he must have a word with Randolf.

Next to her John closed his book with a bang and Teresa observed him from the side, as if having to weigh up the kind of man he was.

'I've got a suggestion for your book club,' she said.

'Aha,' said John, glad a dialogue had been opened.

'An old classmate of mine has written a book. Ruth Ackermann. It's called *The Summer of Canvas Shoes*. It would be nice if your club could read it, and perhaps you could help with setting up a public interview with her in the church, so it becomes a kind of village happening. I think it will be a big draw.'

'Let's have a look.' He picked up the book in front of her on the duvet and first of all took out the clippings, reports by the journalist Kiki Jansen on her journey through Europe with Ruth Ackermann, and newspaper reports that Victor had put in the book for Teresa.

'The novel *The Summer of Canvas Shoes* is a real cocktail of genres,' he read. '*Sex and the City* meets *The Magic Mountain*.' He looked enquiringly at Teresa. 'What's *Sex and the City*?'

'John!' she said.

'Well, I haven't a clue,' he muttered guiltily, and read on.

Deservedly a bestseller. Sales of hundreds of thousands worldwide. The young writer has turned her own stay in a psychiatric institution — the book is a hundred per cent autobiographical — into a humorous novel of manners. Modern life is presented in all its facets. Romance, stress, crime. But where other writers would have given the contemporary developments an apocalyptic undertone, Ruth Ackermann has packaged everything in an ebullient love story that goes spectacularly wrong. This writer doesn't preach, she entertains. Irony has been in her genes since childhood.

John folded the clippings grumpily. '"Has been in her genes since childhood", who the hell writes stuff like that?' he said.

He turned the book over, read the blurb on the back cover and then, growing bored, threw the whole lot onto the duvet.

'What *is* this? We live in a country divided by fundamentalism and racism, where people are being gunned down one after the other, where globalization and the nuclear threat are swamping us like a tidal wave, and all this woman can write is a love story?'

'A love story in a psychiatric institution.'

'In a psychiatric institution. Right. That's something at least, but I do wonder why this of all stories is doing so well at this moment. Isn't it a sign of escapism? Dancing on the volcano? Let's hope we'll gradually get some slightly more serious literature.'

'More serious literature?' Her voice sounded curt.

'Yes, it needn't all be in-your-face current politics, I'm not arguing for pamphleteering, but the idea of coming up with personal psychodrama at a time like this! That's pretty threadbare after 9/11.'

'Why is terrorism more interesting than someone being committed to a psychiatric institution? What on earth is so important about 9/11?'

'What?' said John, flabbergasted. He knew that the age difference between him and Teresa created a difference in perspective, but there were moments when he didn't understand her, had the feeling he didn't know her, couldn't follow her. 'You're joking,' he said.

'No, just go ahead and explain it to me,' said Teresa, and he could see she was angry now. 'What in God's name is so important about a group of idiots who crash an aircraft into a building? Obviously so important that we've been talking about it for years, that we're obliged to write books about it and see films centring on it, without there having been the slightest attempt to take action. All the intellectuals in the world at the same tea-party and still not one step has been taken towards solving the problems. It's because of poverty in the third world, says one. Fine, do something about it. It's because of the Palestinian question, says the other. Well, deal with it. But if you've no intention of changing your personal life one iota, you shouldn't go around sounding off about world politics. And I know' – she raised her hand to ensure he didn't interrupt her, as he was making as if to object – 'that it was a tragedy for New York and for all the families of the bereaved. That stands to reason. And I thought it was all terrible and still do. But now, years later, the loss is no greater than if all those people had died in a car accident.'

'The loss certainly is greater. Not only for the bereaved, but for the country and the whole world. Because what happened is politically charged.'

'That political charge means nothing if no political action is taken,' said Teresa in measured tones. 'The whole of so-called global politics is an excuse for people with no influence or power of decision-making to talk for days about things they can do nothing about, so that they don't have to talk about things they *can* do something about. Men like my father and Jurgen Lagerweij organize interesting-sounding literary meetings where they can raise their profile on the world stage, play with the big boys, and in that way it looks as if they're tremendously involved. In the know. There. When in fact they just continue with their own petty con-tricks: thwarting colleagues, tripping people up, outwitting the tax man, siphoning off money, giving advice to people of questionable calibre. The whole 9/11 thing is an excuse for the politically involved citizen not to bother about anything else.'

'Now now,' said John.

'Now,' said Teresa.

'You're underestimating the symbolic function, I fear. With the politically motivated attacks throughout the world there's more at issue than the event itself. That was true even of the assassination of Kennedy.'

'The assassination of Kennedy!' said Teresa triumphantly. 'Terrible too. Especially for his wife and children. But why shouldn't a young writer be allowed to write about her psychosis because an American president was assassinated in 1963?'

'She's perfectly entitled to,' mumbled John, but Teresa wasn't listening.

'Why are events of which we don't know the background, about which we have no information at all, because no one will ever tell us the whole truth, why is that kind of shadowy murder so much more important that my classmate's difficult life?' She was beginning to repeat herself, and when she realized this, she concluded her tirade with a sigh. 'Why is a man's life more interesting than a girl's?'

'You're posturing,' John ventured.

But Teresa turned her back on him. 'I'm not. I'm angry.' She picked up her pillow, threw it hard onto the sheet and lay down. 'I'm not hysterical – as Petra von Kant would say – I'm suffering.'

He knew that she could be angry and ironic at the same time, a frame of mind that he had never found in anyone else and that he admired.

'Come on,' he said, looking at her back with some alarm. 'You're right. I should show some interest in your classmates occasionally. Just you finish the book, and I'll read it afterwards, I promise.'

But she stopped answering. And not knowing what to do to bring her round, he angrily made the standard quip that Teresa used when she saw him reading his annual accounts and reports in bed: 'Will they find each other at the end, do you think?' But it sounded a lot less nice when he said it.

5

Steam was rising above the hedge. Teresa walked down the quiet avenue to her parents' house, and as she got closer saw the house disappear in the fog. In the odd stillness of the afternoon the fog seemed like the backdrop to an oracular play, the appearance of wood demons, Hamlet's father, or a Greek tragedy. The fog thickened, the roofs of the houses in the avenue vanished one by one and only the branches of the trees still protruded above the clouds. Teresa held her breath for a moment, but then quickened her pace, curious as to where the steam was coming from. As she made straight into the mist with determined strides, towards the neighbours' house, she saw a gardener with a high-pressure hose through the gate in the hedge; he had hung up some garden tools on ropes in the rose pergola and was hosing them clean vigorously and meticulously.

Slightly disappointed, Teresa walked through the wisps of watery mist and suddenly her parents' house loomed up with the clarity of awakening, the thatched roof glowing in the late-afternoon sun from the west, the windows catching the light and gleaming, her mother kneeling in the grass in the front garden. In this theatrical setting the kneeling figure of Iris, with her wild hair and sculpted features, looked even more imperial than usual – the Delphic oracle flashed through Teresa's mind – and her daughter stood looking at her for a moment with anxious awe, until Iris realized she was being observed and looked up.

'Oh, hello,' she said.

'Hello,'

'Did you cut your own hair?'

'?'

'It looks a bit wispy.'

'Thanks.' Teresa walked down the path, into the garden, cut a path through the lavender with her hand and waved a wasp away. How did Iris come up with those things so fast?

'Perhaps I'm going mad,' she said accommodatingly. It was the first thing that came into her head, and she was happy to explain. 'At least, I once read that it's a sign – that you're going insane with a broken heart if your hair is funny.'

'Is your heart broken?' Iris was working furiously repotting a geranium cutting, and when Teresa shook her head vaguely – er, no, no broken heart to speak of – she put down the pot with a thump, and said resolutely: 'That wouldn't be sensible. You won't find another man like John. You're not easy, you know.'

Iris had always taken a fairly orthodox tone with her daughter. There was, she felt, absolutely no reason to be untruthful with your children; untruthful, or soft, which was the same as untruthful. You helped your children get on better by preparing them for the less pleasant aspects of life. Teresa may have turned into an exceptionally beautiful woman, but that didn't mean that life would be easy for her; it was better if she were prepared for the setbacks that would unavoidably follow. So when Teresa was twenty Iris had twice urgently advised her to have a nose job, because with a nose like hers she could expect nothing but problems in the Netherlands. Think of your social contacts, she'd said, friends, marriage: what man would want to marry a woman with a more prominent nose than he had? For a while Teresa became uncertain, but after a few times she refused the offer once and for all; 'as Sophia Loren would say,' she concluded, 'I think I'll stick to my nose' – and in so doing she seemed to have shaken off Iris for a while. Since then Teresa pretended that the whole question of Iris's criticism and comment didn't concern her and so here in her parents' front-garden that was breaking into bud she ignored the remark about her difficult character for now and changed the subject.

'I'm not coming for dinner or anything. John and I are going to the opera in Amsterdam tonight. *Orpheus and Eurydice*. A friend of John's has tickets.'

'I don't know where you find the time.'

'Uh?'

'Well, you're obviously busy. But it doesn't matter, it's very nice you've dropped by today for a few minutes,' said Iris, firming the earth in the pot with both hands. 'I realize perfectly well you don't feel like coming, but we are your parents after all and naturally we like to know how you're getting on.' Teresa wandered off across the grass and Iris said to her back: 'I know you don't want to hear those things, but parents love their children. Even if it's not reciprocal. You'd know that if you had children.'

Teresa strolled down the path past the house. The garden was at its most beautiful now in spring, and at the front the house was smothered in climbing roses, which even this early were beginning to flower. The path was lined with young trees that Iris brought on in pots until they were given a place somewhere at the bottom of the garden. There was something reassuring, something completely safe about this spot, the avenue that hadn't changed in a hundred years, and that every year burst into flower with such enthusiasm as if everything were new and young again. She stopped at the side of the house to look up, to where the sunlight fell heart-warmingly through the leaves of the copper beech. Everything about this house was warm, and now that the earth too was beginning to warm up it was already pleasant here in spring; the early roses and early wasps might be harbingers of a terrifying climate change, but on this spring day the world was eternal and immutably beautiful.

Teresa was aware of her mother's critical gaze on her back. She knew Iris phoned her sister, who lived in a suburb of Athens, every week and for minutes on end complained aloud about her daughter, just to be able to invoke some kind of adversity *vis-à-vis* her elder sister, who hadn't had an easy life. And that was the truth. I'm the justification for her prosperity, thought Teresa, with a loving look at the house, which rose majestically, the rolling thatched roof raised slightly at the side to fit the round window of the bathroom. Every time she was alone and thought about her mother with a feeling of guilt, in the moments when she had shadow conversations with her, in which she tried with all her might to give her side of the story, explain things and exonerate herself, she came to the conclusion that what her mother most needed was a daughter with problems. And for as long as Iris felt the need for tales of woe, it gave Teresa carte blanche for every kind of misbehaviour; all it needed was for her to have an abortion. All it needed was for her to move to town out of sheer rebelliousness and start an affair with a junkie.

Teresa had now walked round the house over the gravel, which at the edges was overlapped by lady's mantle and wild violets, to the back-garden, and Iris had followed her, trowel in one hand, half-full bag of compost in the other.

'Are you staying for tea? The new cleaner is here; we're going to have tea now.'

'How do you like her?'

'I don't know. I'm not keen on her. She steals my shoelaces.'

'She steals your shoelaces?'

'Yes. The young cleaners I've had up to now have never touched my things, but this old one can't be trusted. She opens my drawers, and I'm missing another pair of shoelaces of your father's.'

'He's got shoelaces enough,' said Teresa.

'Yes, black ones, but the brown ones have gone.'

'He hasn't got any brown lace-up shoes.'

Iris ignored this remark. 'It's the last straw when they steal your shoelaces.'

'What good are your shoelaces to her?' said Teresa.

'How should I know?' said Iris. 'Perhaps she gives them away.'

In Teresa's view her mother was doing it on purpose and the slightly crazed edge to her conversation was a kind of coquettishness. Quite clearly Iris needed to play up her exotic origin to the hilt; even when Teresa was a child she had force-fed her on an endless stream of anecdotes about the Greek village of her childhood, a mythical place where life was infinitely grander than in the neatly tended municipal park that was the Netherlands. 'Your grandmother whisked birds off the windowsill just like that and chucked them in the pan,' said Iris to the eight-year-old Teresa, who was struggling with her plate of leeks; and Teresa knew that she should count herself lucky to have a supper that didn't have beaks and legs sticking out on all sides.

'Hm, I don't necessarily need tea, but I'll keep the two of you company,' said Teresa, who was a good daughter, better than Iris would ever realize.

'Fine, I'll call you in a bit, but first I've got to put the pots in the front-garden in position, otherwise they'll all just be left there till tomorrow morning.'

Iris walked back around the house with her bag of compost; Teresa sat down on the wooden bench in the back-garden that stood against the house and looked out over the lawn. The plot was at least fifty metres long and at the end made a curve, where it continued behind the neighbour's house; in that hidden section was a small summerhouse for storing the chairs in winter.

Perhaps it was nostalgia. Teresa sometimes thought that Iris must feel rather lost in this respectable village, with the respectable house and the respectable husband who had positioned himself perfectly on the graph-paper of his career and who made it a point of honour to become increasingly respectable as he grew older.

Fortunately she still occasionally went to Greece on her own for a few weeks. Just as John talked about 'snorkelling in the organization', Iris liked snorkelling in Greek society, with which she had long since become rather out of touch, and from which she always surfaced with new finds. Snatches of language, scraps of culture, the pearl of a strange political belief that she would never have thought possible.

She had remained so Greek all those years that in her own mind she would never become Dutch, but in Greece she stood out as the foreigner she had become, walking by herself in the interior of the Peleponnese, getting lost, after a long walk in inappropriate shoes, and being received like a prophet by two villagers who needed her help – to her great embarrassment finding she could scarcely understand them. In preceding years she had visited only her relatives and friends in the city; swallowed up by the familiar circle of the artistic and intellectual elite with whom in the dim and distant past she had studied. And so she had thought that she simply still spoke Greek. But now she had to conduct a rural conversation with these people that went further than ordering a salad and a glass of wine, she lacked the flexibility to translate the sounds and constructions back into her own idiom. She started stuttering. But the villagers had not been deterred and had pulled her along, one holding each arm; and because she thought it would provide a nice anecdote – what sort of thing could happen here anyway? – she accompanied them willingly to the little whitewashed cottage, which seemed to consist of a single room with a table and a couple of chairs, and a wardrobe and a bed, on which, once her eyes had grown accustomed to the dark, Iris saw a dead man.

'I still understood enough Greek,' Iris told her Dutch friends later, 'to realize why they had dragged me into the house. They wanted me to recite a prayer for the dead man, as they obviously didn't know the words of the prayers themselves, but I couldn't think of anything myself. I couldn't remember a thing. Anything at all. Should I sing something? Or pray. Of course I tried to wriggle out of it politely, but they kept insisting and then I made the sign of the cross a few times at random and sang the Dutch song "Where the white tops of the sand dunes". Crazy, but it was the only thing that came to mind.'

It really was homesickness, thought Teresa when she had listened to this story for the third time. Iris told the anecdote in order to have her position explained to her. Of course there was always a chance that on the basis of this story her friends would see her as a type, or as someone torn between two cultures. But that had not been the reason for her embarrassment. What she had felt was sadness, because she had become so alienated. And at the same time she had realized that as a Greek resident she would never have got into that situation, because the villagers would never have asked her the same favour; she would quite simply never have been in that place at that time.

'I'm glad you're here to keep us company,' said Iris, coming round the corner of the house. 'I'm just stuck here with that cleaner. She arrives every week in patent leather shoes and silk blouses. If you ask me she has ideas above her station. Anyway, I can't let her clean like that, so she just reads your father's books aloud to me.'

'Where is she now then?'

'In the kitchen. She's polishing the silver. As I see it, you can just about do that in a silk blouse. At least if you wear gloves.'

They walked towards the kitchen door. Teresa wondered whether the woman in the kitchen had been able to hear their whole conversation, but assumed that the cleaner was used to Iris by now, and so didn't worry too much; she went in with her mother, and found the new cleaner sitting polishing spoons at the kitchen table with an apron on.

'Have you any idea who Ruth Ackermann is?' asked Teresa, as they were drinking tea at the same kitchen table a little later.

'Why do you bring that up all of a sudden?'

'She's written a book. The odd thing is that I can't remember her; she was in my class, but I can't remember a thing about her.'

'You must ask your father about things like that. He knows more about the people in the village.'

'Yes. I had the idea that he might read the book with his book club.'

'He'll be home any minute.'

'Don't you remember who Ruth Ackermann was then?' Teresa asked again, just to make sure.

'We've got our own book club,' said Iris illogically.

'Yes,' said the cleaner animatedly, grateful to be able to join in the conversation. 'At the moment we're reading Mahfouz.'

Because Teresa realized how absurd her questions were in this setting, with a suspicious Iris and a woman she didn't know, she took up the new theme. 'Mahfouz: I've read some of him. What do you think of him?'

'Nice. Easy to identify with. The man thinks just like me.'

'That's impossible,' said Iris. 'He won the Nobel Prize.'

At this point the cleaner wisely held her tongue, and Teresa got up and felt embarrassed; she decided to wait outside on the bench for another ten minutes until her father arrived, and as she installed herself on it, placing her phone beside her and a packet of cigarettes with the lighter on top, she heard the cleaner take Mahfouz's book out of her bag and start reading about the alley in Cairo where Uncle Kamil sat sleeping on the threshold after sunset until passers-by woke him – 'Wake up, Uncle Kamil, and close your shop.' Teresa nodded off.

She woke up when she thought she heard her mobile

ringing, and as she jumped to her feet she thought the postman was coming down the path whistling, but it was a bird. In the distance the sky was darkening, and high in the trees above her the wind had got up, a sign there was bad weather on the way.

The garden was transformed now the sun had gone, and Teresa looked at the dark ragged fringe of the garden without recognizing a single individual bush or tree; all the contours had disappeared, the summerhouse looked particularly menacing in the dusk and something was lurking under the grim leaves. She packed up her things frantically and turned towards the house. Iris had turned on the lights, the house looked as warm and inviting as ever and Teresa relaxed. But she could not flee indoors, she had no time left to wait for Randolf, she couldn't stay and listen to Mahfouz, she had to go home and get changed for the opera. She popped her head round the door of the kitchen and said goodbye; she nodded apologetically to the woman who went on reading with rapt attention and did not see her.

She had come on foot and if she hurried she could get back on foot without getting caught in a downpour; she would have to hurry, not straight across the rose garden at the end of the avenue, which was the nicest route, but left down Sweelinck Avenue and then on down the high street. She walked briskly, but just as she was walking past the wooden car port on the north side of the house, Iris came chasing after her with a bag of pineapples.

Suddenly Teresa was annoyed by the childish gesture of the pineapples; she was annoyed at the fact that once again she hadn't been able to have a normal conversation with her mother, because the anecdotes, as always, had got in the way. 'New car?' she asked.

'New?' said Iris with a contemptuous gesture. 'You can see it is. It's just a jalopy. I haven't got a fast sports car like you, and I never have had.'

'If I didn't have such a rich husband,' said Teresa, 'who anyway is far too good to me, since I'm just a terribly difficult person, I would never have had a sports car.' The moment she heard herself talking, she didn't like the tone of her own voice.

But Iris had seen her daughter's irritation and patted her goodnaturedly on the shoulder.

'Holding on, letting go,' she said. She rummaged in her collar for a bit and extricated a necklace, which she took off and gave to Teresa. It was a silver chain with a translucent green stone on it.

'Here,' she said. 'If you wear this stone you first go through hell, all the pain surfaces, but in time you notice you're becoming more relaxed and that your mood is enormously improved.'

And just at that moment, when Teresa had given up hope once and for all, Randolf drove up. He got out, more youthful than ever – had he been on a sunbed? – well, he looked good, certainly. She waved to him, as she walked away from him, towards home. 'What,' shouted Randolf with histrionic indignation 'are you off again already?'

'I have to go to Amsterdam.'

'In this weather? Have you got a date with Pluvius?'

Teresa felt exhausted. She saw her parents standing in the drive, and the sadness of it all suddenly hit her so powerfully that she didn't know what she could ever say to either of them again.

III

The Choice

1

There are people who are filled with longings that are not their own. Morphogenetic memory fields extend throughout the world, and via eye contact, primitive forms of communication, primeval behaviour patterns like watching television or films, are transferred from person to person, from one continent to another and from the past to the future. If you consider this constant transfer of longings as a metaphysical question, and study its deeper foundations, you may ask yourself whether all those people who are mesmerized by the longings of others still have their own place in history, but *they* do not ask themselves that question. Quite simply because they are no longer interested in their own lives. They are consumed by the passions with which television has infected them, and there isn't a single longing left that they feel like pursuing of their own volition. That means they need no more history than they already have.

Through forces unknown to him, but which do not concern him, Lucius has become interested in the myth of America, in the upward mobility of American immigrants, and the optimism of the lower classes. He is mainly fascinated by the way the myth impacts on the purchasing power of the average television-viewer, who comes home late at night after working his umpteenth late shift and then watches shopping programmes to see what he wants, who stays up exhausted for an extra hour to see what he can spend his money on.

That is what interests Lucius hugely and what he admires: the American's willingness to live continually on the edge of personal bankruptcy. Three-quarters of Americans live from hand to mouth, from pay cheque to pay cheque, and that readiness to put one's own life in the balance for other people's desires is the foundation of the world economy. Because consumer confidence, that nervous notion that is the basis for investor decisions and government policy, is gauged completely from the greed of the employee who has just been paid and spends his pay on things he can't really afford.

That consumption either goes well or does not go well: individual experiences vary a lot. But whatever happens to individuals, consumer confidence is always restored and the world economy continues to grow. The optimism of the sum of all those individuals is a force that cannot be under-estimated. It is not the top businessmen, not the world leaders, not the thinkers who keep the bubble of progress intact, it is the millions, billions of nameless workers, the workforce, who with their irrational hope for a better life ensure the growth of capital.

There are dissenting voices. In his immediate circle Lucius hears sensible people saying that growth should be controlled and checked; he hears optimistic intellectuals talking about the mission of the West, which must assume responsibility and take account of future developments in the world; he hears pessimistic intellectuals counter by saying that only in the East do cycles of love and friendship last for hundreds of years, and in the West just for the span of an election, and that the West is now simply acting out of self-interest and will have to pay the bill centuries hence. But Lucius has no time for that intellectual discussion, he's not an economist and doesn't understand the basis of the predictions; what he does understand are the primitive passions he sees on television. The spunk, the chutzpah, the vitality of America.

Lucius is gripped by the vitality of the Americans. At night he hears American soap stars saying in television interviews that they once fought a bear; he sees models who grew up in the swamp and live on a diet of porridge and roast boar, and he'd love to have a woman like that as his wife, fragile and elegant, but hurricane-proof. Tough cookies, as Iris would say. And since he saw a documentary about the Cuban refugee Roberto Goizueta, Goizueta is his hero.

'Listen,' says Lucius to his guests this evening, when they are sitting in his kitchen over a bottle of wine. 'True, Roberto Goizueta fled Cuba with only one suitcase, but that suitcase contained over a hundred Coca-Cola shares. And so you can imagine how Roberto Goizueta, soon after his arrival in the United States, was appointed chief executive officer of Coca-Cola.' At this point the guests had better not laugh, because Lucius is serious.

'In his capacity as chief executive officer Roberto Goizueta, who in Cuba had been trained as a chemist, was one of the few people in history to be given details of the secret ingredient 7x. Subsequently a temporary shadow fell over his life when, for commercial reasons, he decided to start messing around with the taste of Coca-Cola. That proved a mistake.

'The day the bottles of "New Coca-Cola" arrived in the shops, America was plunged into deep mourning; a dismayed company psychologist reported to the top management that customers' emotions were identical to those of distraught parents mourning the death of a favourite child.' He always pauses here, but now the guests themselves have become curious. 'Go on,' they say. 'What happened then?'

'Well, Roberto Goizueta gave in. And the day he announced he would be returning to the old recipe an advertising plane circled company headquarters towing the message: THANK YOU, ROBERTO! That same day eighteen thousand people – consumers (or rather United States citizens) – rang the company to express their gratitude and others wrote Roberto letters with declarations of sympathy: "We love you for caring! You've given us back our dream! We are grateful you have made our hard lives easier to bear and have given us a confidence in ourselves to change things for the better." Not long afterwards, when Roberto Goizueta, the Cuban refugee, died far too young in Atlanta, Georgia, flags were lowered to half-mast in all McDonald's branches throughout the world.'

This is an American story, a typically American story about a typically American dream. At night in bed Lucius lies awake trying to think of a similar story for Europe, but there is simply nothing like it. Europe does have shared ideals, but no dream linked to the simple things of everyday life. There is no European folk-myth like the American folk myths about Coca-Cola, about the paper-boy, about apple pie, about the Statue of Liberty or about sport.

And then the cheerfulness with which Americans speak freely on television – 'national television'! – about their material needs and their financial debts. 'Christmas couldn't have come at a worse time,' says a housewife whose savings are gone. Lucius hawks that quote around for a few days, and can't find anyone who thinks it as fantastic a statement as he does, so he stops talking about it.

Not that such things can't be found in Europe. Not that a simple story like that cannot be told – but Europe traditionally resists such an everyday, physical, vital presentation. The European Union was set up to pursue abstract ideals – 'no more war' is most important of these – and at all levels in those old civilizations there seems to be a deep revulsion against translating such lofty ideals into tangible aims and comprehensible dreams.

That may also be because no-more-war is an ideal intrinsically opposed to any notion of conflict, and hence to any notion of competition, rivalry, comparison, individual identity and urge to stand out; Europe actually prefers to sit on the fence as far as possible. And Lucius recognizes that tendency to abstraction in himself, which is partly why he is so fascinated by the world of the opposite.

At night he sees the world of optimism parading past in reality TV and talkshows. In deep admiration he watches Oprah Winfrey as she tells viewers of her daily show about shopping in Paris; in an ostensibly matter-of-fact tone she describes how she and her entourage of friends and assistants were refused admittance to the Hermès store. Of course a terrible row blew up subsequently in America over that refusal, since the suspicion of racism is always lurking in the background, and heaven knows what got into the staff of the store. Fortunately the international management of Hermès reacts adequately, excuses are offered, ruffled feathers smoothed, and when it has all calmed down there comes the anxious question from the viewers to Oprah: 'Is it OK to go on buying Birkin bags?'

Yes, says Oprah.

'Yes, people. Go buy those Birkin bags. Shop, shop, shop, shop, shop!'

Lucius lets out a deep sigh of satisfaction. He sees the world of late-night television as a mystical church whose religious secrets he is gradually getting to know. Tucked up comfortably in bed he experiences in that unknown world not earthly but eschatological beauty. Not real time, but liturgical time. Shop, shop, shop, shop, shop, he mutters just before he goes to sleep.

2

Gabrielle is angry with Randolf. That expresses itself in a moral indignation that makes her voice rise higher and colours her cheeks light-red. She has seen him on television, where, as a regular commentator, he analysed a new privacy bill.

The performance shook her to her legal core and on finding the same attitude in Lucius, she came straight to the point. Her deep seriousness forbade her to show anything but rage now she was angry.

'How on earth can you make a comparison between your DNA and a bank statement? You know that's nonsense, why do you say things like that?'

'Well, nonsense is putting it very strongly.'

'Isn't it nonsense then?'

'All right, I do know it's all slightly more complicated than that, and personally I'm not a great believer in over-simplification, but by the time I've got across every nuance the camera has moved on.'

'And how terrible would that be if for once you didn't

proclaim your opinion while the camera was running.'

'That's a cheap shot. You know perfectly well that I seldom talk to the camera. I spend most of my time in decorous isolation in my study. But I'm having lots of airtime at the moment and when that happens it's handy if you can sort out a few things.'

'You always have lots of airtime and it's true you mostly use it for flying kites.'

Even if she had said this to someone else, and he had not been directly targeted, he would have found this a crazy remark, crazily naïve and busybodyish, but OK, he was willing to try to convince her of his good intentions, although his tone was now unavoidably a little sharper.

'If you can fly kites, but aren't prepared to, you needn't bother to try gaining influence over the way things are run in this country, because you never will.'

Gabrielle had heard the sudden chilliness in his voice and that made her even more indignant, but ultimately she was the one who had the right to be aloof in this matter.

'People who are good at power-games are not necessarily good at anything else,' she said in a clipped tone. 'As long as hunger for power is the only criterion for acquiring influence, the world will be ruled by people who have only one great talent: gaining a position. And once that position has been gained, their talent is exhausted. And so after that they do nothing but defend that position. They sit on a chair and hold on tight to the seat of that chair with both hands. Apart from that they don't do a damned thing.'

'My God! Gabrielle, come on – as if I only do my job to gain a position . . .' He was surprised at her language, which by her standards was unusually terse, and so in his astonishment he continued the conversation which he would otherwise have long since terminated. 'This year, entirely off my own bat, I've set up an interdisciplinary research group that for the next four years will be examining changing views of what it means to be Dutch. As if that isn't a commitment.'

'And what result is that supposed to produce?'

'I don't know yet, but at any rate we've been commissioned by the government to investigate nationality and Dutch citizenship.'

'Well what do you know? Piles of government money for researchers to investigate doors that any normal person can open without any trouble. Have views of what it means to be Dutch changed because of the advent of immigrants? Yes, we find after many years of research. They have. And probably when it comes to it, you lot won't have the decency actually to open that door, because these days no researcher can financially afford to be honest.'

Gabrielle surprised herself, as she wasn't that critical at all of scientific research, quite the contrary, and in any other company she would be generous in support of people striving to realize their ambitions, but the shameless vanity with which Randolf slid in front of the camera as soon as one came anywhere near him, the aplomb with which he presented the stupidest ideas as if they issued from age-old fountains of wisdom, all in her eyes made a mockery of the importance of reliable knowledge and objectivity. The aims that were central to her life, responsibility and account-ability, objectivity and reliability, were being held up to ridicule by Randolf's smug careerism, and, worse still, because he was so successful with his blatant lies, others were encour-aged to make as much fuss as he did to safeguard their own interests.

Gabrielle was proud of her subject. And there were devel-opments underway in the world that confirmed her in her pride and seriousness. On 25 May 2000, when President Clinton made a speech to the House of Representatives complimenting them on their decision to open up trade with China, a decision that was not only good for exports but also for freedom – 'we are exporting one of most impor-tant values: economic freedom' – she had suddenly realized with emotion that she was part of that, of the distribution of freedom across the world. That was a bit different from increasing prosperity or distributing wealth: it concerned a great moral benefit, which transcended ideological consid-erations about money and related more closely to human rights than to capital.

In the years following, a debate on values flared up in the Netherlands, but that was confined to trivialities and nowhere touched that important value to which she was committing her best efforts. The subsequent bookkeeping scandals at Enron and Ahold only reconfirmed her in her task: she must guard the procedures of the exercise of economic freedom, no more and no less. It was a happy mission, because it was a positive mission, one that many people she knew had found such a positive task for themselves. At the same time it was this deep-rooted mission that stopped her being too enamoured of the fashionable tendency among her clients to present her as 'our bookkeeper' (in the same way that they increasingly went to top restaurants to eat pea soup). She wasn't a bookkeeper, she wasn't concerned with the details of the daily muddle, but with clear lines of accountability, lines that she could help lay out.

Randolf shook his head deprecatingly. 'You're exaggerating.'

'I'm exaggerating. Because you're not concerned with your position?'

'Of course it's about the content. About the questions raised.'

'So why do you make such weird comments?'

'Gabrielle, you know me' – as he said this he looked as if butter wouldn't melt in his mouth – 'I have defended like no one else the constitutional ethos of the Netherlands, but you have to be ready to adapt occasionally, in order to realize your ideals.'

'If everyone adapts, there won't be much left of the ideals.'

'Don't be so condescending. I'm just as concerned as you are about the reliability of the debates.'

'Right. So I'm to understand that it's all done out of pure concern. That the moment the television camera comes anywhere near you you start saying things you know aren't true.'

Randolf looked at her for a moment and finally decided she wasn't worth it, that she had perhaps never been worth it, not all the time they had known each other, and not now. He turned away without another word towards John, who was not only his son-in-law but moreover understood the world and knew how things were done in the world for better or for worse.

Gabrielle realized that she had been brushed aside, and because the conversation had ended once and for all, she showed her indignation ten minutes later, when discussion of their new novel began, by throwing her book onto the table harder than usual. She couldn't beat him in this discussion, and precisely because of that, she realized, Randolf was right. He was right because his strategy worked. The more he lied, the more people liked listening to him, and for that reason alone he had no need to justify himself to her. However many convincing and decisive arguments Gabrielle van Dam might have, no one was interested in her opinion.

3

Half-way through April it was still so dark at the time when Lucius usually woke up in the morning and went out to get the paper, that he stood out in the garden for a moment looking up at the mystery of the trees, the dark crowns scarcely distinguishable from the dark sky around. With the paper rolled up in the pocket of his dressing-gown, he listened to creaking and peeping from the branches; at first he thought that the trees themselves were peeping, but then he heard that it was birds, perhaps a nest, or wasn't that possible yet at this time of year? Perhaps the birds had been alarmed by the cat that had walked outside with Lucius and was now looking up at him with interest, curious as to what they were going to do here outside. Lucius shivered.

'Hm?' he said in his head to the cat.

In the avenue at the front of his house the occasional car was already passing. In the distance he could see the lights on in the houses of the neighbours at the back, and as he stood here first the bedroom light and then the down-stairs light, probably in the kitchen, went on in the white-washed village house directly behind his. Lucius went inside, into his own kitchen, fed the cat, made a cup of coffee, unrolled the paper and surveyed the news.

The book club was to meet that evening at his place, to discuss a book about a popular rising in Russia, and it was bloody inconvenient, because Lucius had guests.

It was obviously too early yet for the guests, two German lawyers who were sleeping in the new extension to his house, and Lucius wondered if he would have time to arrange everything with them before he left for court this morning. This evening it wouldn't be possible, what with all the fuss in the house. He hoped at any rate that they would wake up in time.

The cat leapt onto his lap with the obvious intention of lying there all day, but Lucius swept her onto the worktop – which the cleaner didn't allow, but the cleaner wasn't due for another quarter of an hour, and until then anarchy ruled – and with the paper under his arm he went upstairs to get dressed.

When he had checked his morning post and gathered his papers together he went into the shower, before real-izing twelve seconds later that one of the guests was awake downstairs and was running a bath, so he was suddenly standing under a thin jet of cold water. He squatted down and decided to wait like that until the guest's bath was full and hot water was again pumped up by the ingen-ious forces of technology. He soon felt cold. While he calculated how much time it would take to talk to the Germans about their case and then to drop by the office to pick up a dossier, he saw himself sitting there, arms wrapped round his knees, the long black hairs on his legs stuck to his clammy skin; a huge insect almost washed down the drain of the shower on its way to court. I'm curious to know, he muttered in his head, how many magistrates, how many medical specialists and chairs of boards of international companies are squatting in the bathroom at this exact moment while downstairs in the kitchen the cleaner is humming as she makes pancakes for total strangers.

Nothing to be done, the builder had said when the extension to his house was built. It's to do with circulation pumps, hot-water deficit. Something like that. Imagine if you put in a separate boiler for each shower, then before you knew it you'd have four boilers in which hundreds of litres would be constantly heated to boiling-point, and from the shaking of the builder's head he concluded that they mustn't even think about it. Of course, that went without saying, Lucius decided. Lucius paid for the conversion, the water bill of Hydron PLC and tax via the Water Board; he paid for the guests and their breakfast, but still he had to resign himself to the fact a few times a month he would sit going through a brief naked and shivering on the wet tiled floor of his own bathroom. He usually won the subsequent case. That had nothing to do with it.

When the bath downstairs was full and Lucius turned on the hot water again, he soaped himself and washed his hair, as he determined his plan of campaign for the morning. Other people's guilt is always up for negotiation, and he was almost certain that his arguments were sound; as he stepped out of the shower and dried his hair with a towel, he concluded that the day would come right. He tied the towel round his waist and thought reluctantly about this evening; he had promised Teresa that he would bring up Ruth Ackermann's book and when he realized he couldn't get out of it, because the book was coming menacingly closer and closer and one day would be in the middle of the room to call him to account, a hateful feeling rose from his subconscious, not a sense of guilt, but a deep feeling of disgust and dislike.

'The crime is the punishment.' Where had he read that? He let the words float round in his head and then he recognized them. It was a quote from Amos Oz, which Nadine Gordimer had chosen as the motto for her novel *The House Gun*. The crime is the punishment.

He leaned toward the mirror to see himself a nose-length away. But although the window was open and the steam had long since cleared, the glass instantly clouded over, so that he had to take a step back. He looked at himself searchingly, slid two hands across his chest, combed his hair back with fingers spread apart and said what he always said when he talked to himself in the mirror after showering in the morning: 'They should bloody well kick you to death.'

For a while the book club has read nothing but legal novels. The experiment with the genre lasted eighteen months; its bankruptcy became apparent on the afternoon when they were reading Bernard Schlink's *The Reader*, a meeting that ended in a dogged war discussion about good and evil. A complicating factor was that Randolf had read the book in German, which Lucius thought was nonsense – 'there's a fantastic Dutch translation' – so that the conversation turned into furious leafing to and fro between the two books. And while all this leafing was going on (it was a late November afternoon in Gabrielle's conservatory, Lucius reflected on the rhyming imagery between the autumnal garden and the books) the irritation had mounted to such a degree and there had finally been such a dreadful argument about war and peace, crime and punishment, that they had opted for a cooling-off period and for a while read no more novels about legal cases, fascism, or the Second World War. It wasn't that easy. When John was recruited by Randolf and came to his first meeting in Lucius' house, they had discussed *That Awful Mess on Via Merulana* by Carlo Emilio Gadda, and talked rather furtively about Mussolini – Christ, they'd forgotten that book was about the same thing.

'There is a sad truth that when you think about it isn't a truth at all,' said Lucius. He had won his case today. And he had just had time to fix things with his German guests, and he didn't give a damn that Randolf and Gabrielle had obviously had a row before the meeting, that John was constantly checking his messages on his mobile and all the others were stressed-out, hectic, tired, listless, uninterested;

he himself was fit as a fiddle and had a bottle of Sancerre in front of him that was nearly empty, but fortunately there were dozens of bottles of Sancerre in the cellar. He was buoyant, really bouncy.

'There is no reason at all,' he said, 'why poverty should be interesting, or the seamy side. The nonsense that uneducated people are "real" and intellectuals aren't. So why is it,' he said, leaning forward to get the bottle next to Gabrielle, 'that evil always infiltrates the higher world in the shape of juvenile delinquents who rape daughters and damage cars and clamber into houses to spread the elusive menace of the lower classes?'

They had only been going for an hour, but people weren't in the mood and Lucius had decided to broaden the discussion: no longer to talk just about tonight's book, but all books.

'Couldn't we read something about civilization for a change? Something about art and culture?'

He got up carefully from the large dining-table around which they were grouped, walked over to his bookcase and looked intently at one of the top shelves.

'I recently thought of *The Philosophy of Clothes* by Thomas Carlyle. Where did I put it?'

John smiled. '*The Philosophy of Clothes*? That sounds like a manual for metro-man. Or what is he called nowadays? The supersexual.'

'Lucius buys his suits in Italy,' said Jurgen. 'Or in Savile Row, Lucius?'

But Lucius didn't react. 'Ha, here it is. The copy has

seen better days. *Sartor Resartus*, yes, that's the title. And it's about a book called *The Philosophy of Clothes*. It's complicated.'

As he sat down on an old set of wooden library steps by the bookcase with a glass of wine in one hand and the battered book in the other, the mood at the table changed. They had all closed their novels and poured wine for each other with relief, with amused glances at Lucius, who was sitting slightly befuddled on his steps.

'Lucius is our master of triviality,' said John teasingly. 'He prefers reducing things to enlarging them.'

'OK, that sounds very nice,' objected Jurgen. 'But his tendency to let air escape from words is in fact just as pretentious as our tendency to overinflate words.'

Gabrielle began making canapés for everyone; she had got over her irritation and defended their host. 'Lucius at least cuts himself and his importance down to size. It's better to make yourself light than ponderous.'

'Lucius is actually so light he's almost a woman,' said Jurgen.

But the sarcasm was lost on Lucius. He had put down his glass, now empty, and was hunting furiously through the text.

'I can remember there's a passage somewhere about the Dutch custom of putting striped suits on cows when it rains.'

The club members giggled.

'Lucius tends to turn everything into cabaret,' said Randolf goodnaturedly.

'Cabaret? What d'you mean cabaret. I'm not fucking Liza Minelli,' said Lucius. He walked back to the table and chucked the book onto the table.

And while they passed the book round and accepted canapés from Gabrielle, John produced another book, that Teresa had given him to bring, and tapped his glass with the sharp knife that had been lying on the dish with the sausage on it.

'May I?'

They looked at him in cheerful expectation.

'Teresa asked me to talk to you about another book. She thought we might be able to read it. It was written by a classmate of hers, Ruth Ackermann. Perhaps some of you will remember her too.'

Suddenly everyone round the table went deathly quiet. When someone spoke, it was Randolf.

'What kind of nonsense is that?' he said. 'I didn't know my daughter was interested in literature.'

'She's not so much concerned with the book as with the author; she thought it might be nice to talk to her.'

He put the book in the middle of the table, between the dishes of olives, and after a slight hesitation Jurgen picked it up. He turned it over a few times, opened it and started reading a section aloud. After a few sentences Randolf had heard enough.

'That passage could have been lifted straight out of Edith Wharton.'

'So what?' said Lucius. 'What's wrong with Edith Wharton?' His mind was in overdrive.

If John had not come up with the suggestion of reading *The Summer of Canvas Shoes*, he himself would have had to have raised the subject of the book at the end of the evening – and doubtless Randolf would have seriously resented that. Even now, he remained on his guard, not wanting to push Randolf too far, and with a mixture of cowardice and drunkenness he tried to skirt round the edges of the subject. Because he didn't immediately know what to say to support John imperceptibly, he said the first thing that came into his head: 'In life there are quite simply sensations that connect with our mammal brains and sensations that connect with our human brains, so why shouldn't you activate all those brains at once?'

Randolf took the book from Jurgen, cast a vexed eye over it, threw it back on the table, and reached a judgement.

'We didn't set up our book club to read this kind of muck.'

And that judgement astonished John, since even though he himself hadn't much confidence in this private reading tip of Teresa's, he found his father-in-law's opposition totally unfounded.

'Oh, come on now!' he cried, just a little too loud.

Again a deep silence fell. The day was saved by Gabrielle.

'That John,' she said, 'he's always so foul-mouthed, he ruins the whole atmosphere.'

John burst out laughing. And at that moment the decision was made, and no one could back out. But at this moment no one wanted to take responsibility, and so Lucius, after emptying his glass, brought proceedings to an official end with a plan. 'Let's split up into working parties, and in a week or two we're bound to find something to get our teeth into.'

4

The die was cast. Ruth Ackermann was coming. There was going to be a literary evening and Ruth was going to talk in the church. The bookseller had finally managed to get hold of the great writer; that is, he hadn't spoken to her himself, but her publishers told him that Ruth Ackermann was happy to make time to drop in and talk to him about her book. For the first two weeks in May she would be in Germany and afterwards she had to go to the States, but the 18th was still free. The publisher's PR woman said with some surprise in her voice that Ruth Ackermann was prepared to give up a day off to be able to come back to the place where she had grown up. The writer sent the bookseller her best regards, although she didn't know him. And this should have been the moment when he danced round the shop and shouted 'Yes!' in triumph, but the bookseller wasn't that sort of person. He grinned, and that had to suffice.

Up to now he had handled everything on his own, independently of the book club, independently of the volunteers who always turned up when a literary evening was organized – and whom he would shortly need again for coffee and tearing the tickets and looking after the flowers. For fear of making a fool of himself by being turned down by a celebrity, he had become quieter and quieter about his desire to get Ruth Ackermann to come to the village, but now she had said yes, and actually seemed to be looking forward to the evening, he had to hurry and immediately pulled out all the stops. He converted the shop window provisionally into a Ruth Ackermann display-case and placed piles of copies of the book in it. From the store behind the shop he retrieved a stand. It was a dazzling pop-up of the author: a life-size portrait on card. She looked a little uncomfortable, but friendly, and was holding a tray on which the bookseller, if he wanted to, could place books or brochures, or copies of the magazine interview that the publishers had supplied with the pop-up. He decided to position her right next to the till with an encouraging nod of the head. Then he could immediately place a subscription list for the literary evening on the tray.

Lucius sees the odd display on Friday afternoon when he drops in to buy a paper. He takes the paper from the rack outside and carries it into the shop, while reading a front-page report on Belgian undertakers complaining about the nice weather causing fewer people than usual to die in April. When he has paid for the paper and goes outside, Dr Bennie 'The Nose' Driessen is just entering the shop. So he's back too.

The village changes inhabitants from time to time. In the holiday periods children are exchanged between mothers and fathers: the children of the mothers go to the fathers and the children of the fathers go to the mothers, and that means that in some houses the permanent children go in two different directions and that three different cars come to drop the temporary children, and if you don't pay attention you might think you've wound up in a completely different life. On top of that, in some houses the parents also go on holiday with their temporary children and then people from agencies come and stay and look after the cats. To round things off, the owners of the holiday cottages in the woods and the occupants of the caravans on the campsite walk down the high street. So that for a few weeks the village community is completely replaced by an invading population. It could provide the script for a horror movie if it were not all so innocent and so well-behaved; the invading population is obviously more cheerful, and makes more high-spirited use of the woods and cycle paths. The Happy Invasion of the Body-Snatchers.

At a farm on Cross Road they hire out large pedal-carts that will take a whole family and that you can take onto cycle paths and back roads. And that's what the holiday population of the village does. Sometimes when a couple of those wagons meet, the crossroads are blocked, because no one knows exactly how to put a monster like that into reverse. Lucius gets out of his car at least twice a year to help push. Jacket off, sleeves rolled up, and to the astonishment of the holiday-makers, who see a man in a suit getting out of an expensive BMW with his Chopard watch and handmade shoes, he lifts the rear wheels and gives the car a turn, freeing the parents and children to enjoy their holiday. Bye, waves Lucius, and the holiday-makers wave back in surprise.

Perhaps it isn't holiday time everywhere yet, and it's too early for the wagons, but a few holiday children are cycling across the square in front of the bookshop, checking out what there is to do in the street. In search of excitement. Fire. At least Lucius thinks they're holiday children, since they have the expectant faces of children exploring a new world, a hitherto unknown terrain.

He crosses the square, walks to the café for a packet of cigarettes and half-way down the village street, with a detour back to the car he fishes money from his pocket for the homeless people's paper seller, the ever-cheerful Armenian who lives in front of the chemist's door and is an admirer of Alexandre Dumas.

'How's it going?' asks Lucius.

'Well, well,' grins the man. 'Good, bad. Uncertain. I still don't know whether I'm allowed to stay here.' He gives Lucius a paper and for form's sake looks for change. 'You never know, perhaps tomorrow there'll suddenly be a law that deports us all.'

'Let's hope not,' says Lucius, who is in a position to phone the head of the immigration service or, if necessary, the minister, about policy, but won't be doing that for the time being. No, he waves, don't worry about the change. He says goodbye and walks on. He tries to see the man as an incident. There isn't just one parallel world, that of the immigrants occupied with their unfathomable lives, there is a whole line of parallel worlds; the world in which Lucius is walking around is one of them and not one of the worst, he tells himself. And he doesn't know whether that thought stands up morally; he doesn't even know whether he stands up metaphysically, but what the hell. What can you do? Would the homeless people's paper seller want to change places with Lucius? Most probably not. Now Lucius is at his car and takes great pleasure in opening the locks remotely; the lights begin to flicker and all's well with the world.

Naturally Lucius' visit to the bookshop had cast a shadow over this day, and now he was in his car and wondering where to go – he had no appointments, didn't feel like working and could afford to take a few hours off – he decided to do his duty and inform the book club. After making a few calls he started the car and drove to the university campus where, as Iris had said on the phone, he was bound to find Randolf. As he walked across the deserted car park in the sun to Building G, he felt as always grateful for not having to work here. He stretched out his arms to the side.

'Roll out those lazy, hazy, crazy days of summer, those days of soda and pretzels and beer,' he sang.

He squeezed through the revolving door, looked on the board in the lobby to see which industrious employees were still present on this Friday afternoon and hopped up the concrete stairs; the building was deserted, there wasn't a student in sight and on the first floor the door of the administrative office was wide open, the computers secured, the cabinets locked, the secretaries departed for their dirty weekend destinations. He wound his way upstairs to the second floor and turned up the volume. 'Roll out those lazy, hazy, crazy days of summer.' His voice, which was light and melodious, floated through the stairwell with a lovely boom; halfway he enjoyed the effect for a brief moment on the landing. 'Dust off the sun and moon and sing a song of cheer.' Now he was finally on Randolf's floor, where he had to squeeze nimbly round the photocopier in order to reach the constitutional law department through the swing-doors. Lucius stood still for a moment.

The shabbiness of the bare corridor in this new university building took his breath away every time anew. He had only recently seen how different it could be in the film version of A. S. Byatt's great novel *Possession*, the transparent architecture of the London Arts Faculty as seen by a Hollywood director: light design, big windows with a sophisticated view, and the actress Gwyneth Paltrow, in all her distinction, unattainable and irresistible in a beige twinset, who played the part of a scholar. A British water-nymph, in her quest for literary revelation, assisted by a good-looking American with a five-o'clock shadow. *Dempsey & Makepeace* goes poetry. But here in the narrow corridor that led to Randolf, very little of that subtle grace was to be found; here it was just ordinary mortals who had to maintain their dignity beneath the modular ceilings.

And it was all a question of money, Lucius understood

that, peering into the corridor with the frugal neon light. Virginia Woolf had written that universities quite simply need money for deep armchairs, soft carpets, courtesy and vivacity. She was writing at a time when English men could still obviously quite easily scrape together enough money for their faculties and institutes – wine, partridge, sofas and tobacco, and maids with trays on their heads, while English women could scarcely find any money and had to make do with dry crackers and cornflour custard.

Meanwhile, eighty years later, even the men had long since forgotten where to get the money from, and so researchers had become the women of society, living in a culture unimpressed by their unconditional devotion and commitment. The financial tycoons looked the other way and universities could no longer afford the luxury of partridge. Let alone the luxury of courtesy.

Lucius, standing in the bare corridor, thought for a moment with a faint longing of Gwyneth Paltrow. And the reason he had just thought somewhere in the recesses of his mind of Virgina Woolf was because in the film centring on Gwyneth Paltrow he had seen a lesbian walking into the water with stones in her pockets and that, as he thought of Virginia Woolf, had brought him to the conclusion that lesbians always walked into the water with stones in their pockets, and they shouldn't, Lucius had thought, it was a waste. Now he could no longer remember the sequence, but the memory of the university study in the film gave him a slightly uncomfortable feeling, a superficial frisson, and it struck him that Randolf was very unprotected here, without a porter or other supervision.

Recently Lucius quite frequently had had problems with lunatics who maintained that he had put a bomb in their gardens – 'I expect you think you're really something! I expect you think you're invulnerable!' – or had stolen their dossiers from the court and made changes in them. Harmless lunatics probably, but the feeling of menace remained, and became stronger after every incident. If you have a problem with vandalism, just give me the names and addresses and I'll pop round there, the porter of his own practice had said, and that was certainly more protection than poor old Randolf could expect in these bare corridors.

At the end of the corridor the door of a room was ajar. Lucius knocked and went in.

5

Here, in this church of intellectual nonchalance, sits Randolf Pellikaan in all his glory. In his study his nineteenth-century evil aura, that so preoccupies, that fascinates, alienates and at the same time attracts Lucius, assumes the form of modern oligarchy that with axiomatic arrogance subordinates to itself everything in its immediate and distant surroundings. The people that Randolf deals with know he is evil, a fox, a secret schemer, an intriguer who knows his way through the snakepit, but that is absolutely irrelevant, because he is efficient and always achieves what he has set out to achieve. In that respect he is reliable and he can be used for objectives that have to be achieved; his contacts are useful, his profile is high – and protects him, the sum of his positions means that he cannot be ignored and that it is best to keep on his good side. He has the attraction, the sexual attraction even, of men who are invested with power by other men.

Lucius once bumped into him at a reception with a British journalist in his wake.

'Lucius,' said Randolf condescendingly. 'Of course I'd love to talk to you, but this journalist is doing a piece on me for the *Independent*, about social developments relating to integration in the Netherlands, and it's not a good idea if I'm spotted here with someone who doesn't really count for much in that field. Do you mind if I go and have a word with the minister instead?'

It is this completely shameless inner emptiness that fascinates Lucius, the unbridled ambition that enables Randolf to deceive and betray his own friends, and afterwards to come and sit intimately on the corner of your desk with a preposterous self-accusation ('No, that wasn't very pretty') and unilaterally regard the matter as closed.

Lucius sometimes thinks about Randolf at night in bed. On television he sees stars, film-stars, soap-stars, celebrities from the world on the other side of the Atlantic, and he listens to their laments about fame and the emotional responsibilities it entails. 'Success takes you to places where character won't sustain you,' he hears Oprah Winfrey say, talking to her divine guests, raised to unattainable heights, and that quote stays in his mind, until the next morning during a dreary meeting he makes the link to his own divine friend.

Iris once told him how Randolf, when they were on honeymoon in Greece, in the evening on one of their romantic beach walks – moon in the sky, waves lapping at their feet – had written a name in the sand with the toe of his sandal; for the first time for ages he had two weeks off and was at his wits' end. When he had finally finished he looked at her blissfully, and in the sand at his feet was the name 'Randolf'. On that occasion she had reached the conclusion that in this marriage she must take good care of her own soul, because her young, promising husband would not.

Meanwhile, Randolf has no inkling of the fact that his friends and colleagues have mixed feelings about him. Nor would he understand – if you tried to explain it to him – that he owes his social position precisely to the fact that many people don't particularly like him, or at least have very serious objections to him and the superficiality of his character. He amuses himself in the middle of his spider's web. He is satisfied with himself. Satisfied with his achievements, with his natural superiority, which (so he thinks) has got him to where he is now; he finds it perfectly logical that others should think the same.

And that, Lucius reflects at night in bed, is precisely why the great Randolf Pellikaan is so successful – because he coincides completely with the image of himself that he has created. Just look: on the walls of his study there are photos of himself, photos with politicians, writers, important men, a photo with Angela Merkel no less, taken during a conference on European citizenship in Brussels, but also two drawings by Teresa as a child, which he has obviously moved with great care from one office to another as a homage to his own fatherhood.

He is talented; he knows a lot. These days you can't keep up at university unless you make sure you join a consortium of scholars with the same interests, and Randolf is the hub of such a consortium; he is famous for his ability always to strike the right tone in his research proposals. He need make no effort to play a part in the international academic community, where everyone speaks at least six languages fluently and nonchalantly writes sixty books, each of them with the same upright conviction of the recognized expert. He is well-documented; in his choices, here and in his whole life, he has perfected his good taste – he knows that it will impress if above his desk he has not a masterpiece but a little-known etching of Louis XIV visiting a scientific salon, at once a political statement and assertion of a scholarly claim; he also knows that it is better not to listen to too much Bach, or even Mozart, but to prefer Palestrina or Scarlatti; in the course of his life he has acquired an unerring feel for all the nuances, so that he leaves the door of his office ajar in complete confidence when he plays classical music on his PC. And in his early years, the etchings and engravings, and the photos, the music seeping out under the door, and the jaunty smile with which he walks down the corridors (always jovial, always ready to make friends with everyone) attracted a great deal of sarcasm and mockery within the faculty, but gradually they also brought him every possible administrative post and promotion. For however transparent his ambition may be, it is ambition in the correct, well-adjusted and reliable form, which renders Randolf completely harmless to the system and thus preeminently suited for power.

Power? Randolf will exclaim indignantly. God no! You mustn't think that; no, he isn't part of the establishment.

On the contrary he opposes it, doesn't he? Don't forget he
has a Greek wife or, as he says in appropriate circumstances,
an ethnic-minority wife, which gives him street cred on
all his boards of management; and an exotic car, a 1962
Hillman, in which he drives about occasionally in the
summer; for a long time he also had two donkeys in the
field behind the house, which was very funny, and which
at the same time he took very seriously: he bought a number
of books on the subject. What's more, as a columnist he is
more critical than anyone, feared for his attacks on the
powers-that-be, who as a result so admire him for his acute
analyses that they recommend him to each other and enlist
his help and give him positions, without his independence
being compromised.

It is not power that drives him, says Randolf. What matters
to him is gaining an understanding of how the world is
governed and exercising his benevolent influence on it. The
most that can be said is that through the seriousness with
which he carries out his mission he has acquired a deep
contempt for everyone who does not, as he does, do their
utmost to get a grip on the world. Has the MA student
who is coming to discuss his dissertation really never heard
of Karl Kraus? Just think of that! In Randolf's office there
is a piece of paper with a quote from Kraus on it, which
someone sent him and which in all his vanity he has hung
up, since self-irony is also part of the repertoire he has
appropriated by hard work: 'Career is a horse that arrives
riderless at the gate of eternity.'

Everything in Randolf's life accords with the lines he

set out in his youth. He has no need to bite anything back, keep anything to himself. There is nothing hidden behind the eagerness that drives him, and that is what makes Randolf so damned sociable.

Lucius was now standing on the threshold and looking at Randolf, who with his back to him was bending over a table, next to a young woman with blonde hair worn up – Lucius had a strange momentary vision of Gwyneth Paltrow, but when she looked to the side this woman turned out to be less ethereal, this was the usual blondeness of the successful young lawyer, with an expensive suit – she probably came from a law firm or a ministry.

Randolf turned his head to the side at the same time and he was delighted to see Lucius, even at this moment, when he was obviously still at work and would definitely not have wanted to be disturbed by anyone else.

'Come in,' he cried. 'Come in, we're hard at it, but I've got a moment.'

Six months previously Randolf had been appointed chairman of the legal committee charged with producing a report on dual nationality, holding two passports at once: Lucius knew that first he should have done extensive long-term research to gain an overview of the international options. How was citizenship managed in other European countries? What was the situation with dual nationality elsewhere?

And now Lucius started grinning. 'Dual nationality, dual nationality,' he was in the habit of saying to Randolf, 'aren't you getting a bit old for that sort of thing? And does Iris know what you're actually getting up to at the moment?'

And every time that weak joke irritated Randolf immensely, so that Lucius saw no reason at all to stop making it. It was remarkable how quickly Randolf's certainty, outside the protective sphere of his public activity, could be undermined. Randolf, who whenever he entered a meeting room or reception area always felt the knot of his tie, a habitual gesture Lucius always observed with a degree of *schadenfreude*.

But this time Lucius would keep his comments to himself; Randolf was obviously in his element, working on the report, with a young, promising civil servant from the Ministry of Justice at his side. Lucius knew by now that you mustn't be misled by the youth of such civil servants. This was probably a top official sent personally by the minister to help Randolf with the comparison of international legislation, and there was a good chance that the minister himself was keeping in touch with Randolf on progress – relations were different from what they once were. Randolf no longer went to the ministry, the ministry came to him.

Lucius entered the office, and when the young woman who had been introduced to him as an expert on nationality legislation bent back over the table with Randolf, he turned his back discreetly on them and cocked his head to one side, pretending to read the book titles – 'Just fill your basket full of sandwiches and weenies, Then lock the house up, now you're set,' he hummed and took Castells' *The Power of Identity* off the shelf.

Lucius didn't feel like getting entangled in Randolf's projects. Actually, he preferred to keep well out of everything, hanging around a bit, strolling though society, and people who didn't know him consequently regarded him first and foremost as a charming lightweight, a pleasant *causeur* who didn't really count. But because despite himself he conjured up brilliant solutions as soon as problems presented themselves, the civil servants who circulated at receptions eventually started retaining his advice and mentioned his name more and more frequently, put their hands on his arm, on his shoulder ('Lucius, do you know that I don't really belong in these circles either? I'm an outsider, like you'), and then Lucius was happy to raise a glass with them.

It was a point in Randolf's favour at any rate that he had never been mistaken about Lucius. They had known each other since their student days, and Randolf had immediately accepted Lucius' intellectual superiority, so that he called in his help unscrupulously when he found himself in an impasse. Now too he was glad that Lucius was there to go through the problems with him.

He got up and tried to attract Lucius' attention unobtrusively. 'It's really difficult to get the hang of that British nationality legislation, actually you should call in a British legislation lawyer to fathom the finer points, but fortunately I have a bread-and-butter line in Oxford.'

In order to impress the young woman he had obviously

adopted the departmental jargon: the Hague dialect intended to suggest cosmopolitanism. Lucius bit back a comment and started singing slightly louder: 'And on the beach you'll see the girls in their bikinis; as cute as ever but they never get them wet.'

'Do stop it,' said Randolf. 'Will you please stop behaving like a halfwit for once. But anyway, it's handy that you've dropped by, because as we speak I'm working on a complicated passage about the obtaining of a nationality by refugees under treaty and you probably have an opinion on that on the basis of your work for Amnesty. I'll let you read it, it needs editing, so you're getting it quick-and-dirty, but it'll give you an immediate impression.'

'Why are you talking so oddly?' asked Lucius, curious now.

'Do you mind! Haven't you anything better to do than come and mess things up?' snapped Randolf, smacking the print-out down on the table in front of Lucius. (Wounded innocence of an important man.)

'Right,' said Lucius in a placatory tone, 'I'll have a look. There's a good chance you'll get into all sorts of difficulties if you don't first resolve the blanket of fog surrounding the reasonability exception. But you know that yourself.'

The door of the archive cabinet was ajar and Lucius peered inside. Randolf wasn't diabetic, years of tests had shown that, but sometimes such an intense feeling of nausea and vertigo came over him that he almost fainted, and then he had to drink a glass of orange juice immediately or eat a bar of chocolate. That is why there were always Mars and

Twix wrappers on his desk, and there was a box of bars in the archive cabinet, from which Lucius now grabbed one. 'Can I just check my mail?' he asked, tearing the paper off the Bounty and already bending over the screen. Randolf nodded.

Lucius rummaged through his post a bit and Randolf had picked up a handbook which he seemed to be reading, and now the men were so menacingly silent that the young woman obviously felt that her presence was superfluous. She disappeared, saying that she was going to the library to look at some old periodicals that she couldn't find online.

'Oh,' said Lucius.

'Oh,' said Randolf.

There was a short silence; Lucius found himself suddenly dreading the conversation.

'I've just been at the bookshop,' he said.

The announcement did not awake much enthusiasm in the chairman of the book club.

'He was talking about that book by Ruth Ackermann, you know, the Ackermann girl, we've already discussed it. And we were going make a decision as to whether or not we were going to read it in the club. John made the proposal' – he started to falter uncharacteristically because Randolf continued to stare at him without moving a muscle – 'and now it turns out that the Ackermann girl will shortly be coming to the village to give a literary reading. So. We can't really avoid the issue any longer.'

He didn't know how far he could go, on what level of honesty he could talk to Randolf, but just as he was wondering whether he shouldn't put an end to their fossilized conspiracy of silence and bring up the Ackermann affair and make a clean sweep, Randolf burst out in fury.

'God Almighty!' he roared. 'Since when have we read chambermaids' novels in the book club. Because a girl like that once lived in the village, surely we don't immediately have to read her diaries! We do take ourselves seriously as intellectuals, I hope?'

'They're not exactly her diaries.'

'John allowed himself to be put up to this by Teresa. It's bad enough that my daughter systematically refuses to read a book, out of aggression and superannuated teenage rebellion, but she should leave John in peace.' He had his voice under control again and sat down in one of the armchairs grouped around the coffee table, which Randolf – what luxury! – had been allowed to purchase for his room at the faculty's expense. 'Soon, like the rest of the Netherlands we'll be allowing our lives to be determined by the younger generation with its penchant for amusement, pop music in the lecture rooms, *Donald Duck* on reading lists; I refuse to be part of that. You can tell the others that. I refuse to be part of it.'

'The problem is that John is already in favour; and Jurgen, and Gabrielle, and Frans.'

'You can't be serious!'

'Oh yes, they had no objection at all.'

'Fantastic.'

'I don't understand you, it surely isn't such a disaster if we take a look at a different sort of book for a change.

Next time it'll be your turn again. Then we can read *The Man Without Qualities*.'

'I read *The Man Without Qualities* ages ago, thanks. And there's absolutely no need to scoff at the kind of books I read. There's simply a standard that I want to keep up, even if young people think it's too much trouble to read a decent book. Christ, Lucius, I don't wish to apologize for my pedagogical province.'

In a minute he'd start talking about hoi polloi, thought Lucius. Where on earth did he get those words from? From a crossword dictionary? But thank God they were back in familiar territory, his mood improved considerably, he was enjoying this discussion. Randolf fulminating about the havoc wreaked on education and culture, and he himself stirring things up by taking a diametrically opposite view; all he need do was bring up some pathetic reading suggestions like *The Philosophy of Clothes* or *The Transformation of Mrs McTwig*, a book he had once seen crop up in an old episode of *Columbo*, and Randolf would explode. Randolf and Lucius, bound together in eternal friendship, with the permanent irritations and regular conflicts of a bad marriage.

But he remembered in time what a serious mission he was on today, sat down in an armchair next to Randolf on his best behaviour and tried to convince him.

'Come on. I don't understand what's bugging you so much about the book by that Ruth Ackermann. Surely it's an exceptional case. Surely there are reasons why we should read it.'

'And I don't understand why you're even considering it.

175

It's a love-story, for Christ's sake. And not a serious love-story, but a comedy. Why can't the younger generations do anything without immediately turning it into a comedy? Amusement! The world is being brought down by entertainment!'

'Have you ever considered,' asked Lucius, and he really meant it, 'whether our own penchant for amusement isn't much more dangerous for the country and the world? I mean: more dangerous than the fairly natural preference of the young for din and ecstasy?'

'Huh?' said Randolf, momentarily thrown.

'This week I talked to a German colleague about the scandal at Volkswagen in Germany – he's involved in the trial that will be starting there shortly. Listen to this: the cases hinges completely on amusement. On a board of management that brought in great teams of female escorts for the works council; on directors with love-nests paid for by the company; on employees who had their holiday trips paid for by the board. And the same applies to our building fraud scandal. Millions of dollars and euros frittered away every year in brothels and football stadiums. There's not much deep seriousness involved, and yet they're mostly men of our age and our type, Randolf.'

'No. That's the business world; it's a different culture. I admit I don't like that either.'

'Business world or not, it makes no difference at all. In the vast majority of cases it's not the little people, without culture or education, who indulge their yen for cheap amusement. They're top managers, they're management specialists and economists, highly educated, who have more impact on the world's well-being than any politician or statesman, but who are completely detached from the world, who make plans about the social structure of the country and then when they want to relax can't think of anything better than holiday trips to Brazil with a couple of expensive call-girls.'

'Well, that's not right either. But those are incidents. And young people, you must admit, don't abandon themselves incidentally to cheap amusement, they *live* on it.'

'Young people have a different tempo and a different agenda from you. If you give them time they'll turn out to be just as respectable citizens as you are.'

Randolf's phone rang and that was a signal for Lucius to disappear. They got up. And with the tinkling telephone pressed to his chest – he had installed the ringtone of the old-fashioned telephone bell – Randolf came to a personal conclusion.

'Anyway, I'm not going to haggle, not even with my daughter, about the quality of the books we read. Surely we've got principles, I hope?'

'You haven't got principles,' said Lucius. 'You've got a network.'

IV

The Book

1

On his return to the Netherlands the journalist Victor Herwig had found not only temporary work but also temporary accommodation in Amsterdam with a friend who had converted his loft and installed a kitchenette and a shower. The gothic lines of the roof and the slightly curved wooden beams gave the room the look of an upturned boat; all in all, painted papal white and gold, it had a spiritual symbolism that appealed to Victor – for the time being.

He sat here on Sunday morning raised high above the city of Amsterdam, which was swarming at his feet, but which he could not see. The two skylights that had been put in during the conversion were too high up; only if he looked up diagonally from his chair could Victor see the sky, which had been blue every day since he had lived here: radiant and innocent blue. At this moment while the local church bells were chiming – the Westerkerk was close by, he could see it if he stood on a chair and looked out of the skylight. He was starting to whistle along with the tunes of the carillon more and more often – he was sitting on a chair next to his bed, two steps away from the kitchen and three from the shower, and wondering what he was going to do.

How many people actually went to church? In this house everyone was still asleep early on Sunday morning; he couldn't hear a sound downstairs and the balconies of the neighbours opposite, so close that you could easily jump across from the attic window, also remained silent.

The room offered him a pleasant kind of invisibility. No one paid any attention to him. He appreciated that. He preferred to have his visibility confined to his professional status and up to now that had worked well; no one had yet seriously asked him about his life – where he came from, who his parents were, background, social class – and he was constantly amazed at the frequently heard complaint that the modern age was too geared to reality and human interest, a hysterical interest in autobiographical facts, because no one ever asked him anything. Lohengrin, the Knight of the Swan. He came from nowhere. He was no one. No one wanted to know who he was. His friends, his employers, the women he slept with, no one turned out to be terribly interested in him; for them he consisted of his opinion and his content, his work, his achievements, and that was fine by him. Even from this attic room, the whole world was on call, but he himself was nowhere to be found.

There was good reason to mark time here for a while. For ages he had enjoyed commenting on the four corners of the globe – he was restless enough for it, and curious and competitive, Victor Herwig versus the rest of the world, and he seldom lost – but in the last year of his travels abroad he had found himself becoming impressed by himself just a little too often. He knew, and his employers knew by now, that wars and revolts were partly initiated to secure the advertising revenues of the great television stations, and consequently he had set about his assignments with the necessary cynicism – the man sitting here was not an idealist who had returned home disillusioned; but he felt he was crossing a line with his malevolence by acting as if all those problems in those distant countries had been specially staged to allow his intelligence to excel. As if his journalistic intelligence had suddenly become the hub of world politics. Or rather: it wasn't intelligence that he had in greater measure than other people, but a kind of intuitive shrewdness, the talent to see immediately what was wrong beneath the façade of global progress.

There was an additional problem. He was proved right too often, but on too small a scale. Victor, zapping in boredom from channel to channel in his austere hotel rooms, window open onto a street full of everyday hubbub, heard the American psychologist Dr Phil McGraw say repeatedly on his TV shows: 'Pick your battles'; solve your marriage problems, the relationship problems, the elemental fears and insecurities in yourself, and don't fight with each other for years over the best way of cleaning the sink. And Victor knew, as he zapped off the TV, that he should take this on board professionally, since he really could bang on for ages about things that, looked at closely, didn't matter. He didn't get round to the real problems.

He followed the elections, that was his assignment. And every time he managed to give just the right twist to his report by following the day-to-day fate of a street corner that was 'dug up because it was going to be repaired'. Then he enjoyed a personal triumph when after the elections he was able to report that all the blockades had been lifted and that the street corner, without anything having been done, had been hastily filled in again, so that the neighbourhood was a lot worse off after the elections than before. In short, he was becoming more and more accurate and more and more toothless. That had finally led not only to an unpleasant triumphalism on his part, but also to an unjustified confidence by other people in his opinion. He was only just thirty, and every five minutes his opinion was sought about complex foreign affairs; at one moment he was interviewed to his astonishment by Dutch television, the next he was giving talks at embassies, and suddenly it hit him that he must stop doing this work. He had packed his things and gone home.

Staring at the white plastic kitchen block he imagined what it would be like out in the country this Sunday morning. Less quiet than in the city, that was for sure, with the din of the birds, which were still excited by the spring and the commotion of the cyclists riding down the woodland path to the river and taking the ferry to lunch in the Red Lion.

He could ring Teresa. No, that wasn't a good idea.

Then he would first have to think up what he was going to say to her, and at the moment the bells stopped and a serene silence fell over the civilization of the city, he bent to the side, grabbed a pile of paper off his bedside table and got up to turn on his PC. With his foot he fished a chair towards him and sat down at his desk.

The computer was slow booting up.

'I protest against the collapse of decency in the world,' muttered Victor.

Old quotes from old films — he shared his enthusiasm for them with Teresa, he had noticed. Twice a day, when he brushed his teeth, he hit a nerve with the head of his toothbrush above his left wisdom tooth, and because that nerve obviously transmitted mysterious signals to the language centre in the left frontal lobe of his brain, he heard, as he dutifully continued brushing, the voice of the vicar from *Four Weddings and a Funeral* in his head, asking in alarm: '*Do* you? *Do* you love someone else? *Do* you, Charles?' It wasn't that old a film, nor was it a terribly appropriate quote while he was brushing his teeth, but there was no escaping it — every time that vicar was there by the left wisdom tooth: '*Do* you, Charles?' — and at the moment that Charles in the film answered 'I do' and was knocked out cold by the spurned bride standing next to him at the altar, Victor spat out the toothpaste into the washbasin and took a towel from the rack; as he dried his face and then dried his hair with brisk movements, he knew that he would be spared the vicar's anxious question until the next time he cleaned his teeth.

On his return to the Netherlands he had gone along to

the dentist, and the latter, as she took off her rubber gloves after the inspection, came out with an unexpected verdict. 'You have a good set of teeth, that isn't the problem.' If Victor had thought up to then that bad teeth were the only problem a dentist worried about, he now learned that in the world of dentistry, as a result of advances in research, a host of new problems had arisen. Now, for example, he knew that you should no longer, as you used to, brush your teeth two or three times a day, but as little as possible, so as not to damage the enamel. The girl to whom his dentist had referred him, an oral hygienist of twenty-five at most with an impressive array of diplomas on the wall, told him exactly what he had better not eat if he intended to brush his teeth an hour later, and the endless list of don'ts – gherkins, oranges, cola, wine, chocolate milk-shakes, kiwi juice – had confused him greatly. It was becoming increasingly difficult to fit your life into the pattern of health demands.

And the same applied for that matter to all those other demands made of the citizen in the West; new problems were arising everywhere 'You're a good citizen, that isn't the problem' – and you had to make sure that from all the conflicting information that science deluged you with, from all the obligations that developing norms of decency imposed on you, you could derive one or two simple rules for life.

It was Victor's firm conviction that people didn't have it easy nowadays. Because through all the progress the life of the modern citizen might have become grander and lusher than it used to be, wealth had made him more adult and the internet had given him access to the infinity of cyber-space, but his grasp on life, the controls and the overview had not kept pace. On the contrary. The bigger his world became, the quicker the citizen lost his grip. The European has relinquished his political influence to Brussels, to the multinationals, to the collective moral Salvation Army of action groups, to Amnesty, the World Wildlife Fund, Novib, Greenpeace – everything was moving out of sight of the desperate aristocrat that the Western citizen had become. Richer and richer, better and better informed about misery elsewhere, more and more publicly powerless to do anything about it.

So should you eat oranges because of the vitamins, or on the contrary not eat oranges because of your tooth enamel? Should you be against child labour and not buy trainers that were put together in India by eight-year-olds, or should you buy trainers from eight-year-olds in India so that they at least earned something? These days every involved consumer in the West – and 'involved consumer' is another word for 'citizen', Victor was fond of reminding his employers – had to take decisions for which he was not equipped.

'I protest against the collapse of decency in the world,' muttered Victor, as he browsed through the 'Erik de Winter' folder on his computer screen. 'I protest against corruption in local politics, I protest against civic heads being in league with crime.'

In the newspapers the scandal surrounding Erik de Winter had soon been relegated to one of the small items on the home news page at the time, but here in the boundless archive of the worldwide web nothing was forgotten and the whole business surrounding Ruth Ackermann's father appeared at the touch of a button. When he recently began his nocturnal hunt for Erik de Winter, Victor had built up a dossier, which he was now trying to put in order. A few articles he had printed out gave the chronology of events; he put dates in the margin, wrote names in the places where there were only initials, drew lines between the separate facts and tried to check that everything was correct.

As soon as he stumbled upon an old legal question concerning a chemical works, the chemical company Bloem BV, Victor, from force of habit, had thought that he was on the trail of a conspiracy, that he had fallen straight into the entanglements of an old war, had hit the jackpot. Because what was actually going on with that chemical group? Had it perhaps delivered chemical weapons to a criminal regime via smuggling routes and shady intermediaries? But no. It soon turned out to be about a conflict on a smaller scale; his journalist's heart calmed down again, he grunted a little and read on.

First of all it had soon become clear to him what his father had meant on the telephone by 'mess on Haiti'. If you entered the search terms 'Bloem', 'Erik de Winter' and 'Haiti', it produced a torrent of articles all telling the same story, and the case had even been included in the internet encyclopaedias, where the details were omitted, but the plot was all the more poignant in all its simplicity.

The article from Wikipedia was now lying next to his computer. Victor had underlined things in red, and lost in thought had scribbled a drawing of a roundabout on it which he had afterwards – because he felt the roundabout on reflection to be unsuitable – crossed out again. After checking an endless series of texts and articles he had the feeling that Wikipedia's summary was accurate.

Bloem BV, through a series of intermediaries, bought a consignment of 2,300 kilos of glycerine. Before selling the glycerine on, it had a sample tested. Laboratory tests showed that the drums contained only 53 per cent glycerine: the consignment had been adulterated, probably by the manufacturer, with anti-freeze, a poisonous substance which, if consumed, can cause serious damage to the liver, kidneys and brain. Nevertheless Bloem decided to sell the consignment with a USP 98 quality certificate, which indicated that the glycerine was 98 per cent pure and hence was suitable for pharmaceutical uses. Via an intermediary Bloem sold the consignment to a company in Port-au-Prince, which made it into a cough-linctus. Eighty Haitian children died after drinking the linctus. The affair subsequently received little attention in the Netherlands. The management of the company did not face criminal charges; the Public Prosecutions Department decided on a financial settlement with Bloem and the company eventually paid two hundred and fifty thousand guilders. The managing director of

Bloem BV, E. de W., was dismissed as a result of this affair. Bloem BV, however, consistently denied involvement in the death of the children.

Up to that point it might have been an accident, a ghastly accident, with Ruth Ackermann's father the one responsible, but at the same time a victim of circumstances, of his staff who had not informed him, and his bosses, who had fired him without compunction to protect their own business and their reputation. It might even have been possible that Erik de Winter's wife was so distressed by the whole thing that a few years later, at her wits' end, she had stood on the railway line and Ruth had had to rescue her in the middle of the night on her bike.

But a reading of the other documents meant that the victim role was no longer available to Erik de Winter; there was no doubt about it, wrote the investigative journalists, that the managing director had been aware of the anti-freeze in the glycerine from the outset. According to his staff, he was more than a manager: he was a dealer who bought and sold chemical substances direct from his office, ordered personally from laboratories and was generally quite literally the boss of the operation – nothing happened in the Bloem chemical trading company that Erik de Winter didn't know all about. So when the laboratory tests on the glycerine came out wrong, and the stuff turned out not to be suitable for medical use, he had decided on his own not to alert anyone, since, as he stated afterwards, 'he was simply not responsible for the things that happened to the glycerine after sale'.

At this point Victor got up from his chair. Somewhere in the house someone had woken up, because someone flushed a toilet. Victor walked up and down his room a few times, stood on the chair, looked into the flat of the neighbours opposite and saw a boy sitting in front of the television. Sunday morning. The parents would be gradually getting up too. He got down and lay on his bed.

He felt like a coffee. He could make some himself, but it was a more attractive idea to go out and breakfast in the café, then he could have goat's cheese on toast with his coffee. If he remained lying there, it was only because he was still hesitating a little about Teresa; what he would most like to do would be to drive over to see her and tell the stories about the Bloem affair in person. In her kitchen. Over a cup of coffee from the futuristic espresso machine she had, which emitted the ear-splitting sound of an industrial cleaning machine.

He smiled for a moment when he thought of the statement of the Bloem staff; the company had often sold substances with a false quality certificate, they said, and they also mixed new consignments at random with raw materials that they had in storage. Then they dumped the old and new consignments into a lorry, drove about a bit, braked sharply a few times, and by that time everything was sufficiently mixed together. Nice guys. Teresa would be able to appreciate the charm of this story amid all the drama.

It was connected with the lessened grip on life, he thought, the fact that people no longer felt responsible. It was because of globalization with all those network economies and chain companies that people's responsibility was more diffuse than it had ever been. And the citizens, who knew more and more about life, the dangers that threatened them, hygiene and health risks, environmental problems and food problems, the moral danger of a civil war breaking out on the other side of the world just because they bought the wrong coffee – those citizens trusted ever more eagerly in the systems they had once installed for their protection. They themselves had long since lost their grip, but they would be saved from all physical and moral dangers by inspections and government agencies.

He leant to one side, rested his right arm on the floor next to the bed and stretched to get a sheet of paper from his desk with his left hand. Hadn't he just circled the passage in the middle of the night and marked it with large arrows and exclamation-marks? Yes, there it was, that was right, they had had the glycerine tested for purity because Bloem BV had not long before been awarded an ISO9002 certificate – so that they had to meet stringent quality standards. And that was beautiful, the quality standards, the certificates, the laboratory tests to protect people against the danger of poisoning; it was beautiful that there were systems to relieve people of responsibility. The only problem was that those systems didn't work if no one took them seriously.

Victor stared at the beams, painted soft yellow, which bent to meet each other like the ribs of a boat; the primitive shape of the room gave a sense of safety, here he bobbed around as in a soundproof water-tank; nothing could hurt him.

It was not only the certification system that was useless if you didn't take it seriously: the justice system offered no protection either if it failed. That was the most remarkable thing about the dossier on the Bloem affair that lay next to him on the bed. Because the Public Prosecutions Department might have examined the case of the contaminated glycerine, but the civil servants could not find the documents, did not have the autopsy reports, then did have them, then lost them again, and when they turned up again they did not see any causal connection between poisoning and death, subsequently did see one, but suddenly were unable to discover who had been responsible for the purchase of the glycerine.

And so because they did not know who had bought the stuff, they could not hold anyone personally responsible, and so they could not institute criminal proceedings, take anyone to court because of involuntary manslaughter, and so they acted as if it were an environmental offence and Bloem was able to absolve itself from its responsibility for the deaths of eighty children by paying two hundred and fifty thousand guilders.

Victor wondered if Ruth Ackermann had ever seen the documents that persistent journalists had dug up. Product forms, purchase certificates, rental agreements for storage, faxes giving the test results, all carrying the signature of her father, who had agreed to every transaction and had been directly responsible for the deaths of eighty children. Victor couldn't determine from *The Summer of Canvas Shoes* exactly what Ruth knew.

In this case an aristocracy of citizens had been cast adrift in Europe: the systems designed to give protection since people could no longer protect themselves against all the dangers – the certification systems, the quality systems, the legal systems – were populated by citizens who falsified documents and lost reports, and messed things up, and so all in all made those dangers on the contrary greater rather than smaller. 'Received no information', 'seen no reports', 'letters – despite receipt – did not arrive'. When the Dutch civil servants decided to come to a settlement with Bloem BV, they forgot to inform the parents of the dead children on Haiti – they could not find the relevant address.

'I protest against the collapse of decency in the world.' Victor knew there was no point in raking up the case after all these years and he didn't begrudge Ruth Ackermann her moment of fame – why should he make a scandal of her family history if she hadn't done so in her book? He would let the case rest. As a journalist. But he did know at the same time that he was unusually curious about Erik de Winter and about the reason why the village was so anxiously silent about Ruth Ackermann.

And in addition to all this, documents, curiosity, there was still also the question whether he should tell the whole story to Teresa. Teresa, who had looked so serene in her new sunglasses in the High Street, who had made an omelette in the kitchen where her husband rubbed breadboards and chopping-blocks with oil to keep them in good condition.

Victor made an inward bow to her.

'Lighthouses, John: lighthouses in a foggy world.'

Now he wanted to get out of the house, into the open air, but before he went into town – in search of coffee and people to talk to – he put all the articles he had printed out into a large yellow envelope, and put it on the corner of his desk, pending the decision whether he would really send it to Teresa.

2

The Summer of Canvas Shoes is a funny, entertaining book, the critics are agreed. The more serious critics miss topicality and the element of social involvement in the novel, but over and against this is the fact that Ruth Ackermann has a great talent for treating a heavy subject like temporary insanity as if it were an episode from a sitcom. In the view of many, the romance in the institution is 'hilariously written'. According to the journalist Kiki Jansen, who is writing a series of pieces on the writer's European tour, the book falls into two sections. 'On the one hand it's a screamingly funny account of a failed love affair. On the other it is a deeply human confession of a former psychiatric patient. Dostoevsky's *Dream of a Ridiculous Man* meets *I Never Promised You a Rose Garden.*' Slivers of light, shards of darkness.

Randolf picks up the book with great reluctance. Iris collected it for him from the bookshop, where great piles of copies were laid out on tables. And in the window. And next to the till. Very different from what happens with the books they normally read and which have to be ordered specially for the book club from the publishers. The formidable Iris, ruler of hearth and home, has laid it out ready for him as usual on his desk, with the mountain crystal paperweight on it to make things quite clear. He opens it obediently and starts reading. And maybe the story really attracts his interest for a moment, as he reads how the girl loses the power of speech from fear of her own destructive power.

After all, it's quite conceivable (Randolf has also read *The Drama of the Gifted Child*) that a young woman with a keen intuition for the needs of her surroundings should present herself as cleverer than she is and start suffering from fantasies of omnipotence. That she should think it is her mission to save the world. It's also quite conceivable that after a while the omnipotence becomes too great for her and turns against her. The rage surging through the girl's body is so great that she is afraid of scorching the earth with her own words. She is absolutely convinced that people will die for miles around the moment she opens her mouth: children will be blown under the tram; men will jump off high-rise buildings; mothers will burst in to pieces like a fragmentation bomb detonated by her proximity – everything submerged in a single huge explosion of language and text and blood and torn-off limbs, bulging intestines, rolling heads, and it's just as well that the girl is admitted to a psychiatric hospital just in time in great confusion and panic.

But the book does not have the intellectual depth or tragic stature that Randolf expects, because very soon a youthful plot unfolds in which the girl, once safely admitted, falls under the spell of a wildly attractive fellow-patient with whom she begins a passionate affair that is complicated somewhat by the fact that the girl says nothing and the boy hasn't the faintest idea what he wants. Randolf shuts the book in irritation and tosses it onto his desk. He sits staring straight ahead for a while. Then he picks the book up again.

Lucius is lying in bed. It's ten in the evening: he has put a glass of cognac on his mother's old Victorian sewing-table that serves as a bedside-table. At the foot of his bed is a bench on which all his bedtime reading is piled: dossiers, minutes of meetings, a history of English costume, a book on psychiatric patients with Christ delusions, a study of the rainbow by Spinoza; but this evening he has gone to bed especially early to start a brand-new novel. It's comfortable in bed. It has been a mild spring day and Lucius has left the balcony window open, so that a little evening air occasionally wafts in. There is a reading lamp on in the corner of the room, a bed lamp above his head casts a gentle light on the pages. Lucius wears grey-blue silk pyjamas and over the back of a chair hangs a thin dressing-gown with a paisley pattern ready to hand. Should he have a visitor at this point, he can open the door quite decently. But there are no visitors. The rest of the house is already dark and no one would be impudent enough to ring the doorbell if there was only a light on the bedroom. 'Regards to the home front', shouted a vague acquaintance whom he bumped into late in the afternoon on the stairs of the court, but Lucius, thank God, has no home front. All is peaceful; he sighs serenely and opens the book.

In this way it doesn't take long for him to become absorbed in the story of the silent girl who is proposed to by the nervous guy with the canvas shoes and the appearance of a male model. She accepts his proposal of course – and here Lucius takes a sip of his cognac – but a day later his mother comes to visit and after that the guy denies that he has ever seen the girl. How is that possible, asks every lunatic in the hospital. How is that possible, is the question that wafts through the wards. How is that possible, comes the muffled sound from the isolation cell. The sedatives that he takes on the instructions of his psychiatrist, he says, cause acute memory loss. He has simply forgotten everything. Today he has long since forgotten what he did yesterday.

The girl's heart breaks, but she doesn't leave it at that.

Lucius puts the book down on the duvet with a slow movement. Good for you, he mutters. Then he looks searchingly at the photo of the writer inside the back cover of the book.

Gabrielle has been in a hurry all day. She picked the book up on her way to work and during her morning meetings keeps thinking of how she will shortly take it out of her bag and, she imagines, will read it in one go. Unfortunately it has entirely escaped her in the previous months who Ruth Ackermann is. Otherwise she would surely have bought her book before, wouldn't she? God knows, she has thought of the girl regularly over the years and she wonders nervously what she will find in this international bestseller, this letter from another world. It must be a poignant story, if you consider everything the young writer has been through. She thinks of the diaries of a female dissident that she read recently, and from which gruesome details of the stay in an asylum are still vivid in her mind.

Now Gabrielle knows there is a difference between a Western hospital and the terror institutions from the time of the old regimes in the Eastern bloc, but there must be a kind of constant in the experience of madness that is induced by the outgrowths of the political system, be it communism or capitalism, the differences between them are probably not great. Of course no one in the Netherlands becomes psychotic in a deserted courtyard as the snowflakes fall on his face and a mangy dog seeks shelter under his coat and the authorities have already put the necessary stamp on his death certificate, night without end, departure without destination – that was twentieth-century Russia and perhaps twenty-first-century Asia, and, what's more, Western youth culture sounds different from the culture it grew up with – but the essence of alienation doesn't change.

The day passes without her having a chance to take the book out; she only manages to do that at home, halfway through the evening, when the most important emails have been sent and no more big problems are anticipated. Her husband Tobias is sitting in the conservatory watching the football world championships, and she alights on a sofa in the living-room with a cup of coffee and her mobile in silent mode. Then she finally settles down to read, since she has to despite everything, and reads, with mounting astonishment.

The girl, determined not to accept the breach of promise by the guy with the canvas shoes, involves her only friend in the mental asylum via a smuggled letter. All the alarm bells immediately ring for the friend. With the unconditional devotion of one lost soul for another she looks for hours on the internet for the effect of sedatives on the memory, and because she eventually finds out that sedatives have absolutely no effect on the memory, she stands in the garden of the institution to inform the girl of this find via a large text-board:

☹ No Way! No effects! No 1! U2good4him! XU + CUL8ter.

Gabrielle is bewildered.

The fact that the girl's friend is standing in the garden with a text-board has not gone unobserved, and in no time the police arrive. Two strong men jump out of the police van and take the friend, board and all, to the station. There she tells her story with undiminished excitement and indignation to all the police officers. And because police officers have hearts too, and because they find it an old-fashioned romantic story, they release her as soon as she has finished. One of the policemen, a young chap with eyes like Finnish lakes, is actually so strongly moved by the unpleasant love-story of the silent girl that he decides to help her in a personal capacity, and a day later, out of working hours, he visits her in uniform in the institution.

'Jesus Christ,' sighs Randolf.

Lucius, grinning, pours himself another glass of cognac.

In bewilderment Gabrielle leafs further through the book. How is this all going to end?

Because the friend was picked up by the charging policemen so soon after her arrival at the institution, the silent girl didn't see her standing in the garden at all. She now feels so terrible abandoned by her friend and every Tom, Dick and Harry, that she relapses into the great confusion in which she was originally admitted to the institution, and she is fighting desperately with the demons of darkness at the moment the young policeman arrives.

She is in such a bad way indeed that the director of the institution forbids the officer to make contact with her, since that would not benefit her mental health. But the policeman is not someone who gives up easily; four days later he returns and this time he has done his homework; through expert police work he has found out that the girl's father is a top criminal, with eighty deaths on his conscience already, and he explains to the director of the asylum why he must meet the girl without delay: it so happens that the police are on the track of the trigger-happy father. The director reluctantly gives in.

What is going on inside her? What voices speak to her in the darkness? When she looks in the mirror, she sees herself standing there silent. And she sees nothing but that silence. Sometimes she tries to pin down the problem that according to the doctors is behind her silence, but the moment she bends forward in the mirror and searches for the interface between dream and reality, the image that she has of herself bursts into millions of pieces and an icy splinter lands in her heart, so that she freezes; now all she can see and hear is her own silence. The silence is an isolation cell, the cell is made of ice; the slivers of the mirror in her heart and the rods of the railway in her hands, sometimes she sees the track of her blood, sometimes she hears only her own silence, then the isolation cell, with a roar, fills with blood and the mirrors fall out of her hands, how can she hear whispering when she's alone, how can she hear the train passing when she hears nothing, how can she hear time driving along where no clock is ticking, because nothing is ticking, the fact that she nevertheless sees time roaring past and is alone, sees and hears nothing and knives and people with sharp shrill slivers of glass splitting mirrors that are not there, not there, not there, none of them are there and nor is she herself, because she's hidden so far inside herself that she no longer dares to look out through her own eyes.

Then doors swing open and voices mutter and then, saved, floating high above everything through the Siberian seclusion of her hospital bed, she vaguely remembers what the doctors said, that she will only get better when she decides not to keep her destiny so obstinately in her own hands. But unfortunately there is something contradictory about that remedy.

'How is she at the moment?' the young policeman asks the hospital director (two economists are walking down the street, and one says to the other 'How's your wife?', and the other one says 'Compared to what?'), and the director says she's fine, but of course you never know everything that's going on in a person. The young policeman with eyes like clear blue lakes cannot speak freely with the girl, because the director insists on being present.

And here follows the weird scene that has meanwhile attained such cult status on the internet that Hollywood moguls came up with the idea of filming the book. Because in order to pass the friend's message to the girl in coded form, the policeman has to launch into an inimitable exposition on the use of sedatives; does the girl use sedatives? No. Just as well, because in some cases he's been involved in important witnesses have cited memory loss as a result of sedative use, but wrongly, because it's been proved that sedatives have absolutely no effect on the memory.

While the policeman raves on, the director becomes increasingly bored and impatient, but something seems to dawn slowly in the girl's eyes. (At this point the Hollywood moguls thought for a moment of Angelina Jolie, because she played a psychiatric patient so beautifully in *Girl*,

Interrupted, but on the other hand Angelina Jolie is too old.)

Lucius is wide awake in bed and occasionally hisses through his teeth as he reads. On the one hand he realizes regretfully that Randolf will be relieved now the story is taking this idiotic turn. On the other hand his admiration for the young writer is growing with every page. He is impressed by her vitality, her spunk, her chutzpah.

So he doesn't admire her for the book she has written, because although he finds the plot highly amusing, he is fully aware that you have to be young to appreciate the full value of this story – he admires her for the book she hasn't written. The members of the book club know only too well the material she has in cases under her bed, how much subject matter for how many compelling novels, and instead of that she writes an ebullient comedy full of nonsense, which will irritate Randolf, and young girls' jokes that won't make Gabrielle laugh.

It's getting late, but Lucius wants to finish the book before he goes to sleep. He knows enough by now, and he also knows that most of the other members of the club won't read the book to the end, but Lucius is curious. It turns cold in bed and he gets up to close the window, first standing close to the window to smoke a cigarette – he doesn't like cigarette smoke in the bedroom – and looks down at the avenue that, by the light of the vaguely haloed street lamps, stretches away in front of him in the dark like a milky way between the distant mist-banks. Then he climbs back into bed and reads how the silent girl becomes friends with the young policeman, how she points him wordlessly to her armed and dangerous father and how incidentally she wraps up a whole network of top criminals, criminals who occupy high positions in society and enjoy the respect of those around them, but on closer inspection turn out to be nothing but vulgar villains who out of pure indifference to the welfare of others sow death and destruction all around them. He reads how at the end of the book the girl pockets a reward and gains international fame. Then on the last page the guy with the canvas shoes regains his memory and still wants to marry her, but in the final paragraph the girl unexpectedly shakes her head: she refuses.

'Now she was so rich and famous, she decided to leave the lunatic asylum and cautiously to start saying something.'

3

Of course they'd never thought that one fine day one of the children would write a book. And that as a result everything would be brought back to the surface so many years later. They were always determined to forget Ruth Ackermann's father and gradually they forgot their own share in the story. Or perhaps they didn't forget: they managed to live around it.

In the great scheme of things a secret is fairly futile. Of course there are psychologists who think that keeping things secret eventually drives whole families apart and ravages promising young lives. And initially you yourself also think that silence knocks a great hole in your life. But time passes, the hole freezes over and you begin to think that going on living is more important than going on pointlessly feeling ashamed. And so it is.

So they waste whole days trying to be nice. They are . . . What are they? Liberal, democratic, committed, all in the measured mixture that is called right-minded. They salve their consciences with the stupid decisions of which life is made up. In Bangkok a young man is arrested for possession of drugs, they have to defend him; in The Hague the Minister of Internal Affairs asks their advice on civil service integrity; in China a promising manager is waiting for them for a job interview, he's sitting in the waiting-room leafing through a copy of the *Business Management Review*. They must keep going. They cannot afford to admit any doubt about the direction they have taken.

Evil, a famous rock star once said, is a little girl with a blue dress on, playing in the back garden with a red ball. If you were to tell the members of the book club that, they would immediately annex the quote. Gabrielle would note it down in her literary logbook. Randolf would include it in his set repertoire, open his annual after-dinner speech to the class of diplomats with it at least once, and win them over with humour. Lucius would mutter the words sarcastically to himself in one of his sleepless nights, sitting up in bed with a glass of cognac. And the following morning, as he packed his case before leaving for China, Jurgen would call out to his wife: 'Do you know what they said yesterday at the book club?'

No more than that. They don't talk about anything apart from that. The past is another country, that's what they always say, the past is another country.

4

Mid-May. Sun and wind. The maize had already been sown, but because of a fierce north-easterly wind it was immediately blown off the fields, so that the farmers need to resow tomorrow. The nervousness could be sensed even in the centre of the village. Brave people in their twenties were sitting on the terrace in windproof jackets, shouting cheerfully at each other while the wind blew dust in their food. Lucius drove past and had to suppress the impulse to have a drink here on the terrace, before going to the meeting of the book club at Randolf's. The bookshop was already closed, the Armenian homeless people's paper seller had gone home, gone off with one of those nice women in sloppy dresses who like cooking exotic dishes for guests from distant countries. There were moments when Lucius envied other people for the lives they led that were so much more manageable than his.

He drove up Randolf's drive at high speed, partly to send as much gravel as possible shooting in the air. The others had parked their cars further along the avenue, or had come on foot, but Lucius was just a little too fond of asserting himself on Randolf's doorstep. He drove around the house to the car port, parked next to Randolf's ramshackle Hillman (on the point of falling to pieces) and slammed the door of his car shut. The front door was open and he went in, stood in the hall for a while listening to the book club, which by the sound of it was already engaged in serious discussion in the living-room, and went upstairs to say hello to Iris. Her room was right opposite the stairwell, and the door was open.

Lucius liked this room, which, despite the astonishing quantity of carpets, Japanese prints, footstools, nineteenth-century side tables and strange Greek jewellery from a distant past, retained a great lightness and airiness; through the large French windows you looked out onto the balcony with the white-painted trellis on which Iris had hung up flowerpots full of what he guessed were geraniums.

She was sitting at her desk writing an email. Lucius leant towards her and kissed her on the cheek.

'Lucius,' she said with relief. 'God, I'm so glad at least that you're here tonight. Things are coming to the crunch.'

'They certainly are.'

'I must tell you straight that I don't trust Randolf one little bit. If you ask me he hasn't read the book at all. And he hasn't said anything about it.'

'Have you read it?' He sat down on the sofa with the Indonesian patchwork quilt made up of brown and gold sections, on which Iris slept during the day when she was

THE BOOK CLUB

at home. She shut down her email and turned to him, chair and all.

'Yes. It was different from what I'd expected.'

'It's different from what all of us had expected.'

'It's not about anything.'

'No, I like that.'

She looked at him severely. 'Surely it would have been better if that Ackermann girl had raised the matter. As it is, we're stuck with it. Soon she'll be coming here for a reading and what are we supposed to say?'

'We'll say: "Hello Ruth, I knew you when you were ten years old; give my regards to your father."'

'Come off it.'

'Right. What do you want me to do?'

'You can't possibly talk about that book for a whole evening without talking about Erik; make sure that Randolf finally faces up to the fact — that he acknowledges what happened.'

Lucius leafed through a gardening book that lay on the sofa.

'How are your roses doing?' he said.

'Fine. They're early. Do you actually know any plants besides roses?'

'Uh? Yes. Geraniums.'

'Every time you come here you ask about the roses.'

'Listen. I'll try to bring up Erik tonight, although I don't know what good it's going to do his daughter. But if it can cleanse our souls, that will be a nice bonus. Hydrangeas. I know something about hydrangeas too: that

211

you must put a silver fork in the earth if you want them to go blue.'

He kissed her again, tenderly, and went downstairs.

The men were laughing frequently and loudly. The laughter of power, thought Lucius, who sat in the window-nook with a dish of nibbles and was watching the men, who were his friends, from a distance. It was an absolute, uninhibited display of power by alpha males opening their mouths and starting to laugh to show that they were not afraid, that they were in command, at ease and on their guard at the same time. Lucius was not curious about what they had to say at these kinds of moments, because the message behind this defensive line of noise could not be very newsworthy. He wondered, as he often wondered without ever finding an answer, why people without a sense of humour laugh so much more frequently and louder than those *with* a sense of humour. Certainly now John wasn't there and Jurgen, flouting all the rules, had invited two outsiders – a newspaper publisher who lived in the dungeon on the edge of the wood, and a neighbour who was on the board of Laurus – the room was filled with exuberance.

'It was so busy that I almost lost Marijke in the throng.'

'There are more expensive ways of getting rid of your wife, Frans.'

The conversation rolled along hilariously. Lucius felt a wave of tedium, knowing that the mood was unlikely to improve this evening. There was a tension in the air that was not connected solely with the north-easterly wind.

That afternoon he had talked to cab-driver in Amsterdam who was trying to formulate a theory on the difference between space and time. Infinity, said the driver, as he drove along the Rokin towards the Dam, cannot be divided into two. Because if you cut an infinite series in half, each of the two halves will have an end on one side, so you will no longer have an infinite series. Lucius, at the back of the taxi, had observed an astonished silence. He knew that at this moment he should make a clever objection, but he couldn't for the life of him think what. Only now he was sitting in the window seat and recalled the taxi-driver with his crew-cut, did he remember that infinity divided by two is infinity. You didn't need any scholastic arguments for that, just common sense, because, as Lucius said in his mind to the driver, something can perfectly well begin somewhere and have a zero-point and still be infinite. He then imagined an arc, which in the hallucinatory weariness of the early evening soon turned into a rainbow, and started cutting it in half at its highest point, but could suddenly no longer remember whether a rainbow is infinite. It surely must be, he thought drowsily, because otherwise there would be no problem finding the end of the rainbow.

He started awake when Randolf nudged him and offered him a dish of stuffed dates.

'You look tired, Lucius.'

'Haven't had much sleep this week. It'll pass.'

He stayed in his window-seat and ate his nibbles. He was sometimes at a loss as to why he allowed himself to be lured to these kinds of gatherings by Randolf. With these men who constantly talked about the world as if it were their personal project, a business that others knew nothing about. They said it was good to be close to the action. Directors with secretaries who had their own secretaries. Close to the action. Whenever they took a trip to the board-meeting.

Randolf had his exclusive claim on the world. 'Why do you never see a poet or a philosopher in the hotbeds of trouble abroad?' he would say nowadays, aping the Marxist garbage he had learned in gentlemen's clubs. He undoubtedly thought that with his columns and reports he contributed more to the improvement of the world than writers – whose novels he read and discussed with his students, though mainly to prove his own points of view. Randolf's admiration for novels was very selective, yet that admiration had become so much a part of his life that he could plonk Lucius down here on the window-seat and make him read a book with five, six, seven or so people. In this way, through misunderstandings about mutual interests, they had been condemned to each other.

Lucius knew perfectly well that in other circumstances he would have plunged wholeheartedly into this evening's jollity, that he would have got the judgement on the snail and the ginger ale from Randolf's bookcase and would have bonded with Jurgen's neighbour, whom he didn't yet know. But because of the memories of a past he had wanted to forget, a deep sense of desolation had divided him from the others; he wanted to talk to his friends, but he couldn't.

Last night, arriving home from long discussions at the

office, he had watched a repeat of the late news in bed. An administrator of a large hospital was responding outside on the pavement, right in front of the revolving door, to a report in which the death of eight patients was attributed to mismanagement.

'Not culpable,' said the administrator indignantly to camera. 'And what's more, all this commotion is very unfair. Other organizations just batten down the hatches when something goes wrong – we're immediately all over the papers. That isn't just.'

Lucius looked at the man through his eyelashes. He knew him. He knew all these men. And if they happened to be women he knew them too. And he had to say that he abhorred them, but at the same time they were too much like him for comfort.

They should have started their discussions three-quarters of an hour ago, and still no one was making any move towards getting hold of the book; Randolf leant slightly back against the mantelpiece, thrust his lower body forward and launched into a fiery tirade on the advantages of visiting museums in London. So Lucius descended from his windowsill and said rather abruptly: 'You can continue your recruiting drive whenever you like, but now we really should make a start on our book of the month. It's a wonderful book and a huge bestseller. I propose we have a look at what we thought of it.'

The members of the book club and their guests sat down, took out their books and started laughing. While the wind grew even stronger outside, and the exuberance of the

village square wafted through the village, the members of
the book club sat in Randolf's house and laughed.

'Well, we've read it now.'

'How the other half lives.'

'Youth. Youth isn't "the other half"; for that matter, we're
all youth. You were like that once.'

'I wasn't. At least, I can't remember any romantic
policemen coming to the door to rescue me.'

'That's still noticeable as something you missed out on,
Jurgen.'

'I was disappointed, I must say. I recently read another
book about admission to a psychiatric institution, and that
was a lot more convincing.'

'Have you ever read Dostoevsky? *Notes from Underground*?'

'Yes.'

'No.'

'Is that the same book as *Notes from the House of the Dead*?

'The same? Is it the same? No, I don't think so.'

After half a minute they had fluttered away from the
book – 'Can we please concentrate on today's book?' asked
Lucius. But the discussion was too animated to be set back
on track and Randolf got up to fetch Dostoevsky from his
bookcase.

'The Ackermann girl's book is also about Dostoevsky,'
said Lucius trying again. 'About his novel *The Dream*.'

'*The Dream* is a very nice novel,' said Gabrielle. 'But
still more of a digression in his work. *Notes from
Underground* on the other hand – that in a completely
different class.'

Lucius listened for a further ten minutes, but then, astonished at the course the discussion was taking, picked up his glass and withdrew reflectively to his window-seat.The others didn't seem to miss his input and he himself was forced to consider whether he had any input. With his back leaning against the window he could feel that the wind was blowing straight at the house. He drew the curtain behind him to avoid a draught. Through a side window he saw a plastic watering-can rolling through the garden. Lucius hoped that Iris had seen the storm coming and brought in the gardening tools that were scattered about; the bigger things, the cast-iron table, the wheelbarrow, Randolf's bike that was still outside leaning against the shed, would be all right. He was cold. In any other instance he would have suggested lighting the fire, but he sat there in silence and watched the others sitting in Iris's welcoming room in a circle of light.

Shortly after Randolf made as if to end the plenary session (it turned out Jurgen was in a hurry), in an attempt to sum up the evening Frans noted cheerfully that they would survive the literary evening with Ms Ackermann the writer with no problem. And at that moment, as Randolf was taking out his diary from his jacket that hung over a chair, and Gabrielle brought up the question of the next novel, Lucius made a final attempt from his window-seat to open the discussion.

'The book was written by the darling daughter of our dear ex-book-club member Erik de Winter.' He drank a mouthful of wine and was more specific. 'Our dear ex-friend Erik de Winter.'

Randolf turned towards the window-seat and pretended not to have heard the remark; he tried to look as haughty as possible. 'Have you something to add, Lucius?'

'Uh?' said Lucius in surprise, raising his eyebrows: what? me? Did he have something to add? He held his wine glass in the air and spoke in a solemn tone as if he were giving an after-dinner speech over which he had done his very best hours before in the privacy of his own rooms and which he now knew by heart.

'At the back of the cemetery there is a blue, blue tombstone. All those who step on that stone are stepping on Maria. What has Maria on her lap? A child. What has that child in its hand? A book. What does it say? From father and mother, from sister and brother, from niece and nephew, from dog and from bitch.'

He lowered his glass and looked round the circle. Randolf nodded curtly. 'Thank you, Lucius, for the important contribution. Can I now close the meeting?'

A quarter of an hour later Lucius was sitting in his car under Randolf's wooden car port, smoking a cigarette from the packet that he had just grabbed off the table in the hall. He had always thought that he would one day be called to account, but then in Randolf's wake, and if not now, then when? He stubbed out his cigarette in irritation and a few seconds later lit up another. Randolf seemed totally invulnerable to any form of criticism, guilt or shame and Lucius didn't know what to make of it. No, he didn't know what to make of it. The problem was not only that Randolf seemed invulnerable to consequences and reprisals, the biggest problem of all was that he did not seem susceptible to fear.

Perhaps it was time for the professor to get to know fear. But Lucius knew only too well that he wouldn't be the one to conduct his friend through the haunted house of his own past. He now stubbed out his cigarette furiously in the car ashtray and in his impotence thumped the steering-wheel. Failure. The evening had been a failure, and the chance of ever making things better had been lost. He had missed the opportunity. He could blame himself, and he *did* blame himself, but it was also because of the unbelievable scenario that turned this evening into a theatre of diabolical evil, in which the actors had only to open their mouths for uncontrollable laughter to come out.

He wasn't angry, he sniggered helplessly, he was sad. Looking back on his life he was mainly disappointed – the plans they had had, the work they had accomplished, fate, the successes they had enjoyed, everything, everything was a failure. Failed, not because success had been wanting, but because everything was surrounded by a smell of rotting and decay, of deception and falseness which are the result of shutting things off for too long from the supply of fresh air. They had once had the chance of leading a life of value, with the chance of initiating changes, creating a legacy, as the members of the book club would say, but they had screwed it up for good.

It had been the craziest evening he had ever experienced. He started the car and made the gravel fly as he drove home.

5

When Teresa got up and went to the kitchen for the first cup of coffee of the day, the large yellow envelope that had arrived a day earlier was still lying on the worktop. Now she picked it up and turned it round, she saw that Victor had written something on the back. 'PS I wanted to talk to you about this, but I'm just sending you the file.' It was arrogant handwriting, she thought resentfully, and an arrogant message.

Teresa turned the envelope round for a while, uncertain whether to open it, and then laid it aside with an impatient gesture. She wasn't yet dressed: she was walking around in an old black dressing-gown of John's, the sleeves of which she had to roll up to free her hands; a belt kept the rest together, and if she bent a little at the knees she could just reach the pockets that came somewhere halfway down her legs. She felt to see if there were a packet of cigarettes inside, but there wasn't; she extracted only a liquorice sweet and a cutting from the paper, with an advert for volume shampoo. The morning was not her favourite time of the day, and she was in a foul mood, partly because she had drunk too much cointreau the night before; she didn't like drinking all that much anyway, and drinking too much liqueur was the stupidest thing you could do – the syrupy scent of sweet alcohol hung around for days after in your nostrils and sinuses, and sometimes the smell of oranges made you feel sick a week later. Her irrationality was now directed towards the envelope, and she resented Victor's turning up in her kitchen again, with a lofty tone and a presumptuous message; as if she had time to read his files.

The last time he had dropped by to see her, his visit had made her restless and she didn't know exactly why. As long as he had said 'heigh-ho' and sat next to her in the car with his sloppy grin, he had made a familiar impression; but in the course of conversation she had realized that he was more complicated than he looked. The presence of such a forceful, cocksure man in her house, someone she had known since childhood and at the same time didn't know at all, was in itself confusing. But something else was going on too, something connected with Ruth's book.

She looked for aspirin in a kitchen drawer, and then went into the hall to see if there were something in the chest-of-drawers, but all the aspirin in the house seemed to have gone. Obviously they had been in a lot of pain recently. Teresa recalled with amusement the young man whom she had heard a week before at the chemist's asking for three packets of paracetamol and who had then turned to his wife: 'Do you think that will be enough for the holiday?' – she should lay in a sizeable store of painkillers for the summer that lay in prospect. Back in the kitchen she went over to the worktop again and stared angrily at the envelope one more.

The Summer of Canvas Shoes was a nice book. She had enjoyed it tremendously and apart from that wouldn't have looked for any deeper meanings, and would probably have soon forgotten about it if Victor hadn't talked about it so morbidly and threateningly. By the end of the evening he had got fairly hazy and soon she could no longer make head or tail of his stories, but he had sighed so deeply ('Oh, Teresa, that's the way it goes, it's not Disney, that's the way it goes') that she had been automatically impressed. There must be more going on with Ruth than she had thought.

With things that seem superficially stupid, it was as the journalist Kiki Jansen had accurately put it: 'A comedy seems a simple genre, but there are so many snags attached to the writing of a light novel that you as a writer must keep at the back of your mind.'

Teresa giggled.

At the same she had the sense that disaster was threatening, there were rumblings from the distance. She looked aimlessly in the fridge, had no idea what she was looking for, slammed the door shut again, put a cup under the coffee-maker and while the coffee was pouring she opened the envelope. It contained a pile of paper, print-outs, of articles collected via a search engine.

Teresa leafed through the pile and then sat on a high stool by the worktop, with the coffee and a couple of treacle biscuits beside her. She usually breakfasted on almond cookies, flan, shortbread, the German Christmas cakes that were available all year round in the supermarket – as long as she didn't put on weight there was no problem; she picked up a treacle biscuit and read what Victor had written on the first page in capitals with a black felt-tip. 'NOTE: Ruth Ackermann was originally called Ruth de Winter. E. K. de Winter (Erik de Winter) is her father.'

Teresa dipped the treacle biscuit into her coffee and with her other hand turned the pages, looking for a short text, a quick entry into the problem that Victor was trying to present to her, and she soon found a sheet that contained only one short quote.

'Bloem BV itself stuck labels on the drums with the certification GLYCERINE 98 PCT USP, an international designation indicating that the substance may be used in the preparation of medicines.'

Teresa groaned – her head was still hurting and that wasn't something that could be relieved with treacle biscuits – she thought hard but didn't know what 98 PCT USP meant. For all her knowledge of glues and pigments, oil, asphalt and formaldehyde, she knew nothing about medical requirements or Consumer Goods Act regulations, even when they applied to substances she worked with every day. She stared at the garden and scanned the branches of the trees for squirrels: the trees were already too full of leaves again to see them, but if you were lucky they ran right down the trunks and chased the neighbours' cats across the grass. But the trees were empty, the garden was empty, the house was dreary now that John wasn't there, she had to go to Rotterdam in a few hours and she had a headache. She felt as little like reading Victor's file as keeping today's appointments. There was a good chance that he was trying to involve her in his attempts to save the world and banish injustice; she realized she was as unenthusiastic as before. If Ruth's father had been involved in dodgy dealing with chemicals that was highly disreputable, but scarcely a reason to get all het up about it years later.

At that moment the telephone rang somewhere in the house.

Teresa leapt off her stool and with the pile of papers in her hand ran in the direction of the sound.

'Yes?' she panted when she had finally found the telephone among the cushions of an easy chair on which she had sat watching television the previous evening; the running had made the headache flare up and Teresa stood there with her eyes closed, head bent, in attempt to freeze the movement of the pain.

'This is Kiki Jansen,' said a young woman.

'Yes?' demanded Teresa.

'Sorry to disturb you so early,' said Kiki Jansen. 'But at the moment I'm doing a piece . . .'

'About Ruth Ackermann's tour,' said Teresa. The pain had subsided again and she sat astride the chair. 'I know.' Great, there was another packet of cigarettes lying here, she tapped one out looked around her for the lighter. 'You rang me once before.'

'That's right, and at the time you couldn't remember a

thing,' said Kiki Jansen accommodatingly. 'But I'm wondering if I might talk to you somewhere soon.'

'Talk to me?' Teresa lit the cigarette. She shook her head in surprise.

'Yes, the thing is that at the moment I'm working on a profile on Ruth's past. As I told you, the headmaster of the school you both went to gave me an address list of her classmates. As you're the only one who still lives in the village, and because Ruth is coming to the village shortly to give a talk, I thought it might be nice to go to the reading with you. Then I can write about it.'

'I don't think that's a good idea' (letting herself fall backwards into the chair).

'Of course I can imagine that I've taken you by surprise, but we could talk to each other beforehand.'

Teresa blew smoke at the ceiling in boredom, which John hated, because he liked the spotless white space and the illusion of infinity it created, but John wasn't here now. What was Teresa supposed to say to the keen reporter in the meantime? That she had been the belle of the ball and that she really, word of honour, could no longer remember the adolescents at the back of the class? It was quite embarrassing, this complete forgetfulness concerning the best years of her life. Victor had rubbed her nose in that enough, so that she didn't dare tell Kiki Jansen yet again that she had only heard the name Ruth Ackermann a few weeks ago.

She stubbed out her cigarette in the ashtray, turned on to her side and saw the papers that she had thrown on the floor when she picked up the phone. While Kiki Jansen tried to convince Teresa of the absolute necessity of talking to each other over a cup of coffee about the intimate secrets that Ruth and Teresa had undoubtedly exchanged back then in the dressing-room, on the sports field or perhaps even in the shower, Teresa read out of the corner of her eye a passage in bold on the page that had landed closest to the chair. 'Bloem BV still refuses to accept any responsibility and hence also refuses to pay for the operations on the children who survived this drama. The company and its managing director E. de W. have always denied all blame.'

The children who survived? Teresa sat up again and drew the papers towards her with her foot. She vaguely heard Kiki Jansen say something about the importance of human interest, the person behind the writer, a peek into childhood, but she was scarcely listening. With the telephone under her chin she picked up a sheet with each hand and first of all read the text preceding the bold section she had just read.

The glycerine found its way into a chain of customers and was finally used in Haiti in the preparation of cough-linctus; eighty children died after taking this linctus. Other children survived, but had lasting liver or brain damage. Bloem BV denied any knowledge of the contamination of the glycerine, but documents show that the company had definitely had the substance tested for purity in a Dutch laboratory. When it emerged from the test that the glycerine consisted largely of anti-freeze, Bloem decided not to inform its customers, but to sell the consignment on with the certification 98 PCT USP. This implied that, according to Bloem, the purity was 98 per cent; subsequently the purity turned out to be only 51 per cent and the glycerine was hence absolutely not suitable for pharmaceutical purposes.

Below were the bold sentences, which Teresa now read a second time. 'Bloem BV still refuses to accept any responsibility and hence also refuses to pay for the operations on the children who survived this drama. The company and its managing director E. de W. have always denied all blame.'

Teresa stared at the paper without being able to take in the scope of the words in one go. At the other end of the line was Kiki Jansen, and from the silence Teresa could tell that the journalist had asked her a question. 'Er,' she said blankly and turned the paper over. There was nothing on the back and she turned it back to the front.

'So it would be,' the journalist explained again, 'an account of what Ruth used to be like in class and what it was like growing up in the village.'

The headache had exploded, Teresa felt herself becoming nauseous, unwell, and with an angry gesture she grabbed the telephone, which was still wedged between her left cheek and shoulder, and moved it to her right ear.

'Oh, for goodness sake shut up about all that nonsense,' she snapped.

That obviously took Kiki Jansen aback; after her previous phone call she had probably suspected today's mission would be a difficult one, but that didn't mean she was prepared for such a rude and harsh rejection.

'Well, I'm sorry,' she said. 'Sorry to have disturbed you.'

Teresa slowly put the telephone next to her and bent forward to pick the other articles off the ground.

'. . . Bloem BV aware all along that the raw material for medicine which it exported was contaminated . . .'

'. . . the Public Prosecutions Department did not make use of the autopsy reports which show that the death of the children is directly ascribable to the use of the contaminated glycerine . . .'

'. . . parents not informed of the settlement . . .'

'. . . only glycerine that is 98 per cent pure may be given this designation . . .'

'. . . case treated as an environmental offence and settled with a payment of two hundred thousand euros . . .'

'. . . purchase and sale of glycerine largely handled by E. de W, himself; it was he who sent the customers a fax with the certification "98 PCT USP", from which they could conclude that the glycerine was suitable for medicinal use . . .'

Teresa sat at the foot of the chair and lit up a cigarette. She thought of Victor and his message on the back of the envelope: 'I wanted to talk to you about this' – why hadn't he talked to her? Had she given him too little opportunity perhaps? And now she looked back over the last few days and weeks, another question presented itself much more compellingly: why hadn't her parents talked to her? She picked up the telephone and was about to ring her mother, but had second thoughts. Then, to her own surprise, she felt a terrible urge to ring John, who was always so sensible, and so calm, who knew so much of the world and yet was reliable; but although this might have been the moment when a wife could quite justifiably have her husband fetched from a meeting on the other side of the world, or out of bed, God knows what time of day it was or what time-zone he was in, she decided that that conversation could wait until he was back home. He was busy and she hadn't married him to keep him from his work.

She put the phone down again. She had to go to Rotterdam; she had to hurry. Perhaps there was some aspirin in the medicine-chest in the bathroom.

6

Lucius was sitting in a restaurant with a plate of blood in front of him.

A few days earlier he had rung Iris with the announcement that he wanted to take her out to Amsterdam for the evening.

'We'll leave that boring husband of yours at home and paint the big city a pale shade of red.'

'That sounds as if we'll end up in police custody again.' Iris felt a need to over-dramatize the adventure of her friendship with Lucius.

'Not at all. It'll all stay innocent. We'll eat our way up town, and drink our way down town.'

'And then?'

'Then nothing. Then I'll bring you back home, as is proper.'

'If you can still drive.'

'I can hire a student to drive us there and back, if you want.'

'I think that would be better for your career. And for

your conscience. I don't know which of the two you find more important. But as far as I'm concerned you can get a bit drunk. And a student will be a nice extra. I'm getting old, I can't remember when I was last in a car with a student.'

Iris went out with Lucius quite often. She loved those evenings when she was fêted by him and had him all to herself. Not only because of the totally nonchalant way he let such evenings get out of hand, but she also relished the knowledge that Randolf was sitting at home at that moment and worrying. Randolf had always had such sentimental views of women that he couldn't imagine what his own wife had to talk about with Lucius. He could understand Iris having her own male friends, whom she went out with on her own, with whom she shared interests – that was a different generation. But he couldn't understand what Iris got out of Lucius' company, just as he couldn't understand why Lucius preferred to spend his free evenings with Iris, instead of with him. If he worried about their friendship for that reason, he was sensible enough to ask no questions and say nothing about it, but Iris knew that he would be wondering all kinds of things all evening and till late at night. And she liked that thought.

Iris loved Randolf in some respects – they'd been married so long it didn't even matter any more exactly how much she loved him, but she was immensely bored in his company. Sometimes she found his presence in the house so oppressive that she climbed out of the window, to get away for a moment without having to say where she was going.

Because usually – when he was home – he sat working solemnly in his study on the ground floor, and that was so close to the front door that she couldn't slip away unnoticed. That was why she preferred to disappear out of the window of the side room that had once been built as a waiting-room for a doctor and served as a playroom for passing children. Of course he usually noticed eventually that she had gone, but he never mentioned it – because, Iris assumed, he had his own secrets. And they were probably a lot more gruesome than hers; in this marriage it was definitely sensible to leave a number of things undiscussed.

But anyway, Iris's excursions with Lucius were so open that they could not be denied; for Randolf there was nothing for it but to accept them cheerfully, wave Iris goodbye and the next morning inquire solicitously how it had been.

This time Lucius had driven up in a Jaguar. He had the car on trial for a weekend, but didn't intend to buy it – 'I ask you!' – but felt that Iris should make up her own mind about it. Iris was flattered. Lucius in a Jaguar – that was a different class of adventurousness from Randolf in a Hillman. Lucius who always kissed her so pleasurably, smelling very vaguely of something expensive, an aftershave, something that Randolf abhorred; Lucius with his suits, his polished, shoes, his ironic tone that enabled him to talk himself in anywhere, effortlessly. For example, they had begun the evening in good spirits in the restaurant of the Amstel Hotel, where Lucius was welcomed like a long-lost friend, the porter grinned at him and the staff flocked to enquire after his well-being.

'Fine, fine, fine,' Lucius grinned back. 'Everything's fine.'

And he felt fine, and he hoped that lots of people would notice him this evening, because he adored Iris and liked to be seen with her, certainly in places where they knew how to appreciate her extravagant chic at its full value. He wasn't sure if all Greek women resembled Maria Callas (he had never been to Greece), but Iris did at any rate, with her theatrical style and her domineering look. Now she was finally going a little grey, she seemed even more terrifying and she was developing a slightly hysterical tinge to her behaviour that Lucius liked very much. Not a woman to have against you.

Her daughter Teresa had inherited that beauty, but in a more moderate form – undoubtedly due to the calming bourgeois influence of Randolf – and although according to current criteria the daughter was even more beautiful than the mother, she lacked the pontifical self-assurance that made Iris so impressive.

Lucius strode solemnly with her through the room, watched how other people looked at her and installed her solicitously in her place. He chatted to the manager, and made it generally clear that the evening could be entrusted to him with complete confidence. Then he ordered something to drink for Iris, who accepted the service gratefully.

Although Lucius normally never ate pork (he hated the dehumanization of his food), a few days before he had succumbed to his own horror to a suckling pig, and when he got home was up half the night looking for an essay by Charles Lamb – 'A Dissertation on Roast Pig' – that he had once used for a legal article, since it dealt with a shift in culture and legislation, and when he had finally found it, he was immediately hooked again.

For a suckling pig, writes the dreadful Charles Lamb, is the greatest delicacy in the world of food. At least that is so if you are talking about 'a young and tender suckling – under a moon old – guiltless as yet of the sty – with no original speck of the *amor immunditiae*, the hereditary failing of the first parent, yet manifest – his voice as yet not broken, but something between a childish treble, and a grumble – the mild forerunner, or praeludium, of a grunt'.

Although Lucius had hoped to gain absolution by reading the text – as he was deeply ashamed of having sinned against his own principles earlier that evening – it only provoked more sinful thoughts, so that he soon fell into a trance and thought of nothing but roast piglets. That was because of Lamb's language, which was more fiendishly seductive than the taste of pork itself, and which convinced him that the tongue is raised far above the laws of morality. And because he wasn't allowed to think about it, he couldn't stop thinking about it. 'O call it not fat – but an indefinable sweetness growing up to it – the tender blossoming of fat – fat cropped in the bud – taken in the shoot – in the first inno- cence – the cream and quintessence of the child-pig's yet pure food.'

With this guilty dissipation still fresh in his memory Lucius sat opposite Iris at table, and in his mind his plate filled with blood. He seemed to be constantly sinning against his own principles, and with the menu unfolded in front of him he remembered with a start that tonight he had to talk to Iris about *The Summer of Canvas Shoes*, and for a moment it was as if a baby piglet one moon old with its throat cut was lying right in front of him squealing on the white tablecloth.

But the waiter leant over the table to adjust the position of the glasses slightly, and Lucius quickly regained his appetite for this evening: for wine, crystal, table silver, an appetite for everything. As he reread the list of main dishes he suddenly recalled with amused surprise that directly after slaughtering – when that took place on one's own premises and was an innocent and domestic business – his aunt used to eat baked pig's ears; these days the ears were dried and fed to the dogs. He would like to try one of those pig's ears, and Iris was without doubt the best person to get into the car with and go and eat pig's ears somewhere, but not here, not in the capital, where the rules for gourmet tourism were strict and where the tune was called by a reviewer who left the citizenry no scope at all for private adventures.

Despite the thoughts of suckling pig and lamb that occasionally flared up, Lucius was actually definitely not a convinced meat-eater: on the contrary, he had been considering turning vegetarian for years, and anyway he liked little dishes, everything light and fresh, and he loved the taste of lemon. But he could also be made deeply happy by tasting the bitterness of almonds in white wine and believed fervently when spiritual gurus maintained in books that satisfaction tastes of apricot pudding, desire of dates, the afterglow of ripe, dark fruit. When he was fully rested, he liked oysters. When he was tired, like now, at the end of a long week, he preferred to abandon himself to everything that was quivering and rich like cream, everything that foamed and was warm and liquid like butter and jelly and sauce and sabayon, and all in all it was a bloody long time since he had satisfied those desires anywhere else than at the dinner-table.

And just as he was spooning down a morsel of his hors-d'œuvre Iris started talking about sex.

7

'I'm doing the same as that Italian prime minister,' said Iris. 'I'm not having sex till the elections.'

'What about the Italian prime minister?' said Lucius, looking up from his plate.

'Sex,' said Iris. 'He'd said he was abstaining till the elections, and I'm doing the same. No sex till the literary evening with the de Winter girl.'

'The Ackermann girl: her name is Ruth Ackermann.'

'Right, Lucius. I'll repeat my words so they can be taken down in a statement. No sex till the literary evening with the Ackermann girl.'

'What does Randolf think about it? About that "no sex"?'

'I'm not necessarily talking about Randolf when I talk about sex.'

Lucius raised one eyebrow and looked searchingly at her. She was bluffing. Or was she? Iris with the gardener; Iris with the trainer at the gym; Iris, God help us, with the woman who ran the art gallery in the old tram-shed in the woods. It was all perfectly possible and, if you thought about it, even probable.

'Apart from which I haven't told Randolf yet. There's every chance he won't notice. But it's a matter of principle.'

'So what is the principle that underlies your secret boycott of Randolf Pellikaan?'

'I want him finally to tell Teresa what happened back then with the de Winter family, before the daughter comes to sign books in the bookshop in a while.'

'Talk. She's not coming to sign books, she's coming to talk. And not in the bookshop: she's coming to the church.'

There was a moment's silence. The waiter carefully refilled their glasses; at a nearby table a conversation on the apportionment of liability flared up to noisier levels. Lucius took a sip and used the time he needed to savour the wine to think about this confession of Iris's.

'Then you'll have to tell him after all. If he doesn't notice himself, I mean. There's little point in boycotting Randolf sexually if he is in a state of blissful ignorance about it.'

'Have you read *Lysistrata*?'

'Aha, that's what this conversation is about. You've been reading *Lysistrata*.'

For the past few months, and years, Lucius had heard in amazement comments on performances of *Lysistrata* here and there. Through the belligerence of the new millennium interest has suddenly been created in the women in the Greek play who had declared a sex boycott – in order to force their warmongering husbands to make peace. Everywhere there were actors and journalists who thought that a sexual strike like that would again be a good idea, and that Laura Bush should take the initiative. At least, if the word 'initiative' was applicable here.

'Those kinds of playful campaigns make me critical in the old-fashioned sense,' he said to Iris. 'Because if it's really true that the social influence of woman is still limited to the bed, and I've no idea whether that's true, I haven't a clue, but if it's true, then it seems to me that we need to discuss that urgently. Forget that war, or your own domestic quarrels, I'd say, and let's talk about a really hopeless question.'

From a bachelor's point of view, which he adopted on occasion, Lucius didn't consider it was good to understand exactly what happened between the men and women in *Lysistrata*; he'd read the play in the past, but had never looked closely at it. Let them get on with it, with their erections and phantom pregnancies. There was no way that the play could be translated back with any decency into his own life, because in an empty house who was supposed to blackmail whom, and with what?

Lucius was not a radical celibate and in general he ensured that the tension did not rise too high, occasionally picking someone up during a trip, or conference, but establishing ongoing relationships he regarded as a matter for other people. That was something for people who talked about their 'genetic pool', another species, another life-form; a matter for the kind of men who eat tomato purée to ward off prostate cancer, because of the prophylactic effects of lycopene – people with thoughts about the future.

The waiter brought the starter, and Lucius, who took another sip and carefully savoured the fresh fruitiness of the Tokay (slightly sour, lightly bitter, with a hint of aniseed), realized how tired he was. After a busy week full of court cases which he disliked and for which he had had to make a greater effort than usual, the disgust slowed down the operation of his brain, he felt the onset of drunkenness from the first glass. All the glasses of Dutch gin that he had drunk in bed at night this week had formed a reservoir in his stomach. He drank a mouthful and the reservoir overflowed. They were only on the starter and he could already see Iris disappearing.

'Right,' he sighed. 'Sex. That men-and-women thing. Come to that, that's not a bad definition, since it immediately indicates how difficult it is to transpose the situation of *Lysistrata* to any other. The thing is that the play describes an exceptional situation: we are dealing with the presence of two clearly demarcated and by definition mutually exclusive groups, with diametrically opposed viewpoints, two totally conflicting groups, that is, which nevertheless have an urgent and acute interest in intimate association.'

'What?' said Iris.

'Sex,' said Lucius. 'Men and women have an interest in becoming intimate. So how that story is supposed to serve as a model for the relationship between Europe and the American president, between the pope and the Muslim community, is not completely clear. In fact with modern conflicts, like the Iraq problem or Afghanistan, we are not dealing with old-fashioned wars, and those involved do not represent two completely opposed viewpoints, they are not clearly identifiable groups, and it's absolutely not about the need to come closer together. So a sex strike cannot solve all those conflicts, since most married men and women today are probably in agreement at the political level. The dividing lines take a different course. In short, war or no war is not a matter we can settle by kissing and making up, and it's rather awkward behaving as if we can.'

Iris had long since ceased to follow what Lucius was saying, since she had simply wanted to say something about Randolf and the Ackermann girl, but she never felt stupid in Lucius' company, so although she had lost the thread of the conversation, she responded at random.

'I still thought the power of the women in the play was interesting. The economists, John's economics journals, say that women are going to be the greatest power factor of the twenty-first century.'

'OK, OK, OK, OK. That's all very well as long as we're talking about employee power and consumer power and business power. But *Lysistrata* isn't about female power, it's about setting aside the law. What makes the play interesting is the completely natural way power games are played *and* are accepted by everyone. The women don't appeal to principles of justice, they don't take their case to court, they don't follow agreed procedures, they blackmail the men with sex. I can't make it any more respectable than that.'

Lucius took a piece of bread and wiped his plate clean. The waiter bent carefully past his elbow with the wine. The care, the solicitousness of the ritual with the bottle, the serving and the clearing of the table pleased Lucius even more than the food itself; you always had to wait with food, to see if it would bring the moment of rapture you hoped for. The fish was good, but something sensational would have to happen for Lucius to become ecstatic. He leant back in his chair and looked contentedly at Iris, who was saying something about the importance of sex for women. Self-transparency was what Lucius was striving for on an evening like this.

It is illuminating, he thought, the play that Iris has brought up, because the problem that I have and so many people in this world share with me, the difficulty of deciding on a correct view on the conflicts that are raging everywhere, is more to do with power than with justice.

Lost in thought, he tipped backwards on the rear legs of his chair, bad-mannered behaviour that in his childhood had been strictly corrected and forbidden, but was returning now that he was becoming increasingly in control of his own life. He started to explain the question of power and justice to Iris.

'The question of justice is relatively simple. If you want to justify a war, it must meet certain criteria. That is, there are rules *ad bellum*, rules to which you must keep to if you want to start a war, and these are all more or less obvious: you can wage war in self-defence, but in that case all other means must have been exhausted; the war must eventually lead to peace and it must not cause unnecessary damage. And you mustn't start an arms race.'

'We were talking about *Lysistrata*,' said Iris.

'Yes. In his play Aristophanes says the same as Kant, namely that the accumulation of money constitutes a much greater risk of war breaking out than the accumulation of weapons. That's why those Greek women in *Lysistrata* all sit on the treasure chest and refuse to get off.'

'Well, jolly good for those women.'

'Definitely. Jolly good. Provided they subsequently divide up the money fairly. Thus far justice. But politics, including world politics, really doesn't hinge on justice: politics hinges on power, and that's mainly where *Lysistrata* comes in handy. After all, those women throw all considerations of justice overboard and ruthlessly exact peace. That makes *Lysistrata* such an unappealing anti-war play for me. Actually it's arguing for a dictatorship, the dictatorship of the vagina, a kind of sexual feudalism which you wouldn't want our international relations to be governed by in future.'

'Why not, if it's for a good cause?'

'But those women aren't the least concerned about war and peace as a matter of principle; all they're concerned about is securing their own interests. No one who reads the play can possibly present it as a pure anti-war piece. On the contrary, the American president would be delighted: the United States, itself scarcely interested in law, international law any more, can identify effortlessly with those women and their blackmailing practices. If I were Bush, I would have *Lysistrata* read aloud all over the world tomorrow – to whip up support for my wars.'

Something started gently revolving in Lucius' head, and he knew he could only stop the movement by continuing to speak straight out into space. He also knew that Iris had by now switched off and was eavesdropping on the conversations at the other tables. But on the other hand Iris had the rare capacity for following five conversations at once, so he might still have her attention.

How had they actually got on to this topic? Iris seemed to have forgotten her own sex boycott and Lucius didn't feel like reviewing her marriage to Randolf. He was also too far gone for concrete questions and practical problems: he couldn't go into Iris's sexual escapades and the experiences she had had; he had to stay on the safe ground of his abstract convictions.

'Right, as I said: the problem of determining a proper view of war and peace in the midst of all this, in our time, has far more to do with power than with justice. And although I am not an advocate of throwing justice overboard, and consequently don't find *Lysistrata* a sensible anti-war choice, I will admit it doesn't seem that sensible to throw our power overboard either: we might yet be in urgent need of it. The problem with power is just that to a large extent it's difficult to monitor and difficult to define. Every citizen can take cognizance of the law of warfare, because that is by definition public; but we, or at least I as an average citizen, know virtually nothing about the real power relationships. Apart from that, it's very difficult to document yourself, since power relationships are almost by definition not public and it's consequently a tough job finding out what or whom to believe.'

'I don't think I can follow everything any more,' said Iris when the main course was brought and she bent forward to sniff the scent of lemon thyme. She liked lemon thyme.

'Sorry. I'll stop going on about it. One last thing. I'd like to say, I think, that for moral and legal reasons I'm still against military intervention in crisis areas; that means that in a week's time for moral and legal reasons I may be *for* military intervention in crisis areas; *and* it means that I haven't got the faintest idea what is actually going on, so that I mainly feel at the mercy of various military powers engaged in blackmailing each other. In brief, the dictatorship of erections and phantom pregnancies.'

And so Lucius found it difficult to identify with that.

Lucius had talked all evening, and Iris had listened now and then, and if you were to ask her, she would say that she had listened mainly to the statements *beneath* the words. She summarized her conclusion for this evening in a question.

'Don't you do it any more, Lucius?'

'Don't I do what any more?' He took a cigar case out of his inside pocket and turned it round a few times, until he became aware of what he was doing and placed the case in front of him on the table. Iris looked at him severely.

'It. Do you still do it?'

'What kind of question is that?' He sighed. 'I would have appreciated it if you had asked me that thirty years ago, but these days the subject doesn't concern me that much.'

'You can't be serious. I don't believe a word. Aren't you ever tempted any more these days?'

'My God. Temptation. How often does a person even encounter that in the course of his life these days? It surely isn't the case that temptation lurks on every street corner?' said Lucius. He pushed his chair firmly back some distance. 'Come on, that's enough for now. We'll grab a taxi and get a dessert a few streets further on.' He gave his credit card to a passing waiter and tucked his cigar case back into his inside pocket.

Iris reached for the wine bottle on the side table to see if there were anything left in it. The bottle was empty.

'It wasn't good,' she said.

'What wasn't good, my dear Iris?'

'Erik de Winter.'

During the starter Lucius had still had the energy to examine this question, but now he abandoned it in a mood of hazy fatalism. He retrieved his favourite Nietzsche quotation from his memory and talked as usual to his wine glass. '"What is good, you ask. Being brave is good. Let the little girls talk: being good is what is at once beautiful and moving." No, it wasn't good, it wasn't good at all. But now we're going for a sorbet and then we're going to see if there's such a thing as cognac to be had in this town.'

The waiter came back with his card and Lucius fished a few notes out of his trouser pocket, which he gave to the waiter, while trying to look Iris straight in the face.

'Since you've converted to such inflexible principles, we won't bother to book a room for the night.'

The waiter looked blank. He'd been used so often as the witness to advances by guests heading off into the night – the waiter as part of the pre-coital tension – that it no longer affected him.

For a moment Lucius waited for Iris to contradict him, since he loved her greatly and would like to put one over on Randolf and in the depths of his soul one thing merged effortlessly with the other – but Iris was warmly silent.

Only when Lucius got up did he really notice how much he had drunk. Help, my chair is falling over, but it was the waiter pulling back his chair. And then Iris was heading for the door again.

8

Writing, Randolf Pellikaan would say, is a contribution to the political culture of a country.

But Ruth Ackermann would object that from the writer's perspective there is no political culture, no world history and no tragedy, all literature can discover is individual reactions, the psychological salvation of fiction. Writing is first and foremost entertainment.

Yet there are a few readers who have read the book *The Summer of Canvas Shoes* with mounting concern; because what other readers regard as a pleasurable intermezzo, they regard as an urgent cry for help. A psychiatrist who knew Ruth from the old days has written her a letter. He reminded her of the famous poem by Stevie Smith – about the man drowning in the sea, while the people on the beach think he's just giving them a friendly wave. 'Not waving, but drowning.'

Ruth Ackermann wrote back to him. Even if you're

drowning, that's still no reason not to wave cheerfully to the people on the beach. Drowning. But waving. Cheer up.

V

The Explanation

1

'Yes, good afternoon, de Winter here, my wife, my ex-wife, lives with you. And I was used to being sent news about her from time to time, but I haven't heard anything from you for quite a while. Perhaps you didn't receive my change-of-address notification? So that you're still sending the post to the old address?'

Victor was trying to find Erik de Winter's address. It wasn't easy: the name was too ordinary simply to be found in the telephone book or through search engines; there was no point in even trying. Asking around in the village wasn't an option either. Firstly, he didn't want to awaken suspicion and, apart from that, de Winter had probably rigorously severed all links with the village, so it was highly questionable whether anyone at all would know his new address. Victor thought for a day and then came up with the bright idea of ringing the nursing home. He took a chance, asked his mother for information, and to his immense relief she simply gave him, without pestering him out of curiosity, the address of the nursing home where Louise

Ackermann was living after the umpteenth attempt to poison herself. It was highly likely that de Winter was still in contact with his ex-wife – at any rate he had had to leave her behind and hopefully he had had the decency to pass on his address.

So he rang the office and pretended to be de Winter. There was something lugubrious about deceiving a nursing home, but, as Victor told himself in his journalistic zeal, it was in a good cause.

'Your name?'

'De Winter. Erik. E. K.'

'And your wife's name?'

'Ex-wife. Her name is Ackermann.' Victor just hoped she wouldn't ask for other first names and dates of birth.

The woman rattled away audibly at her keyboard. She hesitated. 'You live in Scheveningen?'

'Yes, Scheveningen,' said Victor, thinking fast, 'but do you still have my old address there, or the new one?'

She gave the name of the street.

'Well, that must be right then,' said Victor. 'Odd. I'll have a good check to see if I haven't overlooked anything. Perhaps they're here somewhere in a pile.'

'I see from the notes that we wrote to you some while ago,' said the woman rather awkwardly. 'The thing is, we need to discuss treatment. And obviously we no longer have a current address for your children. I'd like to put you through to a colleague of mine who knows more about it.'

'No,' cried Victor in alarm. 'That isn't necessary. I'm sure it's all correct. I'm sorry for disturbing you.' Before the woman could protest, he rang off. At the same moment he realized that she probably wouldn't let it rest there; he waited for a moment to see whether she hadn't perhaps noted down his number, but she didn't ring back. Well, he thought, it'll probably all sort itself out. He looked up the online telephone directory and entered the name and address, E. K. de Winter. Scheveningen. Gotcha! growled Victor.

After his life had fallen apart, seventeen years ago, Erik de Winter had gone into exile in Scheveningen. From the money that remained after the lawyers' fees and the divorce he had bought a little flat on the beach, with a sea view, in the hope that he would have room to breathe there. The very first evening he knew he had made a mistake. The desolation of the sea in winter overwhelmed him and he felt locked in a marginal existence. Ahead of him he saw nothing but the endless rush of the sea, the nocturnal image of an old television, and at his back he could feel the Netherlands, a community of saints to which he no longer belonged after his resignation and his social disgrace. But since in this final isolation he could think of no urgent reason for moving, he stayed on in the apartment, and year after year looked down in contempt at the tourist population which he saw blossom and fade with the seasons. Uninspiring people, tourists, interchangeable wage-slaves who were content with two weeks' holiday on the cheap promenade, but he could avoid them; he had found the way to the supermarkets where they didn't go, and apart from that he didn't have to have anything to do with them.

When he arrived here he had furnished the flat with the bare essentials: a table, a few chairs, a bed and an easy-chair for falling asleep in front of the television in the evenings. The children had announced after a few years that they no longer wanted to see him, that was easy, it meant he no longer had to get in anything for them, and he wasn't expecting any other visitors. Cooking was consequently fairly simple. He had never done any in his life, but he had soon taught himself to heat up some tinned food on a gas-ring. He hadn't taken to drink in a big way, which was an achievement. His own sin in recent years had been visiting sex sites on the internet, which each time made him feel even more abject than before, but there was plenty of room for those feelings of self-contempt along with the general feelings of disgust and self-loathing; below a certain limit you no longer fight against your own miserable nature.

Unfortunately the original purchase of the flat and some furniture had taken up all the money; so in order to earn his living he had had to look for work and had become a chemistry teacher at a private tutoring college. It was simple work, which didn't interest him, and he did only the bare minimum. When he came home, he closed the door behind him and watched TV against the background of the unavoidable sea. Usually he fell asleep at some point during a late film.

When Victor Herwig rang him, Erik de Winter hadn't used the phone for eighteen months for anything except to order a pizza. Of course he had expected recently that a moment would come when someone contacted him about his daughter Ruth; now she had become hugely famous surely someone at least would become curious about her background. To tell the truth it had astonished him that it had taken so long. But perhaps no one had hit on the idea that a writer of pulp fiction – since Erik de Winter didn't have a high opinion of his daughter's work – had a serious secret to hide. None of his former friends and acquaintances had evidently felt an urgent need to rake up the past. Or rather: it was in their best interests to keep their mouths shut. So, when the telephone rang and a man's voice introduced itself, de Winter was relieved, being certain it was a journalist.

'No,' said Victor. 'I'm not a journalist. That is, I am a journalist, but that's not why I'm ringing. I simply have a few questions: I was at school with her, and a few memories have come up that I'd like to talk to you about.'

'Why should I talk to you about your memories?'

'Because they concern you.'

Silence.

'It's not that I want to pester you or turn your life upside down. I'm concerned about Ruth. There are a few things I still don't understand.'

'And why do you want to understand all about it then?'

Victor decided to take a chance. He had assumed that de Winter didn't want to talk to journalists, but maybe that was a false assumption.

'It may well be that I'll find it interesting enough to write about.'

Now he had said it, he suddenly heard that it sounded like blackmail. But de Winter didn't seem to have a problem with it.

'Do you want to talk about my daughter's book too?'

'Perhaps. If you think it's relevant.'

'I don't think it's relevant.'

'Fine, then we'll talk only about schooldays and everything connected with that.'

'Come over tomorrow afternoon then.'

2

They'd arranged to meet in an Italian restaurant, a kind of glorified snack-bar, which de Winter seemed to frequent; they arrived more or less at the same time. The owner left them alone after de Winter had made a gesture with his hand indicating 'later', a gesture that Victor knew from the Middle East but had never before seen anyone make in the Netherlands. He had the general feeling of finding himself in a spot outside the normal run of things, a neutral zone, in extra-territorial waters, of having landed in the future of seventeen years ago.

Without anything having been ordered, a waiter brought two beers and then disappeared into the kitchen. They were the only customers. Outside it was drizzling and the beach and the streets were empty; there was nothing but the occasional windswept tourist passing, hugging the front of the buildings, too wet to feel comfortable, not wet enough to give up.

Victor would have liked a moment to take stock of de Winter, test out the best direction to take to help the conversation succeed, but the man started talking at once. As if, tucked away in his seaside resort, he had been waiting for weeks, months even, for someone to come along with the right question.

'My daughter had a hard time, I'll admit that at once.' Victor was on his guard. The man was hard to place, his eyes were oddly animated, but he was older and shabbier than Victor had expected. A man in a dated grey suit – very likely he needed to assert himself, in all his insignificance at a pine table, while his daughter was on a tour through Europe.

'You were in her class, I understand.' And he went straight to the heart of the matter. 'Then you may know that at that time some things went wrong with her, and with my ex-wife, and as time went on that escalated, though I believe my daughter did her best to keep things going.' He talked so fast and swallowed so many syllables that Victor had to concentrate in order to follow the thread. Apart from that the man drank as fast as he talked, and his glass was empty after the first few sentences.

'But after that things went pear-shaped for Ruth and she was admitted to hospital somewhere for a while. Anyway, it's all in her book. Even though she felt obliged to give things a cheerful twist. But that's her business.'

Victor had resolved not to start talking about the book of his own accord, but the subject was already on the table from the word go.

'That cheerful twist worked. Given the sales figures.'

'Definitely.' Now de Winter seemed annoyed for some

reason, so Victor decided to let the subject rest again immediately and started talking instead about Ruth's schooldays; that was a subject that had been expressly authorized on the telephone. The waiter came by with two more glasses of beer.

'At the time, when I was in Ruth's class, I never understood what happened.'

'Do you really mean that? Or is that a reproach, a philosophical remark? You don't know what happened?'

'I do now, I've seen the reports.'

'Aha!'

'But it all remains rather obscure,' said Victor, and he tried to put things in such a way that de Winter didn't feel compromised and continued the dialogue. 'I know what happened on Haiti, I know that you gave up your job, to put it like that. And in fact I had the feeling that I'd got quite a good picture of everything from the newspaper articles and the dossiers. But what I don't understand at the moment, after going back to the village a couple of times, is the exact reason why the book club has declared a boycott against your daughter's book.' (Christ, he was back at the book again.)

De Winter burst out laughing. 'A boycott? Funny. I really didn't know that. The things you hear. A boycott. Terrific, I wouldn't have thought they would be so infantile.'

De Winter grinned and Victor knew, with a sudden, physical certainty, that he could easily strike this man. The jauntily displayed lack of interest in his daughter, the carefully studied cynical laugh, it was all in all so sad and shameful that Victor would have like nothing better than to pull the man across the table and hurl him head-first through the glass door of the Italian restaurant, but he knew there would be no point. He also knew he would not do it.

'Perhaps boycott is too grand a word,' he said, and sighed. 'Actually they haven't said anything detrimental about the book, but neither do they seem very keen on Ruth's visit.'

'Visit?'

'She's coming to a literary evening in the village shortly.'

The man was now silent. Outside a few holiday-makers were walking through the rain with their hoods up; there was no further sign of the waiter. Victor began to suspect that this had been a wasted journey. He looked around, at the posters of Venice on the wall, plastic bunches of grapes draped along the window-frame, the cigarette machine in the corner, next to the passage to the cloakroom. When he finally looked back at de Winter, he was just taking out a cigarette, and, with it between his fingers, made a gesture towards Victor as if wanting to underline his words, put the cigarette between his lips and lit it with a match that he tore from a cardboard book. 'The book club are a bunch of bastards,' he said. With an angry gesture he immediately stubbed his cigarette out again in the ashtray, got up and went down the passage to the toilet.

When he came back, he had two new glasses of beer with him.

'It can be useful to have smart lawyers in your circle of acquaintances,' he said, sitting down again. He had adjusted his mood; in the passage where the toilets were the gravity of the events must have descended on him: his cheerfulness had gone.

'I'm not actually terribly interested in literature, but I had manoeuvred my way into that book club. You never know, there are advantages in knowing people who in turn know people; they were good company and I like talking to people now and then.'

He was playing with the menu. Victor stared at the list of pizzas on the back without taking anything in; Erik de Winter had been a member of the book club – that explained at one fell swoop all the discomfort felt in the village since the publication of Ruth's book.

'I'd never made use of them before. But at that moment, when we had received the glycerine and realized that my company was about to contravene the Chemical Substances Act, I discussed things with Randolf Pellikaan and Jurgen Lagerweij at the end of the week. I think we'd just read a classic, *Madame Bovary* or something, and at the end of the evening (it was at Frans' place) I asked their advice. I didn't feel quite right about it. I'd sold the stuff abroad with the certification USP; I knew that that wasn't correct, and so I'd been wondering for a few days how grave that decision was. Randolf called a specialist there and then, a lawyer he knew from the editorial board of a journal, and he spelt it all out nicely. Criminal offence, liability. In retrospect he proved to be quite right. First-class legal advice.'

'And so they didn't try to stop you making the decision?'

'They simply answered my query – as if it were an examination question. I wanted to know the situation, and they told me. There were a number of test reports, so the test I had had carried out wasn't decisive. No, they didn't try to make me change my decision and I don't blame them. We opted for the scenic route, as it's called today: you drive around the block, cut a bit off the journey, and there wasn't that much of a problem. Except that it all went terribly wrong. But well, you have to admit that from a legal point of view the outcome was better than we could have hoped. The company was offered a nice settlement and only had to pay some money.'

'How much? All the reports differ.'

'A couple of hundred thousand.'

'How much is a couple of hundred thousand?'

'A couple of hundred thousand is a couple of hundred thousand.'

'Why was it actually so simple? Why was the case never heard in court?' Victor wanted to ask something about the book club, but didn't know what. So they'd advised de Winter, and they'd not tried to change his decision. And then? What else was there to ask?

'There was no court case because Bloem, or at least Bloem's mother company, had the decency to sack me, and the legal authorities considered that a token of goodwill. And because it was not deliberate. After all, I hadn't intended to cause all that mess. To tell the truth I think they were afraid they had no case at all. I also heard that they didn't want to go to court because such a big case requires a lot of court capacity and because "that capacity is very scarce", according to some lawyers.'

'What does that mean? That this crime was so exceptional, so gruesome, that there weren't judges enough to try it?'

De Winter grinned wearily. 'You're trying to make me feel guilty at this late stage. That doesn't make that much impression after all this time. Does that surprise you? As you can imagine, lots of people have tried to make me feel guilty. I've heard it all before; you can't think of much new to insult me or offend me. I'm sorry. You'll have to vent your moral superiority elsewhere.'

'OK, yes, sorry, go on: the company wasn't prosecuted because there was too little court capacity.'

'They issued a press release; they considered that an adequate signal to society.'

'What was the signal, then? You mustn't poison children, because if you do your name will get in the papers?'

De Winter sighed. 'You think you can still do something about it, don't you? What do you want? What have you actually come here for? I offer you my throat, like a dog, go on, bite, bite me to death – it won't do any good, I'm already dead, I've long since ceased to exist.'

Now Victor got up to go to the toilet. Above the washbasin, where he washed his hands meticulously, he looked in the mirror, and thought, frowning, his eyes focused on an imaginary point at the back of his invisible brain.

Was the outcome of a crime decisive for the degree of moral culpability? Should one come to a different verdict on the members of the club now one knew that the outcome of their decision, taken so lightly between the acts – between *Madame Bovary* and drinks – was death, more than eighty children dead? Yes, it had become worse, much worse, once the children were dead. Victor stopped looking in the mirror, turned off the tap, dried his hands and pushed open the swing-door to the passage with the toe of his shoe. In that position, with the door pushed half open, he stopped. So had it become worse *because* the children were dead? Even if the members of the club could not have foreseen the outcome, even though that was outside their scope and control?

From his studies he remembered a moral rule of thumb that students were presented with by the lecturer in international law: it is not decisive whether you make a decision that turns out wrong, it is decisive how you react after things have gone wrong. Whether this was right in theory, Victor didn't know, but it felt good and had also become his rule of thumb. As he went into the passage, back to the restaurant – the door swung to and fro a few times behind him – he knew what he must ask de Winter.

But de Winter had recovered his composure, his sense of guilt had vanished. He had said what he had to say and was not worried about Victor's judgement; he looked around with renewed lightness in his eyes.

'You have to see things in perspective,' he said, once Victor had sat down opposite him again. They were still the only two people in the place, although at that moment the door opened; a drenched man in a bright-blue cagoule glanced inside, with the rain dripping off his face and the cord of his hood lashing his forehead and chin; but obviously he didn't like the look of the deserted restaurant, as he took a step backwards, closed the door again and joined the group of tourists in identical blue cagoules who were standing out in the street looking lost.

'There's a huge distance between the Netherlands and Haiti,' said De Winter. 'And that's just how it is: there are so many rules that operate well locally, but that on a global scale have no effect at all because the distance between all those involved is too great. So many things are criminal offences in the Netherlands, among Dutch people, but are not criminal offences if you as a Dutch citizen want to do them abroad. Do you think that case of mine was an exception? In the third world there are simply different rules for chemical and pharmaceutical companies, and there are lots of multinationals that are only too happy to take advantage of them. Raw materials you can't sell in the Netherlands you can dispose of there with no problem.'

'Does that make it good?'

'It may be wrong, but it's the law. And when all's said and done, that's how the human mind works too: you don't screw your neighbour, but you do buy organs of condemned criminals without too many scruples. How bad is that?'

'How bad is that?' Victor felt his head spinning from the moral roller-coaster he found himself on. His stomach couldn't take it, he felt he needed to find something to hold on to. 'How bad is that?' He raised his voice in an attempt to regain control of himself. 'Executions of prisoners are increasing worldwide because there is profit to be made from the trade in organs. People are sentenced to death to provide someone else with a liver or a kidney. We're gradually starting to live in a global abattoir.' At the same time he knew that the man opposite him was no longer shocked by the thought of a global abattoir. 'But that's not what I came for,' he said, and recovered his composure. 'What I was wondering was how the book club finally reacted. After it was over, I mean. Were you able to talk to them about what happened?'

'That's a nice thought.'

'Did you still see each other?'

'What are you actually going to write about this? On second thoughts, I don't think I want to tell my story to a journalist.'

Victor saw that the man was making as if to end the conversation; he cleared the table, put the menu back in its stand against the wall, pushed his empty glass to the edge of the table, and half turned round on his chair so that he was now looking at the door.

'If my daughter has chosen not to write anything about it, I'm not going talk either; I could get my own back through her, but that would be cheap absolution – I've already caused her enough misery.'

'And if I promise not to write about it?'

'You're a nice chap.'

'I wouldn't make too much of that.'

'Look.' He turned back towards Victor. 'The book club consists of excellent people: solid business people, bright scientists; they've always done what could be expected of them. They gave me advice, they saw the affair escalate from a distance, and when everything was over, I'd lost my job, my wife had left, they brushed the whole affair expertly under the carpet, then agreed with the general judgement and decided it was better if I was no longer part of their company. Randolf Pellikaan came and told me so at home one evening; I was staying temporarily with my sister in Bilthoven. Randolf was as friendly as could be and appealed to my common sense and my empathy; I could imagine of course, he said, that matters were sensitive and that it might be better if we could insert a cooling-off period. Randolf, who on the threshold of the house turned to me again, put his hand on my shoulder and said: "Nothing personal you understand, we've talked that out sufficiently."'

Victor snorted, and his face contorted into a grimace. De Winter looked at him sarcastically, drank a mouthful of beer and got up to ask for the bill for Victor in the kitchen.

'Don't laugh,' he said.

But Victor said: 'I wasn't laughing.'

3

Obviously they were on the same wavelength, because on the same day, at the same time that Victor was having his conversation in Scheveningen with Erik de Winter, Teresa went to visit Iris.

She found her in a nostalgic mood. All the doors and drawers of the walnut cabinet were open and the table in the front room was covered in photo albums. In folders there were loose snaps of holidays, trips with Randolf and Teresa, solitary excursions to Greece, visits to every possible relative in Athens and California – and in the albums her lost youth in Greece had been stuck in its place. Iris sat sprawled on the sofa in the niche that she called 'the canoodling corner', and was bending in fascination over a page full of summer photos.

It was as if Iris were still growing – not getting fatter, because she remained steadfastly at the same weight, but larger, more imposing, as if her nose were continuing to grow and she were getting more and more hair that she had to tie forcibly back in a knot. She preferred to wear expensive linen skirts which flowed out gracefully in all directions, and now she was sitting on the sofa she towered above it, not like Anita Ekberg in the Trevi Fountain, but like an eighteenth-century aristocrat in a painting by Fragonard. Teresa studied the image from a distance and started as always – she saw her mother and started – but the distance she felt now was greater than usual and suddenly she could not shake off her dislike of Iris's smugness. Did she actually love her mother? She doubted it.

'Look,' said Iris, when Teresa sat down opposite her in a serious mood in an uncomfortable high chair. She didn't notice that her daughter was more thoughtful than usual, or if she did notice she was obviously determined not to have her mood ruined by it. 'These are photos of our trips to the coast when I was little. I can actually remember this. Your Auntie Katerina was with us then. And Giannis, a few years before he went to university. Look, look, look,' she said enthusiastically and tapped the photo with her fingernail. 'Here you can see precisely where we always sat. Mother attended to the picnic and the chauffeur fiddled with the car a bit.' She leafed through the album further and held it up triumphantly to Teresa.

'Look how many photos were taken of me at that time. Mother must have been crazy about me.' For a moment she looked in reverent silence at her own girlish figure, and then said, putting a good face on it, 'Well perhaps that's just normal. As the new cleaner is fond of saying: "You think your own kids are the most beautiful, even if their heads are on sideways." I expect there are just as many photos of the others.'

And when Teresa still said nothing, she added guiltily: 'There are lots of photos of you too, you know.'

'That's great,' said Teresa, and it came out sharper than she had intended. Iris shut the photo album and looked straight at her. Always the same thing, the disrupted relationships between mothers and daughters. You could try to escape it yourself, to do your best to build a normal relationship, but the trap was merciless and always snapped shut at the moment when you weren't paying attention. What had she done this time to upset her daughter? Iris knew that Teresa wouldn't bring it up herself, so she just went on talking.

'I was going to call you to pass on the address of someone who's looking for some art for his office, statues for the garden or something. But I'd mislaid the piece of paper I'd written it on. I thought I was going senile, I turned the house upside down looking for it. But it finally turned out there was a good reason why I couldn't find the piece of paper, because a pigeon had picked it up and taken it to its nest.'

The odd thing was that Iris didn't make up all these things; sometimes they actually happened to her, though Teresa didn't consider that any kind of excuse. She frowned and shook her head rather pityingly. 'So have you got it back now?'

'No, we can see the piece of paper up there clearly, but we can't get to it.' Iris leant forward to put the photo-albums on a side-table. 'Do you know who's really starting to go senile? Fietje, and she's only a few years older than us, for goodness sake. I went to visit her the other day and she suddenly started on about the war, I'm not sure *which* war, and then she said very anxiously: "There are children walking through the room. They're from the government. Who are they in heaven's name?" I simply said that the children were all right, but all in all it was an odd afternoon. Well, I hope your father manages to keep his marbles for a little while longer, because it strikes me as very confusing to have to live with someone like that. Then at a certain moment you've absolutely no idea what's happened to the pieces of paper. Would you like a glass of port?'

'No thanks.'

'According to your father I've been getting increasingly careless with my stories recently. Yesterday we were at Jurgen and Machteld Lagerweij's and then I appear to have got up (well I can't remember a thing about it) and appear to have said (so he says at least) that Napoleon's chamber-pot was once captured by an English regiment that took it to Peking, where after important banquets people still drink port out of the thing, and that's strange, because I had no idea that I knew that.'

'Oh.'

'Why are you so quiet?'

'I came to ask you something. Do you remember that I asked you not so very long ago about my old classmate, Ruth Ackermann?'

'Oh yes – Ruth Ackermann.'

'You said at the time you didn't know her, but I think you really do know her.'

'Oh, know, know, I've probably seen her a few times.'

'And you also know that her father murdered eighty children.'

'Come on, Teresa, that's a merciless summary of the facts.'

'Why did you two not tell me anything about the whole business? For Christ's sake, I've come especially to ask about it and I've got John to read that book. Can't you simply brief me on the massacre that took place? John still doesn't know a thing about it, and Ruth will be coming shortly for the reading. Isn't it time to tell us what's going on?'

'We don't like talking about it any more.'

'That strikes me as an understatement.'

'It was a weird time.'

'And?'

'It simply didn't stop.' Iris sighed. She tried to order her thoughts and tell the story properly, since her daughter looked as if she wasn't going to let it rest. 'It was complicated. For ages new things kept emerging about the business. It started when you were still at primary school and it didn't stop until long after you were at high school. First there was the disaster with the children themselves. Then it was decided that Erik and his company would not be prosecuted. Parliament got involved, and the Minister of Justice intervened when a report was leaked saying that Erik had known everything in advance.' She now started waving her hands restlessly. 'More and more reports kept appearing, autopsy reports, and then there was a complaint by the lawyers, until the Public Prosecutions Department decided that there were no new facts and the complaint was denied. Only then did it stop.'

'Why is it that we knew nothing about it at school?'

'You must have heard something, but probably you didn't make the link with Ruth. I think she was already called Ackermann when she joined your class.'

'And why did you two never say anything about it?'

'Randolf was very upset by the whole thing, and didn't want to talk about it at the time, or even now. And I found it mainly shameful, too shameful to burden you with. The families of the children were given compensation, I remember that. Seven years after what happened they received compensation from the Dutch government. Mainly because the United Nations applied pressure, I believe. At the time a big UN human rights conference was being planned; before that the matter had to be cleared up and the Netherlands had to pay compensation. It didn't amount to much, a few thousand euros per family, and even then via some Unicef fund or other. It cost about half a million in all, but in the Netherlands it was proudly announced on television as a gesture, a gesture of the ministry's – I remember that distinctly. That spokeswoman standing in the street outside the door of the ministry and proudly speaking of a "gesture", with which the matter in her view had been wrapped up.'

'Wrapped up!'

'I wasn't too fond of the choice of words either.'

'And all that while the company refused to pay for the operations.'

'That was because the cause of death remained vague. According to the Public Prosecutions Department, you see, you couldn't establish whether the children had actually died through taking the linctus. Experts from America said you could, that it could be deduced from the autopsies, but the PPD lost those reports from the Americans, and forgot to summon them for interview; then they also lost the information from the American lawyer representing the parents, and then they no longer knew how to get in touch with those parents, and finally, I believe, they lost the whole dossier and concluded that they couldn't prove anything.'

'But surely there were questions in parliament? So why was there never a prosecution?' With her questions Teresa was checking whether she had the account straight in her mind; every time that Iris gave an answer that was obviously right, she ticked the question mentally and went on to the next.

'Well, that's all I know. If you want to know more, you'll have to ask Lucius, because he followed everything closely at the time.'

'Why Lucius?'

'Lucius is free-floating,' said Iris. 'A free-floating intelligence, and he has a different relationship with the matter from anyone else. You mustn't try to interpret him. I don't know why Lucius does the things he does. But anyway, he followed everything to the end. The others didn't: at a certain moment, they wanted to have done with it. And then Erik left the club.'

'The club? Erik de Winter was in the book club?' At this point Teresa's voice shot up in pitch in astonishment.

'Yes, didn't I tell you?'

If Teresa had thought that she knew the pattern of events, that she had gained a clear picture of the affair from Victor's dossier, that picture had now changed into a completely new pattern, as when one turns a kaleidoscope: nothing looked as it had a moment earlier and she had to refocus, try to get a grip on the lines, the relationships in which reality now presented itself to her. Erik de Winter was not a vague acquaintance of her parents', he was a friend of her father's.

Iris did not notice her daughter's confusion. 'When Erik disappeared from the club,' she said, 'I had a very long conversation with Randolf, and I know for certain that he felt very guilty for a long time.'

'*What?*' Teresa now saw the patterns shifting at lightning speed, she tried to understand what Iris's statement meant, but everything was spinning round, forming a new constellation for a moment, and then disintegrating into different, into dissolving images of a past that she had thought she knew, and that now lay before her in a chaos of slivers of glass.

'Yes, Randolf felt guilty, I think. Because he knew beforehand that there was something wrong with that glycerine. I believe that Erik asked his advice, and that Randolf rang someone whose back-garden bordered on the back-garden of someone who knew about those things.'

Iris shook her head.

'No, I think it was definitely indelicate of your father not to want any more contact with Erik de Winter.'

4

Going back in the car Teresa had been able to fight back her tears, but now as she walked into the kitchen at home, she could feel them almost overflowing her lower eyelids and her face contorting, eyebrows knitted, lower lip protruding, although she did her best to put on the sort of cheerful face John would expect. There was absolutely no excuse for a sudden breakdown. She tried to smile.

'Are you OK?' he asked. He had never seen her so distraught.

'Yes. I'm a bit thirsty.' She sat down on a high stool by the white marble worktop of the kitchen island with the thumb and forefinger of her left hand pushing her lower lip back in against her teeth. John went over to the tap and came back with a glass of water.

'What is it?' he said.

Because he was talking to her in an attentive tone that was unfamiliar to her, she felt for a moment that she could tell him everything that was weighing on her heart. The thought calmed her. From her handbag, which she had put on the chair next to her, she took out a paper handkerchief and reflectively blew her nose. Meanwhile she tried tentatively to find the best angle from which to approach the story. She knew he would prefer it if she kept the conversation objective.

'Do you believe that gods, Greek gods, I mean, perform actions?'

John looked at her in surprise, but after some hesitation replied. 'They'd be very odd gods if they didn't perform any actions at all, don't you think? What good are gods if they don't do anything? At the very least they have to punish us poor mortals for all the things we do wrong.'

'Yes, but that's precisely the problem. I talked to someone here about it recently, and they said, and actually I'd never thought of that, but they had a point, they said you can't possibly call people free agents if the punishment and reward for all our actions are fixed in advance in carefully measured proportions.' She was looking for an explanation that would quickly compress events for her into a rounded story.

John laughed. 'I don't think that the Greek gods were very worried about our freedom. That's more a modern concern. The Greek gods were simply old-fashioned reactionaries.' He took the glass from her and refilled it at the tap.

Teresa now became slightly confused and could no longer remember very well what Victor had said. Somewhere there must be a link with all the other things he had told her. She tried to recall his reasoning. Now she thought about it, it looked as if Victor had argued for the abolition of

punishment and reward, but that must be the exact opposite of what he meant. Hadn't he said something about
knowledge of the universe? Freedom as the obligation to
act in accordance with . . . with what?

'You know,' said John, 'I'm a dyed-in-the-wool liberal.
And I'm well aware that in recent years everyone has suddenly
gone conservative, with your father in the van, with theo-
ries about the family and the leadership of the intellectual
elite. Society changes and before you know it you're suspect
if you cling to something as frivolous as moral autonomy.'
He now filled a glass of water for himself and looked in a
kitchen unit for nuts. 'But for now I take the view that
first of all we must take ourselves in hand. And that subsequently we must act as if everyone is responsible for his
own actions. Forget all that stuff about Greek gods, and
divine laws, and eternal obligations. Even if man's responsibility has no basis, it's still practical simply to hold everyone
responsible in this earthly life. That means: we may not be
free, but it's better if we act as if we are.' He sat down
opposite her and took a handful of nuts from the bowl that
he had placed between them. 'But why are we talking about
this? Where have you been? Who is it you have been talking
to so grandly about the Greek gods?'

Teresa returned to the moment and immediately felt a
rising wave of horror.

'I was at my parents' place.'

'And?'

'Their friend Fietje is starting to go senile.'

'Aha?'

'And they don't give a damn.' And when John looked at her with slight astonishment, she shouted furiously: 'They don't give a damn. They never give a damn about anything!'

She didn't know where her rage suddenly came from, but she could feel that she was on the point of losing her self-control completely; she tried to think, to draw breath, but all her thoughts were suddenly churning through her head and swept along by that force she grabbed the bowl of nuts in front of her and threw it furiously through the kitchen. As if only now, now she was talking to John, did the full implications get through to her.

For a second John had been flabbergasted. What he always admired in Teresa was the rationality in which he found other women greatly lacking, and now he failed to understand the cause of this new hysteria. He was shocked and irritated. But he soon had himself under control again. This was a blip. He was immediately prepared to forget it. And because he knew Teresa was susceptible to appeals to her sense of propriety, he thought that by far the most sensible thing to do would be to take her to task about the theatricality of this behaviour.

While Teresa wrung her hands like a goddess in an ancient tragedy, he got up and picked up off the floor the tin of nuts, the lid of which, being welded to the plastic bowl, had fortunately remained in place. He said in a businesslike tone: 'Your parents have a friend who is going senile and they don't give a damn. That really isn't very nice of them. But don't turn it into such a drama.'

Teresa's thoughts faltered. As if from racing along she had

been brought to a standstill. She slid back on her chair and put on her normal face. Though she must still be beside herself, because she saw herself sitting in the kitchen, controlled and aloof, and at the same time she saw herself from far away: at the same moment that she was sitting there, she was also standing outside helpless and desperately knocking at a gate, watching a window above her head open and a bucket of cold water being poured over her with a determined swing. The latter was a pathetic image, and the moment she realized that, she saw Victor's sad face, she heard her mother talking about a financial gesture, she remembered the old school building where she had smoked cigarettes in the window-seat on the second floor. At this moment she could think eighty things at once, she understood everything, she saw through the double betrayal of marriage, when one says nothing and the other asks nothing, her brain was going flat out, while she stood on the step wet and cold and the water poured down her face. And in that one second in which she thought everything over, she swallowed her tears again and said: 'I put your post on the stairs.' For a moment John looked intently at her face, which was as calm and balanced as always, left the kitchen, and she was alone.

Teresa sat on her chair. Never in her life had she thought so clearly. The worst possible thing is true, she thought, the worst possible thing is true. She drank some water, took a deep breath and to her own astonishment began weeping, silently and unstoppably.

5

Lucius woke with the cat in his arms. The night seemed endless, sleep had come in waves, something was hurting, an old sorrow connected, he thought laboriously, with things he had forgotten and at a higher level of consciousness he knew that dreams give meaning to what you yourself are, but in these images of drenched streets and mist-cloaked gas-lamps he recognized nothing that reminded him of himself; again and again he saw a man in a floppy hat coming downstairs into the cellar and he heard black taxis driving through the puddles, the splashing of the water under the wheels sounded close and threatening; after waking for a moment, he went back to sleep, started awake again and was finally not sure if this was a good dream or a bad one.

It was already getting light and he could see the face of his cat, lying in the crook of his arm, with her head on his shoulder. It didn't surprise him to find her somewhere in bed. But up to now she had never come so close that she had abandoned all her usual suspicion, put herself at his mercy. Usually, just before he fell asleep, he felt something slight scuttle across his body and a second later he would know it was the cat, looking for the best place to sleep – she padded around for a while to assert herself and then nestled in the hollow between Lucius' right calf and left shinbone. When he woke in the morning, she lay with her full weight on his legs, so that he first had to free himself before jumping out of bed to go down to breakfast.

The cat had not been at Lucius' house that long; she had turned up one night a few months ago. When he got back at two in the morning, she was sitting by the garden door and wanted to go inside with him, no objection to that. Slightly amused, Lucius had opened a tin of tuna in the kitchen and tipped the contents on to a plate; the cat had wolfed everything down in a trice and had gone upstairs with him to the bedroom and lain on the bed as if it were the most natural thing in the world. Two hours later Lucius was woken by a blood-curdling scream that seemed to be coming from downstairs. He charged downstairs, ran into the room and saw the cat standing by the garden door in a state of obvious pain and distress. When Lucius opened the door in alarm, she flew outside, took a mouthful of grass and started vomiting up her food with athletic movements. Her whole body was shuddering and it was as if she needed all her strength to get the tuna back up from the depths of her stomach. It took a while before the stomach muscles gave up the struggle and the food came out. The fact that Lucius was standing here in the garden in the middle of the night in his silk pyjamas and in his bare feet beside a puking cat was an odd phenomenon that he himself observed from a distance with some surprise. And when a little later they were back in bed together and the cat looked pensively at him, rolled itself into a ball and went contentedly to sleep, for the first time in his life he realised he was responsible for the welfare of another creature. It moved him and at the same time the idea was repellent to him.

'Silly puss,' he growled, 'stupid little predator.'

While the cat slept, Lucius began to worry. First of all, he hadn't a clue what you did with a cat. What did she need to eat, for instance? It didn't occur to him that he should go to the vet the next morning to check if she had been reported missing, if she carried a chip, because now someone had called at his door, individually and under their own steam, he fully respected that decision. If the cat wanted to leave again, she would certainly go of her own accord. There was nothing you could do about that either.

He lay awake for another hour and tried to remember the documentary on capuchin monkeys he had once seen; he had forgotten most of the facts, but he did remember that monkeys born in captivity obviously sensed automatically and without further instructions that they must chew heads of garlic and then smear the mixture of garlic and saliva over their whole bodies. Now he simply hoped that the cat would know when nature required something similar of her. Perhaps though there were also manners and customs that he should teach such a young animal. He would call the home-help the next morning; she knew a lot about that kind of thing.

The cat was impeccably beautiful, which also won Lucius over. She had now learned how to get in and out of the house via the cellar window – the bars kept out the burglars but not small pets, and God knows what animals got in while he was out. During the day she led a very independent life, but every evening she came running from the fields as soon as Lucius got out of his car and then hopped around him until he went to bed. There he read a bit, or watched television, and she washed herself with busy, brusque movements, feet intertwined criss-cross, so that Lucius could sometimes scarcely make out a cat in the shape. On one of the first evenings after the beauty ritual he drank a toast to her. 'The Owl and the Pussycat went to sea.' She seemed so interested that he went on a bit.

'In a beautiful pea-green boat,
They took some honey, and plenty of money,
Wrapped up in a five-pound note.'

Now the cat sat down specially to listen and looked intently at his mouth. Lucius drank a mouthful of wine, raised his glass a little higher and boomed through the silence of the bedroom:

The Owl looked up to the stars above,
And sang to a small guitar,
'O lovely Pussy! O Pussy, my love,
What a beautiful Pussy you are,
You are,

You are!
What a beautiful Pussy you are!'

And from then on the cat wanted to hear it every night.

There was the mystery of individualization. Not the species, but the individual. Not the cat, but *this* cat. Lucius discovered a developing bond of friendship, which he hadn't anticipated, because he had never been very interested in animals, but which was now issuing from their closer acquaintance. Every day the cat and he had more history between them, new rituals, fixed agreements: they were long past the point where the cat could be exchanged for another animal without his noticing it – and suffering. The cat in her turn would not be so comfortable sleeping on someone else's bed, or at least, so Lucius hoped, unable to bear the thought that he was nothing but a representative of the species to her. His individualization had been ensured, he told himself, on the night he had stood barefoot next to her in the grass. He had tackled that well. And without knowing what he was doing at that; as if he had instinctively smeared himself with garlic and saliva. He too obviously had a nature, a human nature that preceded his socialization into an adult man, a caring and protective maternal nature that he had never noticed in himself before.

At the same time, despite this promising friendship, he remained conscious that he was in bed with a predator. That the claws and jaws, however small and elegant, could really injure him in his sleep, since a cat is quite simply an unpredictable nocturnal animal. But he also became increasingly convinced that he in turn could just as well harm the cat, that the creature that had surrendered herself so unconditionally to his care must wait and see whether Lucius was actually to be trusted.

Looking at the sleeping feline face, Lucius thought about himself. Once, years before, on a walk, a psychiatrist friend had told him the story of one of his patients detained under a hospital order. The man, having found his way to the clinic for treatment after years in prison, had explained guiltily to his psychiatrist during one of the first sessions that while he was simply a nice man, sometimes, without being aware of it, he turned into an out-of-control tidal wave of urges and that, without being able to do much about it, he had to seize something small in the gloom of night, something small and soft and then squeeze it until it was dead and no longer moved.

That story had made a greater impression on Lucius than all other stories about crime that he had encountered in his career, since then when he read the newspaper he always thought of the violent inclination to grab something soft and squeeze it until it was quiet – and searched for that tendency in important moments in world news. In his own life the nocturnal danger had taken the form of a small body that slept in the hollow of his legs and early in the mornings licked the inside of his wrist with a rough tongue. 'Small, dangerous, vicious predator,' he muttered, but he still didn't know which of them was actually in most danger.

This morning the cat had crawled upwards and was lying

in the crook of Lucius' arm, with her head on his shoulder, so that, now he looked at her, he could see how incomprehensibly beautiful she was: the perfect nose, the upright ears, the hairs meticulously distributed over the coat, everything painfully pristine and pure. Lucius knew that he would never be able to harm her. But he also knew that the greatest danger lies not in the criminal urge to grab something small and squeeze it until it is dead. God help me, he thought, I wish the cat had found another house. He lay still and did his best to breathe as little as possible.

6

Because Lucius knew that Teresa was coming – she had rung him – he had brought out his old video-recorder. With some difficulty he connected it to the television in the living-room. He needed a scart cable and couldn't find one at first; in a drawer containing leads and plugs he did find an old dictaphone with a tape in that he started listening to, until after a few minutes he decided that wasn't getting him very far. He went into the cellar and in a plastic box found the cable he needed.

When the video was working, he fetched from the top shelf of the bookcase in his study a brown envelope containing a videotape that he hadn't seen, let alone watched, for nine years and when everything was ready, the tape rewound to the beginning of the broadcast they wanted, he put a bottle of red wine on the table, with the corkscrew next to it. He had no idea what etiquette required in these kinds of circumstances. He didn't want to offend Teresa by putting the wine out open, even though he knew she was already offended. And there was nothing to be done: at the end of the evening she would be feeling even worse. Now she would be able to see that they had happened, all those things which by now she knew had happened.

Up to this moment, for Teresa at least, there had always been a way out from the guilty awareness, she could still retreat, shrug her shoulders, assume she had imagined things, that her friend Victor had been exaggerating, that the newspapers had put a spin on things, that the whole matter had rightly been immediately forgotten, swept under the carpet, blotted out; grow up, these things happen, such is life. But after seeing the video there was no way back and she would be responsible for the knowledge she had. When she rang the bell, he gathered up his courage and let her in.

Teresa, on an upright chair facing the television in the bachelor pad she had known since childhood (which had always reminded her of a mountain refuge – an extreme luxurious mountain refuge – with the bare floorboards, the faded kelims and the two wooden bookcases without keys that she had tried to open as a child), watched tensely as Lucius fumbled with the video. He got confused about the remote and so they hopped from one television channel to another and for a few seconds watched a Roman Catholic church service, a detective film about a Canadian mountie, a stand-up comedian, a CNN report on floods in Pakistan, the stock-market bulletin, a documentary on Coco Chanel, and they were in the middle of an ad for cheap mortgages when the video suddenly came on and a presenter appeared whom Teresa didn't know. The man announced a documentary on the Bloem affair, which had wrongly received little attention and was now running into the sand.

'Attorney Alex Hamer,' read the presenter from the sheet of paper lying on the table, 'representing the next-of-kin in the poisoning case on Haiti, has announced that there will be no new criminal proceedings again the chemical company Bloem BV.' Now he looked up and continued earnestly to camera. 'Eight years ago that company supplied impure glycerine for cough-linctus, as a result of which at least eighty Haitian children died. According to Hamer the case has now been finally closed.'

As he read on from the autocue Teresa tried to read a judgement from his face, as if her own opinion depended on the way he viewed the affair. She was still hoping that there were excuses and that the affair would turn out on closer inspection to be based on a misunderstanding. But the presenter read grimly on. There seemed to be little chance that he would come up with any mitigating circumstances, let alone with a happy ending.

'Haiti has many problems,' he said. 'The population has to contend with poverty, political instability, repression, lack of education, lack of freedom, and all in all little seems to have been spared the Haitians. But eight years ago the assault came from a very unexpected quarter. Ninety-two families were hit by a sudden tragedy when children fell ill and died, sometimes two or three children in one family on the same day, or within a few days. And it took a while before the parents, the doctors and nurses who rushed to help, the pathologists and medical researchers discovered the cause. Initially attention turned to nearby factories, rubbish tips, to possible contamination of the water supply. There was great astonishment when after rigorous investigation the cause was identified as the bottle of cough-linctus that was in each home, simply in the kitchen next to the tap. And at first it was incomprehensible to the parents, the doctors and people in the street who heard it from passers-by, that it wasn't local swindlers who had poisoned the cough-medicine, con-men, gangsters on the make, but that the cough-medicine had been mixed with anti-freeze in the utopias on the other side of the world, where the houses are big and the streets are lined with expensive cars. Even more incomprehensible was the news that there was no question of an accident, but that the raw materials had been deliberately sent from the Netherlands to Haiti in a contaminated state and there traded.'

Teresa now knew that the presenter had formed the same judgement on the affair as Victor, and she herself, after she had read the press reports. There was no more reason for uncertainty and alarm, the axe had fallen and it was over. Further resistance was pointless, she could simply stay and watch the mess unfold before her eyes. She took a deep breath, and oddly enough it sounded like a sigh of relief.

'We have spoken to a number of the next of kin,' said the presenter. 'Parents of children who died in the tragedy. In this country their legal options have been exhausted, they can do nothing at this point to instigate criminal proceedings against those responsible for the deaths of their children. The Public Prosecutions Department has arrived at a settlement with Bloem BV in the case: because the company has paid 250,000 guilders to the Department, it can no longer be prosecuted. It is true that the court ruled that that settlement should never have been made, but the case has still not been reopened. Attorney Hamer has one chance left of bringing criminal charges against the company. He could take the case to the European Court in Strasbourg. But today Hamer announced that the next of kin have decided against. The parents are not giving him a brief to go to Strasbourg. The case is closed. It's over.'

The presenter disappeared from the screen. A voice-over took up the story from where he had left it and began a reconstruction. 'Today in this report you will hear the story of one of the Haitian parents,' said a woman's voice.

And as the names of the children who had died began to roll across the screen – Leonel, Guysanto, Jean-Baptiste, Carline, James, Estelle, Josiane, Georges, Esmeralda, Antoine, Otis, Joseph, Alfonso, Patrick, Ambroise, Gracía, Apollon, Bernabotte, Clifton, Louise, Margarette, Noelle, Pierre, Roy, Yantha . . . – in the background images were shown of a wide expanse of white beach, green hills with lush vegetation, and then the camera dived from a great height down to the slums of Cité Soleil, where there were shacks with corrugated roofs. It produced a colourful picture; from the gutters of the houses hung clothes, trousers, dresses, blouses tied to the beams with rope; the streets were strewn with mysterious sacks, buckets, pots, and by each house stood jerrycans connected by hoses to large oil drums full of water, all in the brilliant colours of poverty, red, yellow, white, aquamarine, the multi-coloured jollity of street life.

Then, while the voice-over went on talking about the legal proceedings, the camera switched to an unpaved street corner in Port-au-Prince, where a man in a straw hat was selling lottery tickets; his kiosk was right underneath a huge toothpaste ad that had been painted in garish colours on the canary-yellow wall behind him. It was boiling hot in the street. There was a buzz and hubbub. Nearby you heard a dog bark, and you could almost see the earth trembling, from all sides boys in baseball caps came running yelling towards the camera and in the background a few young women walked slowly past with large plastic washing baskets on their heads. The camera zoomed in on a tall, slim woman who had tied a red cloth round her hair. She was wearing a snow-white blouse, the white of washing in the tropics, and a flowered skirt. With one hand she held the basket that was balanced on her head; she walked on imperturbably, and a moment later you saw her turn the corner, into a smaller street, where she stopped in front of a house painted a cheerful turquoise, the door slightly askew in its frame. She pushed the door open with her foot, put the basket on her hip and inclining her head, went inside, straight into the living-room, where she put the basket away in a corner, pulled a chair from under the table and sat down.

'This is Marilène Vaillant,' said the voice-over. 'She's thirty-six years old, she has three children, and eight years ago her seven-year-old son Clifton died of kidney poisoning after ingesting a number of spoonfuls of cough-linctus.

Marilène and her husband Bertrand are among the group of parents who have decided not to take the case against Bloem to a higher court, because after eight years of legal tug-of-war they lack the mental energy.'

The camera zoomed in on the face of the woman and obviously she was given a signal off camera, because after a short silence she began to speak; her voice was soft and she spoke a French so transparent that Teresa could understand her without looking at the subtitles. Listen, said Teresa to herself, listen.

7

'I understand perfectly,' said the young woman, 'that you want to know why we have decided not continue with proceedings against the factory. That does indeed seem strange and incomprehensible. I can imagine that parents in the Netherlands want to know what kind of people suddenly abandon their children eight years after their death, as if they'd never existed. Eight years of legal proceedings. And then suddenly nothing more. If you think about it properly it's hard to explain. Perhaps people believe that we've gradually forgotten Clifton, because it was all so long ago and because we achieved so little in all those years.

'I myself have occasionally been frightened in the last few years that we would forget him. He was seven years old when everything happened and if he hadn't died he would have been fifteen now, bigger than us, noisy and cheeky; I probably wouldn't recognize him at all if I were to meet him now. When he was little, just born, when he was a little creature with soft hair that I carried with me in a sling against my body, I sometimes fantasized about

what he would be like when he was fifteen. I fantasized
about the conversations we would have. Yes, it could have
gone wrong, could have been difficult, I know all the worries
that parents have about fifteen-year-olds in this city, but
Clifton never made much of a fuss, he was calm and
thoughtful, and I think he could have grown into a big
boy, a man.

'Perhaps he wasn't even coughing, I think looking back.
Just as you're inclined to blame yourself in retrospect, because
the events are even more difficult to comprehend if others
are responsible. So I wonder, when I think back, how badly
he was coughing. He was a bit hoarse. That was actually
all. As a rule he had a lovely voice. I'm not just saying that
as a proud mother, it was something that immediately struck
everyone about Clifton, he had a lovely voice, and a lovely
singing voice too, he sang in the choir of the church further
down the street. So perhaps it was because of that singing
that I was worried about his cough and about the fact that
he sounded so hoarse. Or perhaps he really didn't feel well.
Actually I can't remember, and I blame myself; I should
have taken more care, thought more carefully about whether
he really needed cough-linctus. When I try to remember
events, I always have the feeling that he had a bit of a
temperature, had a cold, a slight flu, but it may also be that
I imagined it all.

'So I bought cough-syrup. He took it a couple of times
precisely in accordance with the instructions on the paper.
And he got ill. He was already a bit listless, I think, and lay
on his bed for a while, but once he'd taken the cough-

medicine he got really ill, terribly ill. At the time of course we didn't yet know that it was because of the cough-medicine, how *could* we have known that? But anyway, to start with I wasn't really alarmed. Children are sick all the time, and then you worry a bit, you growl a bit, you moan a bit, and secretly you also enjoy it, the weakness, the need-iness, suddenly the child is no longer a seven-year-old boy, but a toddler. But he had a headache and that was rotten. And he vomited up all his food. We tried to get him to eat and especially to drink a lot, because it's dangerous if you lose too much liquid; we're always warned about that if children have gastric flu and are sick. But very soon he couldn't keep anything down and the headache got worse. Then I became alarmed.

'Later, when we heard that the cough-mixture came from Europe and that it had been poisoned there and sent to Haiti, I realized that my alarm and my worry was all for nothing. At that moment there was nothing more I could have done. There are disasters that swamp you like a wave with a force you can't resist, they bowl you over, sweep your house away, your family, your happiness, and you don't know where they come from. There are roots of evil that begin on one side of the world and emerge on the other side, and sometimes you see them in time and sometimes they remain invisible until it's too late.

'But I didn't know all that then. I was sitting on the bed with a sick little boy, trying to get him to drink. It's true that children get ill quickly, more ill than adults, but some-thing else was happening here, that soon became clear.

There was something wrong with Clifton. There was something fundamentally wrong. And my God we sent our neighbour for the doctor, but she couldn't find him. When we finally reached him hours later he was just coming from Gracía and Alfonso's house, children from Clifton's school, and when the doctor came to us Gracía was already dead.

'You mustn't think we are relentless people. We believe in God. Since childhood I have believed that God created the universe and that His hand is hidden in the world. My parents taught me that all things have issued necessarily from His goodness. God wanted to create everything that He thought in His perfection actually with the same perfection, that's what my parents told me and I believe, but sometimes it's difficult to go on believing it. That's why I'm not sure if we're capable of forgiving. For that matter we don't know *who* we're supposed to forgive, we've never heard anything from the people who sent the cough medicine.

'Then, eight years ago, here on his bed, Clifton had an unbearable headache and the stomach cramps were becoming more and more violent. He vomited up every glass of water that we gave him to drink, and in his intestines and stomach blood was churning and from my beautiful little boy came a poisonous stream of bile and slime and blood. I tried to reassure him, I washed him, put a damp cloth on his forehead, told him that God would protect him, until I almost believed it myself. And yet, how irrationally relieved I was the moment the doctor came in. Now everything will be all right, I thought in my innocence, and for a few seconds despair turned to hope, until the doctor put his bag down and looked at me. Of all the terrifying moments in the last eight years that was the worst: the doctor looking at me and knowing with instinctive certainty that he could no longer do anything; he knew that Clifton was going to die and that's why he didn't even unpack his bag.

'And I held that sick boy to me, his head hanging down on my left shoulder, his hand resting on my leg, I could feel that his breathing was going too fast, as though he couldn't keep up with what God had in store for him, he was panting, I pressed his head against me. Then I begged the doctor to make Clifton better, but the doctor, who knew all the children in the neighbourhood, who had set Alfonso's leg when it was broken, the doctor had already seen two children die and he sat here in the room and he cried, because he hadn't slept for nights, because he had rushed completely pointlessly through the city, and then he said he had promised to return to Alfonso. After he had gone we were completely alone with the dying boy in our arms. And in that black night, when everyone on the planet had abandoned us, Clifton died.

'Perhaps the people in the Netherlands are angry with us, perhaps they think we don't want to do anything for our son any more, just as we did nothing for him then. But that's not how it is. We loved him. He was ours. He was a beautiful boy of seven, with little teeth with slight gaps, which looked funny; he had curly hair, ears close to his head and had a rather shy look. After he sang in the choir of the big church he was given money by the priest, from which he had bought a watch from the kiosk on the corner with a light in it, which lit up when you pressed the button. He always wore that watch and he was wearing it when we buried him.

'People mustn't be angry at us. If someone doesn't understand why we don't want any more court cases, I can only try to explain that we don't want any excuses or any stories from the Netherlands, because we're tired. The management of the company must answer to God and that's all I want to say. I think Clifton will understand.

That's the whole story. The lawyer, who has done his very best for us, advised us to go to court in France, but we said that we can't bear any more court cases. I've only agreed to talk to you today so that you don't think and the people in the Netherlands don't think that we don't miss Clifton. We don't want to hope for news from Europe any more, but that's not because we don't miss him, we miss him terribly, because Clifton was the most important thing in our lives, he was our dream, he was my eldest child, my firstborn. And sometimes I can no longer quite remember the sound of his voice, because he's been gone so long, and that's the worst thing of all. But I can call up the picture of him at any moment of the day, then I sit here on this chair and I think of him, of the shy way he laughed. He had a sweet face. And he had a watch with a light in it, which lit up when you pressed it.'

'When the titles came on Lucius turned off the television and finally dared to look sideways at Teresa, who the whole time had sat motionless in her chair a few paces to his left. She was silent. With her hands on the arms of the chair she pushed back against the back of the chair in order to stay seated. Lucius took a deep breath, looked away from her and for a while looked aimlessly into the spring garden. It's all right, he said. It's all right. And he couldn't get up, because the cat had jumped onto his lap and, purring gently, had fallen asleep on his left thigh.

8

The 18th of May arrived, and it was again an almost summery day. Everyone in the village had woken up with the expectant feeling that something pleasant was about to happen and some knew, as they swung their legs out of bed, that it was the day of the interview with Ruth Ackermann in the church.

As soon as everyone was up, the day had great difficulty in finding a suitable tempo: for some people the hours raced nervously by, for others they passed obscenely slowly; and so some people began to hurry, while others continued calmly with their work, with no thought for the present of going for a meal or getting changed. It was as if the village had two different time-zones, which intersected somewhere in the front porch of the church. But it was all a question of points of view and temperaments: here the sun shone unsuspectingly; there the moon was already rising with a thoughtful air, and it was simply a question of how much you wanted evening to fall. And yet, although beforehand not everyone felt easy about it – a few people it seems had personal reasons for not particularly looking forward to the meeting with Ruth Ackermann – they had all come to the church on time and there they now sat on the hard wooden pews waiting for it to begin.

Lucius in a new lightweight summer suit, Randolf who successfully projected the cordial message that he was not above coming to hear a discussion on chicklit like this, Iris next to him, with a colourful shawl around her, John with the whole population of Armazon in his inside pocket, Teresa, Gabrielle, the other members of the book club, the pupils from the high school, the wife of the baker, the baron's daughter-in-law, the string-quartet of the doctors' collective, the customers of the bookshop, the elders and the vicar, the landlord and landlady of the bar – a complete cross-section of the village community.

Those who sat here in the pews every Sunday morning felt at ease. They waved to each other and called out to friends and acquaintances on the other side of the aisle, close to the altar or next to the pulpit. Only for Victor, who was leaning against a wall at the back of the church, and Teresa, who was sitting poker-faced at the front next to her husband, had the distance become too great for them to be able to greet each other enthusiastically. The church smelled as it always smelled, and because of that, you recognized eternity in it.

When everyone was properly seated and the coughing and shuffling had subsided, Ruth Ackermann entered, with her Dutch publisher, a PR woman and a few other nondescript types who according to the PR woman belonged to the entourage – and at the back of the small procession came the journalist Kiki Jansen, who was writing a report on Ruth Ackermann's tour through Europe.

The audience, who up until now had known only the stylized photo on the back cover of her book, saw a delicate, unassuming young woman with casual clothes and the clumsy movements of a calf. For a moment she seemed not to know quite where to sit and was already walking towards an empty place in the front row, giving the people at the front a close-up glimpse of her nervous features, but the publisher took her by the arm and pushed her in the direction of a long table, where she was received by the bookseller. The audience heard a loud crackling sound as a microphone was pinned on to her and then all the hubbub slowly ebbed away, the entourage dispersed into the auditorium, and the PR woman came to a halt. Everyone looked at the famous writer, who looked back with obvious curiosity, along the rows of faces, searching for the expression on vaguely familiar faces, details that she had not yet written down and which one morning a few years later might return to her memory and form the germ of a spectacular new book.

The bookseller waited until the last whispers had died away and turned respectfully sideways to the writer, who sat down next to him at the table. He tried to judge whether she was sitting comfortably, whether she needed anything, whether she had perhaps been annoyed by anything that had crossed her path in this village environment, a bump, a pavement, a wrong word that had caused her to stumble – but she seemed content, and with some relief he turned his gaze back to the audience.

'Ms Ackermann, it's an honour to welcome you here this evening. We all know how busy you are these days.'

He looked at the piece of paper he had slid under his glass of water. 'But we also all know that you grew up here, in our own village. So you may have come back to some extent from curiosity and nostalgia.'

Now he turned back to her again, with an admiring look, and broke into a cautious laugh. 'Although to tell the truth I can't really imagine how a lively mind like yours was able hold out so long in a sleepy village like this. How did you actually survive?'

A start had been made, the first question had been put and now the bookseller and the audience waited expectantly for an answer. Ruth Ackermann nodded, leant forward towards the microphone and coughed as if she were frightened her voice would not hold out.

'How I survived?' she said. 'I had to survive. I'm far too shy to die.'

Relieved, the audience, who had been apprehensive about the seriousness of the literary evening, started laughing – there was a mighty roll of laughter through the church. And it was precisely that laugh that the journalist in the front row recognized unerringly as a warm bath in which the young writer finally came home after the great international success of her irresistible début.